ESCHPE FROM PERIHELION

DIEGO TOVAR

For those who believe even the smallest orbit can change the course of a star.

PART ONE
SHACKLED

Sacrifices must be made for the endless pursuit of progress. Mines are not mere pits of labor but rather the foundation upon which society is built. The toil of a few empowers the prosperity of many.

—VICTOR KOL, FOUNDER OF TERRALUX MINERALS

1

ARAYA

The cracked pavement threatened to snap Araya's ankles with every step. Nova Angeles didn't bother hiding its malice. The city was a tin carcass, rusted shacks thrusting up like broken teeth.

Her lungs burned, as if the air itself meant to brand her from the inside. Dust scraped her throat raw. Heat dug into her chest and refused to let go. Strands of hair snapped across her face and packed grit into her mouth and eyes. Her lashes burned but she refused to blink.

Sweat carved tracks down her cheekbones. Heat needled her warm umber skin, and old bruises lingered as faint shadows under the surface.

She ran, all wiry muscle and tight focus, petite enough to vanish in a crowd yet carrying herself like someone who already outlived worse than Nova Angeles offered.

What's ahead? Who knows. What's behind? No question at all. Death. Don't look back, Araya. Don't you dare.

One wrong turn dumped her into the plaza and killed her cover. Too many eyes. Too damned open.

The crowd clogged the space, all elbows and noise, and whoever tracked her stayed close, swallowed by the press of bodies. Merchants, beggars, and scavengers packed shoulder to shoulder and clawed at what little the world still offered. It wasn't much.

Stalls pressed together under sun-faded tarps in sick reds and browns. Fire pits smoked in the gaps, gray threads climbing into the jaundiced sky.

Smoke from old fat and charred crust drifted through the food stalls and settled on her tongue. *Ignore it. Hunger makes you stupid, and stupid gets you killed.*

She ducked her head and barreled into the crowd. Hunger pulled at her gut and she crushed it down. Sleeves scraped her arms, fabric biting like sandpaper. Plastic scraps and dyed rags flashed at the edge of her vision as she forced a path through bodies.

The sun hammered the plaza and made shade worth fighting over. Shadows sliced off leaning stalls and crooked poles in thin strips, never wide enough to hide her. Bargaining shouts slammed her ears, tangled with fire crackle and boots thudding through sand.

Under the noise, her pulse held steady. That was hers, and real. The only rhythm this town hadn't taken yet. She needed a place to disappear, and she needed it fast.

Araya scurried with the other outsiders, tangled in their slow shuffle, all of them serving the same silent sentence of abandonment. Somewhere out there, there had to be a future. She just hadn't found where it was hiding.

Her robe snapped in the wind like a banner, and the thought almost made her laugh. Nova Angeles hadn't flown a banner in years. Nothing here deserved saluting.

This was one dust-bitten town among dozens, scattered across the desert like scraps. They survived on the idea of civilization, even after the world went dry.

Only one place lay rich with water and green space, and she would never touch it. That was for insiders, and the inside was off limits for people like her.

Los Angeles glinted above the dune crests, a silver blemish on the horizon where insiders lived and where they dragged her people when resource quotas ran thin.

"Stop running," the insider said.

Her foot caught on a splintered pallet. She pitched forward and grabbed a crate before it toppled. Fruit split under her fingers. Rot-sweet stench surged up her throat and she gagged.

The insider tipped the brim of his field hat. His other hand rested at the pistol on his hip. "I'll use force if I have to," he said. "Let's not make a mess when there's no need."

You're making a need for it. You people always make a need for it.

He stood apart from the fray, untouched by the grime that clung to every other face. His gray uniform was immaculate, boots spotless, skin unscarred by the sun that carved years into children before they turned ten.

His smile was a practiced curve of control, polished into teeth. Nothing human in it.

She held her ground. Sweat burned her eyes, and she dragged a sleeve across her brow. The sting steadied her. Pain was simpler than fear.

"Please," she said, voice cracking before she could stop it. The sound scraped her pride raw. She'd given him exactly what he wanted. "I don't mean trouble."

The messenger stepped in and pulled his hand off the pistol at his hip. "Carmine Kurier," he said. "You can call me Mr. Kurier."

He offered his hand. She ignored it.

"You're more elusive than most," he said. "And you're not in trouble. Far from it."

His insignia flashed at his collar, gold and three-pronged, ringed in crimson. Metal stamped into authority. Power boiled down to a symbol.

"You're a messenger," she said.

"You state the obvious. We both know how this works."

Unfortunately, I do. The crowd looked away. Eyes slid off her. Shoulders turned. Silence locked into place. No one challenged an insider and lived.

Araya straightened and locked her spine. "My name is Araya Santera," she said. "I have a family."

"A family. My intel doesn't list motherhood as a key attribute to your profile."

Dignity bent but refused to break. "We want to. Very soon."

"I want to be lounging by my pool *very* soon." He scoffed and rolled his eyes. "That won't cut it."

Fingers curled into her palm. Nails bit deep and left crescent moons. "Please," she said. "I beg you. From one person to another."

"No child, no exemption." Mr. Kurier withdrew an envelope from his coat. Plain paper, plain seal. But nothing plain ever came in those envelopes. Nothing merciful either.

"Congratulations," Mr. Kurier said. "TerraLux Minerals has selected you for service."

Araya took the envelope. The paper carried an impossible

weight. Her tongue went dry. She tried to speak, but nothing came.

He kept talking, reciting lines like scripture. *National service... civic obligation of outsiders... the enduring pride of contribution...*

They blurred together like static in an empty room. A broken transmission replaying in a place already forgotten.

"Fifteen years of labor on Mars," he said. "That's the standard term to meet your red lustronium quota and repay your civic debt. The ore powers Los Angeles, and whatever is left trickles to the outer wastelands you call home. In return, you will be granted housing within the grand dome of Los Angeles. Post term, of course. You may designate up to three family members to join you."

"I don't have a family. You made that point clear."

"Perfect. You won't have to choose who stays behind. Lucky you."

Lucky. He meant it. He actually meant it.

The sincerity in his tone twisted her gut. Messengers like him believed they were doing the world a favor. To an insider, the world consisted of the city of Los Angeles and no one else.

"Are you still at the same address registered under your name?"

She nodded. What else could she do? Tears pricked hot, grief burning against fury, but she held them. Not in front of him. Never in front of an insider.

When her voice finally surfaced, it gurgled like mud in her throat. "I hope you feel ashamed."

His face didn't flinch, but civility peeled away, leaving something colder in his tone. "Don't take it personally, outsider. We all have a role. Yours is to serve. Mine is to collect."

"You can walk away." The plea came out exactly as desperate as she meant it to.

He chuckled. "Why would I walk among you in a world built for me to soar above?"

For a long moment, she stood in place.

The plaza churned and shifted, and he vanished into its hustle. Yet the burden remained, a phantom pressure she couldn't shake, proof that freedom here was nothing but a story the broken told themselves to sleep at night.

2

ARAYA

Sandy shacks and tin awnings streaked her peripheral vision as Araya sprinted home. The wind committed assault. It fired grit at her face, and dust devils skittered across the road like they had somewhere important to be.

She dropped her chin, squinted, and pushed harder. Breathing through her nose was a great way to inhale half the street, so she kept her mouth tight and tasted sand anyway.

A cluster of teenagers lounged on the curb ahead, doing that universal teen thing where boredom becomes sport. Here it went by Devil Dodge.

Devil Dodge was simple. Find a dust funnel. Pick a passerby. Accidentally shove them toward the spinning column of pain. Then act personally wounded when the victim failed to say thank you for the exfoliation and berated the little twerps instead.

Araya clocked them, adjusted her path, and crossed to the other side of the street without losing speed. As she passed, she gave them a one-finger review.

They yelled after her. She laughed, because if you couldn't

laugh at dirtbag teens trying to weaponize weather, what could you laugh at?

The sun set. Rays toasted her back like someone held a space heater to her spine. Long shadows shrouded narrow alleys, stretched between shacks and stacked scrap. Araya zigzagged through them anyway—left, right, hard left—until her home snapped into view.

By the time Araya reached home, the only place she lowered her guard, panic leaked away. Not all of it. Just enough to function.

The room was basic: one bed and a wash bucket, and two woven chairs that survived far longer than she expected. Her home smelled like mold. In Nova Angeles, that qualified as aromatherapy.

Nova Angeles lacked plumbing, and Waste Wednesday was born. Everyone hauled their business to the outskirts of town and dumped it in a communal monument of poor infrastructure.

A shit pit. Sewage baked at one hundred and ten degrees. That was a worse smell than mold.

Nova Angeles was poor. But the outsiders who lived there were far from it. Araya certainly felt that way. She had Zaheen. That put her comfortably above empty.

Zaheen Mandisa leaned in the doorway with her arms crossed. She was taller than Araya and didn't bother pretending she wasn't. Her eyes—dark, coffee-brown, and way too observant—raked over Araya like a checklist and landed on every new scrape and bruise.

Her locs were pulled back, threaded with scavenged copper wire and strips of cloth. Half function, half flair. Nova

Angeles was where you made do and made it look good. Zaheen did both. Really good.

"We agreed you lie low," Zaheen said.

Let the birthday festivities begin!

Twenty years old. Two decades in sand. Araya's reward? Insiders chomping at the bit, anxious for their messengers to scoop up lottery drawn addresses. The worst birthday present of all time sat in her robe. "Left pocket."

Zaheen reached for the envelope. "It can't be."

Araya nudged her head against Zaheen's chest and listened. Her heart raced. "Playing the drums in there?"

Zaheen rolled her eyes. "Jokes, even now?"

"Life sucks sometimes, and there's no way out of this. I won't let them take my joy." Araya lifted her chin and kissed her on the lips. A second time for good measure. "Stay strong, Zee. Build a life. Don't wait for me."

"You are my life. Let's run. Far from here."

Araya found her reflection in Zaheen's pooling eyes. "Our reality's sealed."

Zaheen grabbed her hips, and Araya blushed. "You won't even try?"

"This isn't forever." Outsiders shipped to Mars rarely came back. Those who did ended up in body bags or with severe PTSD.

"It should've been me," Zaheen said. She wiped tears. "I wish it were."

Damn it, Zee. I'm trying to hold it together.

"That's sand rot," Araya said instead. She snatched the envelope and crumpled it. She opened her palm and glared at the purgatory paper. "They come at dawn."

Zaheen snatched the crumpled sheet and flung it across

the room. "You want to know what's sand rot? Imbecile insiders who want to control our lives. That's sand rot." Zaheen grabbed her satchel. Drawers flew open. A water flask went in. Spare clothes. A cloak. She slipped on her boots.

"No." Araya grabbed her wrist. "Zaheen. Stop."

"They don't get to take you," Zaheen said. "We leave tonight."

Araya shook her head. "They'll find me. They always do. Hell, they found me today."

Zaheen met her eyes. Her chest rose and fell like it was arguing with gravity. "Then we fight."

"Fists and sticks are no match for rifles. If we run, they execute you for interference. Not on my watch. I'm going, because it keeps you safe."

Reality sank. Zaheen dropped the satchel and slid off her boots. "We've always survived together."

"When I'm back we'll reunite. Find a better path inside."

Zaheen scoffed. "I refuse to let our future child be an outcast for spoiled insiders to laugh at. Outsiders who work in Los Angeles are second class citizens."

"If our kid sleeps at night without the worry of choking on dust, let them be an outcast. Who gives a shit." Araya sighed. "Look...our circumstances box us in. But boxes have corners, and we'll figure out how to cut a few. I'll be back before the standard fifteen. Somehow, someway."

Zaheen stared at her like she was trying to decide whether that was wisdom or stubbornness.

Araya took her hands. Soft as sagebrush leaves. "You're pissed. I'm sure as hell pissed, but don't burn rage today. Save it. Aim it. Let it be fuel for the future."

"Fuel," Zaheen echoed, bitter. "Yeah. That's what everything is to them."

She had me there.

"Araya, promise me something."

"Anything." Araya meant it.

"When you're back, we'll change the world."

"I cross my heart"—Araya traced an X over Zaheen's chest and pushed her on the bed— "and hope to die. Let's not waste our last night."

Araya went in for another kiss.

3

VICTOR

Victor Kol grinned.

From his rooftop jacuzzi, Los Angeles glowed beneath glass and steel. The artificial sky held a flawless sunset—perfect gradients, calibrated warmth. No smog. No dust. The dome worked exactly as designed.

The city was sealed. An endless party for people who preferred not to think about what waited beyond the walls. Exactly his kind of party.

The jets hammered his back in steady pulses. He sank until the water reached his shoulders. Cold armrests bit into his forearms. He raised his martini and sipped like he had all the time in the world.

Steam drifted across the terrace garden, briefly smearing the city into abstraction. Mist clung to his beard—dark hair threaded with silver—and beaded along the sharp line of his jaw. Victor had the kind of face people trusted when he smiled and feared when he didn't. Tonight, it stayed neutral. Satisfaction didn't require theatrics.

A mild breeze stirred the palms and ferns lining the terrace. Imported, of course. Salvaged from what little remained of the equatorial rainforests. Their leaves whispered, a sound that reminded him of balance sheets and shipping manifests and how close those ecosystems had come to complete liquidation.

Below him, his city spread outward in clean geometry. Streets lit like circuitry, towers rose, and from this height, it looked like a metallic old growth forest. That illusion pleased him.

Every street, structure, and glowing artery of commerce traced back to TerraLux Minerals. His empire. Proof that extraction didn't destroy the world for those who bent to what it was transforming into.

In Victor Kol's mind, the design was simple: live your life around his wishes, and he'd return the favor. That was the line he liked to use. His loyalists understood it perfectly, and they cashed it in for penthouses and fancy greenhouses in a world made of sand.

The click of heels cut through Victor's quiet.

He sank lower in the jacuzzi until the water rode up to his shoulders. "It's impolite to disturb a man's peace," he said without turning.

His aide stopped at the edge of the terrace.

On second glance, she was new. He cycled through staff fast. The good ones learned the rules and stayed invisible. Most couldn't handle what Victor demanded.

He studied her without meeting her eyes. "Care to join me?"

"Sir." She kept her gaze down. "Director Sorev insisted it was urgent."

"Director Sorev can insist all he wants." Victor finally found her viridian eyes. "Put the phone down and come."

The phone rang again.

"It's Director Sorev," she said. "I shouldn't get in the way."

Victor plucked the phone from her hand and flicked his fingers toward the penthouse like he was shooing a fly. "Go."

She disappeared inside.

Victor put the phone to his ear. "What could possibly be so important?"

"Sir, we have a security breach."

Victor exhaled through his nose and rubbed his temples, as if the gesture could scrub stupidity from the world. Director Sorev wasn't even on the same planet and still managed to be irritating.

Victor had a system for irritants. The worst ones got stationed on Perihelion—far enough away to be useful, miserable enough to be motivated. If they proved their worth, they earned a reward that consisted of a parcel of green and a permanent address inside Los Angeles. If they didn't, they stayed out there until they stopped being a problem.

Director Sorev was pushing any chance of return. He was becoming less a colleague and more a recurring defect, a scab resurfacing no matter how many times Victor tried to patch it.

Victor vaulted out of the water and paced. Wet footprints darkened the expensive tile. "I'm starting to think you want to stay on Mars forever."

"Sir, the situation is violent. An uprising has formed in tunnel three."

Victor pinched the bridge of his nose. Incompetence.

Pure, expensive incompetence. "Am I to do your job for you?"

"Absolutely not, sir."

"What's your plan?"

"All three tunnels are accounted for. We've sealed One and Two and returned the outsiders to their barracks. Everyone in Three is locked inside until we can pacify them."

Victor almost laughed. *If everything were accounted for, you wouldn't be calling me.*

"You know what sits under those tunnels," Victor said. "Red lustronium is the reason this place has light and air and a stable temperature. Every shard we pull from Mars buys us another day. Perihelion must not fall."

His voice remained calm. Calm carried further for the anxious types like Director Sorev. "The grid drinks it. Without red lustronium, the artificial sun flickers. The shields thin. And we all get sand."

Silence sunk in.

"I don't tolerate loose ends, Director Sorev. Insiders are gods among peasants. Remind the workers in Tunnels One and Two of their place."

"How would you like that done, sir?"

Victor leaned on the railing and lowered his voice. "Tunnel three will never learn. Expendable bodies are everywhere in the dunes. We will find more to send your way. Exterminate the strikers."

Sorev's reply crackled through the line—agreement, excuses, Victor didn't care which—and the call dissolved into static.

Victor lowered himself back into the jacuzzi. The water

curled around him, warm and perfumed. A luxury designed to calm the nervous system. It didn't work.

He stared out at his city. Built from ambition, engineering, and a carefully maintained narrative. He remembered the first days of the dome, when it was nothing but scaffolding and raw metal ribs against the sky. He walked the unfinished rim with a harness cinched at his waist and a line of engineers behind him. They whispered about infrastructure worry. Thermal cycling. Cooling failures. The manpower required to keep the dome operational.

He heard every word and fired all of them. Fear was contagious, and he would not bow to it.

Even now, years later, the same problem resurfaced. The system only looked stable until the moment it wasn't. One pocket of workers deciding they'd rather die angry on Mars than live obedient, and the illusion would shatter.

Victor sank deeper.

The dome could not falter. Not because it was beautiful. Because Los Angeles was load-bearing—in every sense that mattered. Without blood and ore, he too would be floating in an ocean of sand.

4

ARAYA

Nerves churned in Araya's stomach, upsetting what should have been a peaceful Sunday morning. She loved Sundays. Their simplicity was the point.

She never went far on Sundays. Long ago, she and Zaheen agreed it was their time: no scavenge runs, no water hauls, no bartering. Just the two of them with whatever they'd managed to gather during the week.

She'd sleep in, and wake to Zaheen's comfort at her side. They'd walk the town's outskirts and sit on the dune crests above Nova Angeles, imagining what the land had been like before it turned to sand.

Dreaming was what Araya did best. She held on to it; somehow, she always found a pocket of peace. Just not today.

Light filtered through the thatch in fractured beams, catching dust adrift like a small constellation. Heat pressed from all sides, creeping across Araya's irritated skin, beading sweat in her palms, loosening her grip on Zaheen's hand.

Their fingers tangled, tight as roots under scorched soil. They sat on the edge of the bed—splintered wood, a thin mattress barely keeping the steel from biting their legs. Araya rocked forward, then back, caught between now and the door that would take her away.

She stared at the thin stripe of daylight beneath the door, watching each passing silhouette slide across. "Zee, one of those shapes is going to take me. Promise you won't forget how much I love you."

"I'll never forget," she said, and Araya believed her.

Zaheen reached into her pocket and revealed a gold-inlaid necklace, coiled in her palm. Its pendant was a shard of desert glass, cloudy along the perimeter and clear at the center, as if it still carried a trace of the sandstorm that shaped it.

Araya was at a loss. Untarnished metal was as rare as a full cistern in the desert.

You never fail to surprise me, Zee. Endless surprises... this won't be our end. "It's stunning. How did you—?"

"Happy birthday, my love." Zaheen clasped the chain around her neck. "You're beautiful."

Araya tucked the pendant under her robes. "A piece of our world to carry with me."

Fists rattled the door, and Araya went still, like prey under a hunter's eye. Her heart lurched. For a breath, she couldn't feel her hands.

Zaheen pressed her lips to Araya's cheek. Araya held the warmth like the last light on the dunes before a long night, trying to memorize the shape of it, the feel, the way Zaheen's breath brushed her skin. Zaheen didn't pull away until the door burst open.

Two insiders stormed in, silver-armored, batons out. "Araya Santera," one of them demanded.

She jumped off the bed, and blockaded Zaheen from view. "You're looking for me."

Mr. Kurier slid in between his guards. He was pale in a way that didn't happen naturally out here—insider pale. The kind you get from spending your life under a dome while other people do the sunburning for you.

"There's my newest employee." Mr. Kurier said. "How are you this morning?"

"Worse now," Araya said. She eyed him and glanced at the guards. "These tin cans your protection in case I decide to heat you up?"

Mr. Kurier ignored her question and landed on Zaheen. "You must be so proud of her."

"We had tomorrow," Zaheen said. She stepped out of Araya's shadow. "You're here to steal it."

He lifted a brow, unsure whether to find her amusing or pathetic. "I checked your record, Ms. Mandisa. You'll be twenty next year. If you're lucky, I'll pull your address again and you can join Ms. Santera on the adventure of a lifetime."

His smirk curdled milk. "Or...shall I say fifteen years."

Zaheen scoffed. "All you bring is misery. All of you insiders are the same filth that I find on the bottom of my shoe."

"Misery is this sand pit you sleep in." Mr. Kurier rolled his eyes and checked the time. "Ms. Santera it's time to depart."

Araya pulled Zaheen close. Everything dropped out of scope. Just Zaheen. The rise and fall of her chest. The smell of sun-dried linen and woodsmoke caught in her hair. Skin against skin. "Until we meet again, my love."

The guards yanked her away. Araya forced a smile in case

this would be the last time Zaheen saw her face. She wanted Zaheen to remember her joy, not terror.

"Enough," Mr. Kurier said. He slammed the door shut, and separated Araya from her center of gravity.

The guards flanked her like they expected Araya to sprout wings and fly away. She slowed on purpose. Not a lot. Just to be annoying. They answered with the old reliable two-person shove. Left hand, right hand, like they'd practiced it in a seminar titled *Escorting Difficult Outsiders 101*.

She stumbled, caught herself, and decelerated again.

Sand clung to everything—her robe, her lashes, the polished armor of the guards. Even the messenger wasn't spared. He sneezed, then scowled at the dust.

Where are the Devil Dodge teens when you need them?

Araya pictured it anyway. Two burly guards. One innocent-looking dust funnel. A tragic misunderstanding involving a quick push and momentum. She almost smiled.

"Disgusting place," Mr. Kurier said, sniffling. "How do you people breathe?"

Araya hardened her face. But inside, something bright and petty flickered. She enjoyed his dismay.

They passed peddlers dragging fabric carts with one good wheel, and people clutching empty sacks, still searching like persistence alone might conjure food out of sand. Nobody stopped to watch Araya. Hunger didn't pause for the taken.

By the time they reached the outskirts, the market's noise faded to a whisper. The alleys opened into barren land. Araya pulled her robe tight as wind slapped grit across her face. Behind her, everything she knew was swallowed by haze.

Beyond the dunes, warped by heat, the dome of Los

Angeles floated on the horizon. A pale arc of steel. In the right light, it glowed like a second sun.

She and Zaheen had run this way once. Teenagers with bad judgment and too much hope. They chased the train, legs pumping, sand spitting, and screamed at a thousand tons of steel for it to stop.

It didn't.

The engine thundered past and the wind off the cars slapped them sideways. When the last carriage cleared, they just stood there, bent over, sucking air, hands still locked.

Now the dunes rose like fossilized surf—wave after wave, frozen mid-crash. And perched on the highest ridge sat the train.

A chain of metal cars flashed in the sun, each one clipped to the next. The engine belched smoke from its chimney in a smear that dirtied the sky.

This was the artery between Los Angeles and Nova Angeles. People went on the train. Resources came out. Araya spent most of her life trying to make sure she never got close enough to count the bolts.

The guards marched her to the front car.

Inside, the air was stale and metallic, like hot coins. Only a few outsiders sat slumped in the seats, eyes gone flat, bodies arranged like someone paused them mid-cry. Each one had a messenger at their side—upright, alert, watching with the patient attention of a person guarding cargo.

Mr. Kurier took his seat and crossed one leg over the other. "The escorts are staying. They have more of you to catch."

Araya took the window seat and watched the dunes. She prayed to see sand again.

The train lurched, and metal screamed as the wheels found the rails. Nova Angeles smeared into haze and dust. The town thinned to memory.

"Do you enjoy this? Taking people from their families?"

Mr. Kurier shrugged in the window's reflection. "It's a job. Everyone needs a job."

"You ruin lives for a living." She couldn't bring herself to face him.

He flagged the attendant and ordered a drink. "It's business, Ms. Santera."

Araya held her tongue. Words were liabilities. She watched the dunes and daydreamed of Zaheen instead.

5

ZAHEEN

The door groaned on rusted hinges and Zaheen slipped into Holly's bar, as if it wanted no part of the grief coming through. She pushed back her hood—sweat-matted hair stuck to her temples, sunburn brightening her cheekbones. Her shoulders sagged beneath a weight she could barely hold.

The place reeked of stale liquor and despair. Dust drifted in the air like smoke after a fire. Alcoves carved into the crumbling brick walls held the ghosts of lives unraveled, stitched back together, and unraveled again. The mahogany counter was chipped and stained, dark grooves worn deep by trembling hands, desperate fists, and time.

Zaheen sank onto a stool and traced the scars in the wood as if she could read the stories carved there.

Behind the kitchen door came a thud of hurried footsteps, and a sharp gasp. Holly burst through, one hand pressed to her chest, breath caught somewhere between a wheeze and a shout.

"Zee, you can't sneak in like that," Holly said, laughing, but scolding. "You're going to kill me one of these days."

She turned away, rummaging through cabinets stacked with mismatched glassware. Holly's sun-browned jittery hands were quick. She pulled down a copper stein, its handle carved with curling vines and set it in front of Zaheen. "The usual? Insiders brought in a new shipment of fruit scraps last night."

Though Holly paused and crossed her arms, the sleeves of her faded bone-colored robes tightened over muscles shaped from years of hauling crates in and out of the bar. "What's wrong?"

Everything. There isn't a part of me that isn't breaking.

Zaheen opened her mouth, but nothing came. She rubbed her temples; her heartbeat fluttered like a trapped bird against her ribs.

"Araya." She forced back the image of guards tearing her away. Mr. Kurier's grin was the cherry on top of a terrible sundae she never wanted to taste again. "She's just... gone."

"Dome dirtbags," Holly said. Frustration etched fresh lines across her weathered face. A quick puff lifted her ginger curls into a fiery halo. "You're not going to be taken. I won't let that happen."

Zaheen gripped Holly's outstretched hand, anchoring herself in the steady presence she'd long relied on. Holly had always been there—when TerraLux soldiers killed Zaheen's parents for refusing Mars relocation, and in the late nights after, when she all but raised her. Holly was the grandmother Zaheen never had.

Holly laid her other hand over Zaheen's. "I'm so sorry, Zee. Truly."

"I can't shake the feeling that I'm useless."

Holly lifted a blood orange from a wooden crate. "When

my son was taken twenty-two years ago, I believed he'd come back."

She squeezed half the orange, as if wringing the last drops from a storm. Red juice ran down her fingers and across the counter. "But as I've gotten older, I've realized how foolish I was to believe the lies Victor Kol spews."

Holly drove the knife into the remaining half. Zaheen could almost see her picturing Kol at the other end of the blade. Holly set a thin slice on the stein's rim and slid the drink to Zaheen. "We're disposable to him. Don't you ever forget that."

Zaheen wrapped both hands around the stein and took a sip, letting the bittersweet taste sit on her tongue. She set it on the coaster, and a soft clink broke the quiet.

"I didn't know you had a son." She'd always felt close to Holly, but that was a large piece to keep hidden. She looked down at her drink and let the question go. Some truths were better left alone.

"This is really good," Zaheen said, smile faint but there.

"Of course it is. I made it." Holly wiped down the counter with the rag tucked at her waist. "I never had a reason to talk about my son. Thinking of him only reminds me of what I didn't do. Which is why I won't repeat those mistakes with you."

She wrung the rag out and tossed the juice-soaked cloth into a nearby hamper. "You can't repeat my mistakes either. Victor Kol *will* come for you next. He comes for all the young ones. I was lucky. When I was your age, there was no lottery. She won't come back unless we find a way ourselves."

Impossible. Even for you, Holly. Zaheen's eyelids dropped

like heavy drapes. The thought of Araya trapped on another world pressed her flat.

"I'm grateful you want to help, but we can't bring her back on our own. We're two specks in a desert," she said. Zaheen drained her drink in one pull.

Holly slammed her fist on the counter, and Zaheen flinched. "Where's your fight? Are you willing to sacrifice?"

"You know the answer." Zaheen couldn't summon anger at Holly for doubting her.

"There are more of us, Zee. Many more. I can start conversations and make introductions. No promises. But a chance. That's what I can offer."

Possibilities sparked through Zaheen's mind, dangerous and exhilarating and bound for trouble. Holly watched her and set the stein down more gently than before.

"You remember what I've told you about the uprisings that ended the old wars between Nova Angeles and Los Angeles," Holly said. "One town after another burned until Los Angeles offered the one taking system. One body instead of entire streets. They tell it like we gave up. They leave out that some of us keep going."

On any other day, Zaheen would've smiled. Holly only ever sounded like this when she was about to drag out her favorite story.

"I was young, maybe a little younger than you," Holly said. "Our people of the Sand Alliance were desperate and hungry."

Holly's eyes flicked toward the door as if the old memory stood at the entry. "That year, the trains ran heavier. Supplies from Mars, extra rations for insiders, new tech for the dome. We studied the schedules for weeks. One night, when the guards were lazy from the heat, and the dunes were shifting just right, we made our move."

She tapped her chest with two fingers. "We buried metal plates under the sand, right along the tracks. When the train passed, the ground buckled, and the first car tilted just enough to scare the guards into jumping ship. Not a soul died, but the train came down like a beast falling to its knees."

Holly chuckled at her memory, and Zaheen wished she could see it too. "We broke open the storage cars. Grain, dried fruit, water tablets, even medicine. Months of supplies. We hauled it all back before dawn. Fed the whole town. Kept people alive."

Her voice softened. "They called it an uprising. The Sand Alliance called it never ending rebellion."

She sat back, shoulders heavy but unbowed. "We're still here, old and tired, but not broken. Never broken."

Zaheen's mouth set into a hard line. The task loomed, but the image of Araya in her arms kept fear at bay. "When do we start?"

Holly grinned. "Right now, of course."

6

ARAYA

Araya watched the dunes slide past the window until they didn't. One second, they were there—rolling, peach-lit, familiar—and the next they were gone.

Darkness took over.

Time stretched. Seconds blurred into minutes. However she measured it, the answer was the same. Zaheen was farther away now.

The window became a mirror.

It can't be. She can't be.

A woman stared back. Hollow-eyed. Too thin. Big eyebags. Bony fingers. Like someone who'd been surviving instead of living and was losing that battle.

In Nova Angeles, warped glass had been kind. It softened her edges, kissed her skin with borrowed light, and let her pretend she looked healthy off rations of old scrap. This window showed her every sharp angle and quiet loss.

The lights snapped on. The reflection vanished, replaced by concrete rushing past. A tunnel. It had to be.

The train jolted. Her head smacked the seat and pain

rippled down her spine. The engine groaned, slowed, and finally stopped. Cold air leaked through the seams, crawled up her sleeves, and settled.

Mr. Kurier clicked his harness free and stood. "Shall we?"

Something cinched tight in Araya's chest. She hadn't known what an insider would feel like up close, but she hadn't pictured *this*—the casual, polished detachment. To him, she was a parcel with legs.

His smirk didn't help. It scraped at her nerves, right up there with the static hiss of the train's speakers. The PA system leaked a buzzing drone that drilled into her skull and settled behind her eyes, where it bloomed into a dull headache.

"I don't have much choice."

"True," he said. Mr. Kurier stepped into the aisle. "A path to a better life awaits."

And so does the path from my fist to your nose.

He walked ahead. She followed, because the alternative involved batons and beatdowns.

The corridor swallowed them. Then another corridor swallowed that corridor. Same stone, same gray, same straight lines that went on long enough to make her wonder if the train had secretly delivered her into an architecture student's depression spiral.

Gray blocks. Gray blocks. Gray blocks.

At regular intervals, a door would interrupt the monotony. Each door came with a guard posted beside it, baton resting in their hand like a comfort object.

Noise seeped through the seams as they passed. A muffled sob. A ragged cough. Someone shouting a name, over and over, and went unanswered.

The sounds stacked on top of each other, layering into a thick, vibrating hum of panic. It wasn't one person's fear. It was *everyone's*, collected and recycled until the hallway had its own pulse of misery.

They hit a checkpoint. One every twenty seconds and they walked for ten minutes.

Scanners hummed. Red lights blinked. Systems logged her in with little chirps and beeps, like she was baggage getting tagged at a terminal.

At last, they reached the facility entrance. The doors hissed open, and the building inhaled a reluctant breath. Araya pictured something out of an insider brochure. Tall columns. Polished floors. A motivational slogan about *Opportunity* stamped into the wall in tasteful font.

Nope. The walls flaked, and the corners were rust streaked. She inhaled a breath of mildew and hot machinery.

Lights scrubbed shadows out of corners and left nowhere for anything—bugs, lies, or people—to hide. Araya squinted and immediately missed the dunes.

Cameras clicked as they pivoted, soft little ticks that said, *We see you. We're logging you. Try something cute.*

But it wasn't the lights or the cameras that hit her. It was the people. They stood in rigid lines. Backs straight. Eyes forward.

Their clothes matched hers. Threadbare scraps, torn seams, fabric that had survived purely out of spite. Some were barefoot, and Araya was lucky to have shoes. Their faces looked sun-worn and dirt-caked. The harsh reality of the outside.

These people, her people, had been stripped down to essentials. And then stripped again.

Araya never saw so many empty faces in one place. The worst part was recognizing the expression. *Oh. That's me.*

Mr. Kurier stopped at a red line painted across the floor. "This is where I leave you."

Araya froze. She hated his smirk and pompous voice. But once he walked away, this stopped being transitional. There would be no one left in the building who knew her name.

Something in her face must've cracked, because Mr. Kurier sighed.

"Good luck, Araya. I mean it. I hope to see you on the other side."

For half a second, she almost believed him.

"We'll need more lower-class citizens in Los Angeles to maintain hierarchical civility."

There it was. Mr. Kurier fully confirmed. The man she intended to uppercut someday, if fate and basic survival instincts ever aligned.

He turned and disappeared into the flow of uniforms and messengers unloading the next shipment of outsiders. She tried to follow, but he dissolved into motion and bodies and noise.

"Outsider!" A guard jabbed a finger at her. "In line, Now."

She complied. Rules were gravity. Ignore them and plummet.

The man ahead of her turned in line with wide eyes. "Have you seen my son?"

She shook her head.

"Please," he said.

"I don't know you," Araya said.

The man grabbed the collar of her robes. "Have you seen him?"

A baton slammed the man's back.

Araya clenched her jaw. Every instinct screamed *do something*. Instincts were terrible planners for the future of her survival. She remained still.

"No talking! Face forward!"

The man folded to the floor. The baton fell again. And again. And again. By the fourth strike, Araya stared at the ground. By the fifth, she shut her eyes.

When it ended, the guard dragged the man away. His body left a thin red streak, like someone had tested a paintbrush on the floor and decided against the color.

Araya relinquished the sight. Locked it up. Told herself she hadn't seen anything.

Zaheen would've helped. Or at least refused to look away. Araya didn't let herself imagine the look Zaheen would give her now.

Thirty minutes passed. The line shrank. Eventually, Araya stood at the front.

A security officer waved without interest. "Move through."

Araya stepped under the arch of the body scanner. A red laser snapped on and crawled over her in a slow, methodical sweep—head to toe, toe to head. She crossed to the other side and waited.

The officer behind the console typed on her computer, fingers hammering keys in a staccato clatter. "Araya Santera. From the Nova Angeles settlement?"

"Yes, ma'am," Araya said. Though the woman looked barely older than she was. Her hair was neatly braided. Her uniform was pressed and spotless, like it had never met dust in its life.

And still, the telltale stuff was there up close. The tired pinch at the corners of her eyes. The stiffness in her shoulders. The posture of someone who'd learned the fastest way to survive was to do exactly what she was told, exactly when she was told.

"Proceed through the door and remove all clothing."

Araya nodded because nodding was what bodies did here. She wasn't a person inside this facility. She was inventory. A scan result. A compliance box waiting for a checkmark. A life being peeled down to the parts that could be counted for someone else's profit.

7

ARAYA

The door shut behind Araya.

The room was barely larger than a storage locker. White walls. Hard light. Nowhere to hide. In one corner sat a bin with its lid half open, vomiting fabric onto the floor. Some stained dark enough that guessing felt unwise. Others were shredded, torn clean through, surely an outsider who tested the limits of disobedience.

The intercom crackled. *"Remove all clothing and place it in the designated bin."*

Araya tilted her head. A tiny lens winked at her from a seam near the ceiling.

Her breath tightened. In. Out. In again. The next breath stalled, and pressure settled in her chest like a misaligned gear.

Araya wiped her face with the back of her hand. *Enough.* Tears were inefficient.

She unfastened her shirt one button at a time. Fabric slid from her shoulders. Pants followed. She folded each piece and placed them in the bin, careful, as if order still mattered. She suspected she wouldn't see any of it again.

Bare feet met cold tile. She stood rigid, arms locked at her sides.

"That includes jewelry."

Her fingers found the chain at her throat. Instinct screamed at her to curl around it. Protect it. Protect the small, stupid hope hanging from her neck.

She slid her fingers under the clasp and worked it loose. The chain pooled into her palm. It looked harmless. That was the problem. Outsiders didn't get to keep harmless things.

She dropped her only possession into the bin. Her birthday gift landed with a soft, final clink against whatever rags and histories lived down there.

"Thank you for your cooperation. Step forward and enter the door in front of you."

The door ahead split open, and Araya stepped onto a rubber conveyer belt. Her foot skated. She grabbed a handrail before gravity finished the job and introduced her face to industrial flooring.

Tiled walls closed her in, and vents along the ceiling exhaled. A chemical spray slapped her, and her eyes watered on impact. The mist clung to her skin in a thin, oily layer. She lifted a hand to wipe it away, and the ceiling opened. Water slammed down in sheets.

Araya sucked in air and got punished for it. The cold punched straight into her lungs. Her body responded with instant betrayal: goosebumps, chattering teeth, locked muscles, and frozen fingers.

She wrapped her arms around herself. It didn't help. The belt carried her forward through humiliation.

She tried not to think about warmth. She failed. The sun on her face. The scratch of her robe. The bite of sand against her ankles. Zaheen's hands. Zaheen's voice. Memory stung worse than icy water.

The conveyor shuddered and slowed. The spray thinned, turned patchy, and stopped. Araya blinked water from her lashes, and regained vision.

Another doorway waited ahead. Panels slid upward from floor to ceiling.

"Step into the designated changing area. Dry off and put on your uniform."

The next room looked like a copy-paste error. Same white walls and sterile quiet. This one had a towel and a clothes rack. Araya grabbed the towel and wrapped it around herself.

She dressed fast. Black pants. Snug but flexible. A long-sleeved shirt that fit like it had been measured off her without asking permission. Socks. Boots. They slid on easily. Last came a gray vest.

The door slid open, and a guard stood on the other side. "Step forward, outsider. Follow me."

Araya slid her hands into the vest pockets and gave a small nod.

The hallway opened into a theater. Rows of outsiders filled seats in identical uniforms as her own. Araya passed hunched backs and vacant faces, eyes that lifted for half a second and snapped away.

The guard stopped at the nearest empty seat. "Sit. No talking."

Araya lowered herself and obeyed.

The woman beside her sat coiled, bracing for delayed impact. Her skin, a deep polished dusk, softened the harsh overhead light instead of throwing it back. Short coils framed her face in a tight ring, and her eyes never stopped moving.

She tracked every guard like a variable in an equation that could change without warning.

Her fingers twisted against each other in small, restless knots, giving fear nowhere to settle. She leaned forward, planted her elbows on her knees, and stared at the screen as if focus alone could protect her.

"The name's Skye Amaru," she said without turning. "Watch the guards. They're looking for a reason."

"I'm Araya Santera. If they find one, it might be their last."

Skye flicked a glance down the aisle. Araya followed it just in time to see a broad figure drop into the seat on her other side. The guard repeated the same flat instructions and marched off without waiting for acknowledgment.

"I'm from Nova Angeles," Araya said.

"I'm south of that," Skye said.

"Deadlands?"

"I was alive there."

"Sorry," Araya said, and winced. "Force of habit. Insiders drill those silly names into us until they stick."

Skye held out a calloused hand. "Let's stick together. Whatever's coming, it won't be easy. You've got spunk. I like that."

Araya hesitated. Pacts meant obligations. Her hand hovered, but she reached out. "A dune's stronger than a single grain."

Skye shook. "Flowing sand can be deadly in the right element."

Araya opened her mouth to answer and got interrupted by a tap on her shoulder.

The stocky man smiled at her. "Dante. I'm from the old

refinery blocks. Northwest corner of Nova Angeles. I fix ships. The dome, too. Pretty much whatever breaks. It's a hell of a job."

"You're telling me because..."

He leaned in. "I don't break easily. I'd be useful to have around. Another grain in your growing dune."

The screen burst on. Patriotic music boomed into the room. Araya plugged both ears but removed her hands just as fast when the guards marched by.

The drums beat over footage of collapse. Bombs tumbling end-over-end. Buildings folding in on themselves. Soldiers sprinting through smoke so thick it looked solid. Corpses scattered across blackened ground.

The music swelled. The audience leaned forward together, a synchronized flinch. Spellbound.

Araya leaned back. They wanted awe. Fear. Unity. She gave them posture and silence.

Onscreen, the sky went orange. Fire rolled across coastlines. Triumphant fanfare blared. World leaders in spotless white suits smiled in the aftermath. They shook hands in front of a dome planted in the middle of a desert. Los Angeles.

The video jumped to Mars. Laborers with grit on their faces grinned for the camera while they shoveled glowing red ore into carts.

Red Lustronium. The narrator said. *The lifeblood of society.*

Araya tapped Dante's shoulder. He jolted, and dragged both hands down his face, hard, like he could wipe the propaganda off his brain with friction.

"Have you thought it over?" he asked. "I don't have anyone."

"We'll have to protect each other," she said. "Where they're taking us... even that might not be enough."

"Sounds like here." The narrator's voice on the screen tried to drown Dante out with glory and brass and promises, but the words landed anyway.

Araya hated how accurate Dante was.

"I don't expect either of you to protect me. And I doubt you'll need mine. But we all need something. A way out. What we build now could be our shot. If escape's even possible."

"Together then." She caught Skye's attention. "He's with us. Dante."

Dante smiled.

Skye answered with a quick dip of her chin.

The screen blinked and the propaganda gave up, replaced by training videos. Araya forced her focus forward.

A worker swung a pickaxe into red stone. The caption listed a quota. A diagram of the human body was displayed. Common bruise sites. Another showed burns stippled along a forearm. Another explained how to wrap a bandage. How to splint a leg. How to spot lung strain from dust and fumes.

Rules followed. Curfews. Chains of command. What to say. What not to say. Punishments, spelled out with the same tone as the bandage tutorial.

The screen went black. The overhead lights snapped on. Araya blinked like she'd been pulled out of sleep.

At the far end of the theater, a steel door groaned open.

Desert sunlight poured in and hit Araya. The glare bleached the room, turning faces into silhouettes and her eyes watered. A hot gust of grit showered her with sand. It brushed her skin and for half a second her body tried to relax, muscle memory recognizing home.

Guards stepped in unison from the perimeter in clock-work formation. No batons now. Rifles at their sides, casual as tools.

A command rang out across the room. "All outsiders, proceed to the transport zone."

Araya jumped out of her chair and obeyed, because that's what she did when armed insiders commanded instructions.

8

ARAYA

Araya reached for her hood and grabbed air.

This wasn't the outside she knew. Her people belonged to sand and heat and smog. To grit that stuck to skin and lungs. After the spotless uniforms and the insiders' refrigerated grip, she wasn't sure she belonged anywhere.

The thought broke apart under a low buzz covered in clouds.

The sound swelled, a mix of vibration and pressure. It crawled through her ribs and teeth as a shadow slid across the sand. A silver cruiser dropped from haze—flat-bodied, wings locked wide, eight engines hammered in flawless synchronization.

The ship settled. Its belly split open with a metallic cough. Panels clattered. Vents hissed. Hatches snapped open one by one. Ladders slammed down and kicked sand in miniature explosions.

"Everyone aboard the light cruiser!" a guard shouted.

Araya stuck to her rules. No eye contact. No hesitation. And quiet compliance. She ran with the pack. Araya was quick enough to disappear in the group, but not fast enough to lead.

Skye and Dante kept pace on either side as they jogged for the ladders.

Araya saw plenty of machines. She'd seen the refinery's hulks from a distance, heard their guts grind and hiss when the wind carried sound the right way. But this was something else. Outsiders didn't build things that hovered. Outsiders built things that broke.

She doubted anyone from Nova Angeles, besides those on Mars, had ever set foot on anything like this. Not her. Not Skye. Not even Dante, with his refinery know-how. Their world ran on rusted tracks and wagons pulled by starving horses.

She reached the ladder. The sand under her boots pulsed in broken waves from the engines, as if the ground couldn't decide whether it was solid or liquid. She curled her toes anyway, as if she detected the dunes through the rubber.

This might be the last time she felt sand, and she hated herself for thinking of it like a goodbye.

If it was her last step on the sand, it wouldn't be the last for her people. Nova Angeles thrived under burning skies, fought for water, choked on dust, and somehow persisted on a diet of stubbornness and hope.

A guard barked for the line to move. Araya grabbed the ladder. The metal was hot and slick against her palms. She climbed, each rung lifting her farther from the dunes, from Nova Angeles, and everything that had ever made sense.

When she pulled herself into the belly of the ship, the desert vanished.

Inside, the air was thin and frigid, cooled by pumps

cycling coolant through the hull. Outsiders packed into narrow rows, backs rigid, eyes too wide. Crates lined the aisle, bolted to the floor, their metal skins scarred and dented by years of hard use.

Araya didn't need labels to know what they held. Food. Medicine. Tools. Supplies for insiders. Always for insiders. Never for people like her.

Two rows back, she spotted Dante and Skye and slid into the seat beside them.

Sweat darkened Dante's brow. "I hate light cruisers, and anything that leaves the ground."

Skye yanked the safety strap over her shoulders. "You work on these things, and you hate them?"

"Never flown. Fixed plenty," Dante said. "Once an insider made me test an engine. I had to crawl under while it was still glowing hot." He swallowed, eyes locked forward like looking at Skye would make it real again. "One wrong move and the exhaust would've taken my face off."

His fingers cinched around the edge of his seat. "Metal over my head. Fire at my back. That was enough insider tech for me."

It's still safer than where we're going, Araya wanted to say.

One by one, the ladders retracted into the cruiser's belly. The hatches sealed with a heavy clunk. The windows slammed shut and sliced away the desert glare and replaced it with dim red strips along the floor.

The ship rumbled. Vibration ran up the walls and into Araya's legs. Bolts groaned in their sockets. The floor shuddered. Crates creaked as they settled harder into their clamps.

The cruiser woke up, and Araya had no way off.

A jolt hit the cabin. A chorus of screams followed as the

whole world tilted. Horizontal became vertical. Her heart sought to stay in the dunes while the rest of her body went with the ship. Gravity slid sideways and snapped into a new direction like a bad decision made permanent.

In the dark, with the engines howling and her body pressed hard into the seat, her mind did what it always did when it had nowhere left to go.

It ran to Zaheen.

The memories came in flashes, choppy and imperfect. Zaheen's forehead against Araya's. Her birthday night where they promised to change the world when she returned. Araya clung to those moments. A lifeline didn't have to be pretty. It just had to hold.

The cruiser tore upward until the shaking eased and the roar steadied into a constant, hungry hum. Then the windows slid open again.

Araya expected more desert. Instead, she found an endless void—black and bottomless—stretching past anything she'd ever known.

"Our planet used to be such vibrant greens and blues," Skye said. She chuckled and nudged her chin toward Dante, whose eyes were screwed shut. "Poor guy's missing the view."

"I've seen better," Araya said, a smile sneaking its way onto her face before she could stop it.

"I always wanted to see space," Skye said. Her gaze locked on the stars like they might blink back. "Just... not like this. Happy belated birthday to me, I guess."

"When's the big day?"

"June fifth. Twenty-nine seventy-nine."

Araya laughed. "You're kidding. Twins."

"Almost triplets," Dante said, cracking one eye open. "June sixth."

"Baby brother," Araya said, and this time the smile stuck.

She turned back to the window. Earth lay colorless and broken. A planet reduced to a bruise.

From orbit, the damage was impossible to miss. Oceans had collapsed into dull gray basins, cracked and empty, their beds veined with jagged scars where rivers once pushed water instead of dust. Old coastlines lingered as pale rings tattooed the surface. Sand rolled over everything and buried what remained in waves.

The ghosts of cities clung to the land. From this height they looked like rust blooms on metal, civilization ground down and scattered until it barely registered as pattern. Dark craters punched holes through the surface where something had burned too hot. Farther north, dust storms twisted in tight spirals, storms without rain, without endings.

And at the center of it all sat a blemish. One dome.

It glowed faintly against the dead planet, a smooth circle of steel and glass wrapped in a ring of light. Rail lines spiraled outward from it like veins, all feeding the same greedy heart.

Araya recognized it immediately. The place Mr. Kurier had promised.

Home, he called it.

That wasn't home. Home was sand and choking smog. Broken land and stubborn life. As Earth receded and Nova Angeles faded into nothing, Araya closed her eyes.

Please, she prayed. *Don't let Mars be worse.*

She already knew it would be.

9

ZAHEEN

Zaheen lingered at the edge of the dunes, miles from Nova Angeles, where the world bled into emptiness. Around her, the sand lay in vast, pale swells, caught mid collapse, as if the whole expanse held its breath.

Far out on the slope, a rusted shipping crate jutted from the earth. Dunes had bitten deep into its sides, nearly claiming it. Sun glare warped the metal, and heat rippled off it in wavering sheets that turned Holly into a shimmer, more mirage than woman.

Even from this distance, Zaheen heard Holly's fists hammer the steel, each blow cracking through the heat like rifle fire.

The brightness was blinding, and Zaheen raised a hand to shield her eyes as she squinted toward the crate. "Are you sure he can help us?" Her voice carried farther than she meant. "Because this feels like inviting trouble."

Holly spun from the door, eyes blazing, hotter than Zaheen had ever seen. And Holly had had plenty of fierce, cause-lit moments. "Zee, if there's one thing I know about this man, it's that trouble trails him wherever he goes. That's exactly why we're here."

Zaheen scanned the eerie quiet. "Maybe there's someone else. Somewhere else."

"No one else." Holly shook her head. "Jude Dray is a runner for the Sand Alliance. He has ties and identifications most in Nova Angeles can't even imagine. He's our guy."

Holly planted herself in front of the crate's door, feet spread in the sand and leaned close to the warped metal. "You hear that, Jude? I'll camp out here for days if I have to."

Zaheen opened her mouth to protest, but the latch clicked. The door eased open, darkness pooling at Holly's feet.

A low, smooth voice slipped out. "What do you want?"

He stepped forward just enough for the desert light to catch him. Tall. Lean. Sun-baked like everyone else. His sand-stained robes clung to him like a second skin.

But it was his eyes—bright hazel, startling in the harsh light. There was something coiled in the way he moved, a quiet, careful tension, like a snake waiting to decide whether to strike or slip away.

Holly planted herself right in front of the open crate, arms folded, blocking the door with her body in a way that made it clear she'd done this before.

"This is how you greet former clients?"

"Holly..." Jude stepped out another inch, his gaze darting between her and Zaheen. "I don't appreciate surprises."

Distrust rolled off him. It hung around Jude the way grit clung to the folds of his robes—every shift, every breath, every glance. Zaheen felt her spine stiffen under Jude's stare.

"This is a friend," Holly said. She nudged Zaheen forward

with an elbow as she stepped beside her. "Zaheen is one of us."

Jude shifted back a step. "I said no guests. How do I know she is who you say? How do you?"

"She's not an insider," Holly said with an eye roll. "She's local and family. If I planned to use you, trust me, you'd know. We're on the same side. Zaheen included."

A dry, crackling laugh rasped from his throat. "Sides. Very black-and-white of you. Just because I helped you once doesn't mean I will again."

Holly only shrugged and turned her back. "I thought you were someone who wanted real change." She glanced over her shoulder, winking at Zaheen. "Shame, really. A man who talks justice, letting two allies vanish into the sand. No better than an insider."

She hooked an arm around Zaheen's shoulders and steered her away. "Come on, Zee. We'll find someone who actually gives a damn. He's not one of us."

"Stop," Jude said. He hauled open the rusted door. "You've forced my hand. I'm too curious for my own good."

Holly spun on her heel and strode back to the crate.

Zaheen followed. A man who lived this far from the settlement had reasons. Secrets. She wondered how many would pull her straight into trouble.

Never trust a snake in its own den. Her mother's warning had kept her alive more than once. *No matter how sweet the call, the dark hides fangs you won't see coming.*

Jude locked eyes with her.

Zaheen turned away before he could read her.

Inside his home, strings of wooden beads hung from the ceiling, swaying faintly and breaking the space into uneven rooms. He gestured toward a corner where four worn chairs hunched around a beige rug, its edges curled like dead leaves.

"Sit," he said, flicking on the lights.

A faint yellow glow seeped from floor-level solar lamps. The room remained mostly concealed, offering fragments instead of its whole shape. Everything else dissolved into murk. Zaheen suspected Jude preferred it that way, controlling what she saw and what she didn't. She found it ironic. The insiders operated the same.

She took the chair beside Holly. "I've heard stories," Zaheen said.

Jude settled into the opposite scat. Something like a chuckle tugged at his mouth and died before it formed. He folded his arms with the slow deliberation of a man who could outwait the sun.

"Let's see if your fairytales are true."

Zaheen leaned forward, elbows on her knees. "That you kill for the right price. Insider or not."

Holly gripped her forearm. "We're guests. Act like it."

"I'm not offended," Jude said. "I find it fascinating. Rumors paint me as cold, intimidating, detached." A breath slipped out, more sigh than exhale. "But that's not who I am. Why are you here?"

Zaheen opened her mouth to speak, but Holly cut in. "Someone close to her was taken."

"And that involves me how?"

Holly held his gaze. "You still want TerraLux Minerals to fall?"

"Of course I do," Jude said. "But I don't take business trips to Mars. The Perihelion facility is a death trap." He looked at Zaheen. "No offense."

Jude returned his focus to Holly. "And if I did, it would cost more than you can imagine."

"I'm not asking you to retrieve her," Holly said. "We want a movement. Liberation."

"Ambitious. How do you plan to pull that off?"

Holly shrugged. "Money's the usual answer. But I've got something more tempting."

"Do tell."

"We take down Victor Kol's entire mining empire." The words pulled a short, incredulous laugh from him.

Zaheen sprang to her feet. "I'm desperate to get her back. Whatever it takes."

"I've met your type," Jude said, the laugh draining away, a careful mask sliding over him like armor. "The ones who talk about systemic change. I always ask the same question, and they always disappoint me. I'll ask you to see if your answer is like everyone else."

Zaheen eased back into her seat. "Ask it."

"Are you willing to die for the cause?"

She didn't hesitate. "If my death brings her back, I'd die a million times."

Holly shot her a look Zaheen knew too well—the look of caution, of quiet warning, of knowing she couldn't keep her safe.

Zaheen answered with a small tilt of her head, steady and unblinking. *I'll be fine. We're always fine when we stick together.*

"Interesting," he said, thumb brushing the stubble on his chin. "Because I have a plan. One that might catch the attention of someone with real stature. A government figure.

Respected. Influential. Someone capable of rewriting the rules for those inside and those out."

"And what plan is that?" Zaheen asked, piquing interest.

"Are you familiar with Chairman Malik Sahar?"

Holly's foot began to tap. Then her fingers joined in, drumming the armrest in a rhythm that sounded like a warning. "Involving the chairman could spiral fast. We're talking consequences way beyond what we can control."

"You came here asking for a path to change," Jude said. "I'm offering you an opening. Whether you step through it —" his gaze locked on each of them in turn "—that's on you."

Zaheen didn't look at Holly. She didn't need to. "I want to hear him out."

"We use his son as leverage, and force the chairman to vote against TerraLux Minerals. We drag corruption into the light. Once our people are safely back on Earth, we release him unharmed."

Zaheen's pulse hammered. A dangerous man with dangerous solutions. "That sounds like ransom," she said. "Terrorism, even. Are you trying to get us killed?"

Jude lifted a brow. "Victor Kol built an empire on slavery and exploitation. Chairman Malik Sahar let it happen. Call it what you want. I call it balance."

Silence fell like a curtain.

Jude rose and paced, hands held behind his back. "If we do something this extreme, it has to matter. It must mean real change."

Mid-step, he stopped. "If we fail, we're dead."

Zaheen's thoughts slipped to Araya—afraid, trapped on a cold ship with no horizon. Zaheen would trade places in a heartbeat. Anything was better than leaving her to a fate worse than dying of thirst in the desert.

"That's how this works," Jude said. "High stakes, higher rewards."

Zaheen shifted in her seat. The plan churned her stomach, but so did doing nothing. "Why not go after Victor Kol?" she asked. "Why waste time on the chairman's son?"

"Victor Kol is nothing without protection," Holly said. "And we don't want a martyr."

Jude nodded. "Chairman Sahar's committee signs off on every one of Victor Kol's proposals. If Sahar says no, Kol might light the fuse himself, and in that chaos, we step in and fill the power vacuum. That's our path to victory."

"Men with big wallets tend to have bigger egos," Holly said. "Compensation's a hell of a hobby."

Jude dropped back into his chair. "Though if Chairman Sahar chooses money over family, we lose before we even start."

Zaheen had no choice. "If we do nothing, we've already lost. Tell me what you need me to do."

"She's got the same flame," Jude said to Holly. "That kind of fire is dangerous in a world built to snuff it out."

Holly smirked, the corner of her mouth lifting with old defiance. "Then we burn brighter... brighter than they ever expect."

Jude turned to Zaheen, and the smile he gave her was too knowing for her comfort. "We need a spark. A thorn in Victor Kol's side. Someone who can make people pay attention and rally the ones still hiding in the dunes. It has to be you."

"Why me?"

"They'll see themselves in you. The Sand Alliance put me

on an assignment inside Los Angeles. If I speak too loudly, I'll be compromised. Holly's bar is the only community space we have left. If she becomes the loudest voice of our movement, the insiders will shut her down in a heartbeat. That would kill our momentum before it starts."

"And what about me?" Holly asked. "Where do I fit in your grand plan?"

"Mentorship," Jude said. "Guidance. You know the ins and outs better than anyone. You built half the backchannels in this town. You're our grand connector. If Zaheen is the body, you're the spine. You teach her what to avoid. Where to strike. When to hide."

Holly exhaled, gaze drifting toward the ceiling as if searching for patience.

"Ground rules," Holly said at last. "No using this campaign for personal gain. We run everything on a vote, so I can keep tabs on everything we do. You hear me, Jude? I've watched too many movements burn their own people."

"I know. Just because I've forged every kind of identification card in Los Angeles doesn't make me an insider. Politicians, corporate elites, TerraLux executives... their signatures are easier to copy than their morals. But I've never sold out our own, and I'm not about to start today."

Holly studied him. "Fine. That much I believe."

"You would give everything for justice alone?" Zaheen asked.

Jude's eyes drifted upward, toward the dark line of the ceiling, as if he were searching the shadowed rafters for the right words. "My family was taken too. Long ago," he said. "I fight for memory."

"I'm sorry," Zaheen said. The words felt small, swallowed

by the hollow opening inside her. Grief here was shared currency. Everyone carried a coin.

"Don't be." Jude looked back at her, his hazel eyes glossy, something fragile and long-hidden pushing at the surface. "Tonight, I'll hold up my end. I'll bring the boy to Nova Angeles."

10

MALIK

The committee chamber buzzed like a marketplace where nothing was truly for sale, yet everything had a price. Whispers slipped between clenched teeth. Hands met under the table, fingers closing around promises no one dared speak aloud. Favors shifted in nods and polished smiles. The constant, quiet bargaining drilled into Chairman Malik Sahar until his temples throbbed.

From his seat at the highest tier of the crescent table, he watched the nine councilors arranged below him. Their crimson-upholstered chairs gleamed under the artificial lights, worn by years of posturing.

Beyond them, glass panels framed the dome's immaculate skyline—towers rising in blue and silver, an engineered peace held aloft by lies. Malik drew in a steady breath through the filtered air, tasting coolants, perfume, and the faint tang of metal polish. Scents no outsider would ever imagine. Scents the council relied on to believe they were civilized.

He lifted his gaze. The ceiling was a festival of gilded frescoes, Los Angeles reborn from ruin. Crowds lifted their hands to a shining dome. Workers smiled as they laid the first beams. Not one of those painted faces belonged to an outsider. No dust on their skin. No strain on their backs. The light caught the gold leaf and glittered back at him, so bright it stung.

It was a lie fixed in place. Every stroke of paint scrubbed clean of the miners in the tunnels on Mars, the laborers in the dunes, the bodies spent so this room could shine. The murals looked down as if amused by the performance, smug gods presiding over a farce, and Malik could not shake the thought that he sat in a hall built on the lives of others.

Malik saw the truth beneath every flourish. This was not governance. This was a battlefield, one where no one bled where others could see. Here, wounds were dealt in grins, ambushes hidden in polite phrasing, blades sheathed in ceremony. And today, every one of them was aimed directly at him.

He tapped the gavel twice. "Order."

Silence spread, brittle and reluctant. He swept his eyes over the members. They glittered like peacocks drowned in gold and gems. Beneath the polish, he saw only dolls—painted, empty-eyed, waiting to be posed.

The silence gave him a moment to feel the weight in his own body. His back ached from nights spent bent over reports and complaint records that no one else bothered to read. The lines at the corners of his eyes had deepened, etched by years of arguments and meetings that changed nothing. His olive-toned skin, once smooth, now carried the faint sag of too many sleepless cycles. Short, dark curls threaded through with gray at his temples, and his neatly trimmed beard could not quite hide the tired set of his mouth. He knew he looked older than his years. Responsibility aged faster than time.

They settled into their seats around the crescent table, but their attention stayed on themselves. Tablets flicked. Sleeves were smoothed. Phantom lint was brushed aside as if the room revolved around them. They mistook boredom for sophistication.

Malik remained at the podium above, yet the power did not flow downward. It bled sideways, backward, into dim corners and into pockets already heavy with favors.

Behind the committee, the public seats loomed. Rows of empty, scrubbed wood. No one ever came to these meetings.

Malik knew why. Victor Kol spent years building a city that made politics feel unnecessary. The lights stayed on. The air stayed cool. Food arrived on shelves. As long as the dome held, people believed the system worked without them. It was easier to stream filtered news and glossy TerraLux broadcasts than to sit through policy sessions and budget fights.

That was Kol's quiet victory. A population numbed into comfort, stepping back while the same hands tightened around every lever. The emptier the gallery became, the more crowded the bureaucracy felt with Kol's influence.

A committee member with lacquered lips and knife-edged cheekbones lifted her hand. "Chairman, what exactly is so urgent? This session feels...performative."

Several heads bobbed.

Malik set the gavel down with care, though he itched to hurl it at their powdered faces. "Did none of you read the report?"

Of course you didn't. Silence followed. No guilt. No shame. Only complacency that boiled his blood.

"So many lost," he said, words gathering force. "Tunnel three is a graveyard, and you don't even care."

Unease flickered across a few faces, but vanished.

"TerraLux Minerals must be held accountable," he said, swallowing the urge to sneer at their vacant eyes. "Victor Kol, too, if necessary."

A tall man in a navy suit leaned back, languid as a cat, and rolled his eyes as if the matter were beneath him. "We can always send more outsiders. Problem solved."

Another member draped in turquoise pendants—so many that they dragged her chin down—smiled thinly. "I, for one, concur," she said. "Sacrificing a few from outside may serve the greater good. Fewer mouths to feed means fewer shipments to dead-end places like Nova Angeles."

"Outsiders serve one purpose," said another, glazed in diamonds. "To provide for us. Their demise was inevitable."

When Malik first took the chair, he had allies in these ranks. Victor Kol saw to that but wiped the slate clean. He traded loyalty for obedience and was clever enough to leave Malik where the public could still see him. The head of the snake, decorative and harmless. In truth, Malik was only a cog in a machine already rusting through.

A chair scraped. A woman rose, chains of gold draped across her chest until she looked less like a person and more like something hammered out on a forge.

"We should care," she said, chin lifted, voice clear as a bell. "We should care because if outsiders keep dying, the pool will run dry. When that happens, we'll be forced to send our own."

"They may be nobodies," she said, eyes skimming her colleagues, never quite lifting to Malik. "But we are somebodies. If we want to keep it that way, we act now, before the death toll grows high enough to walk through our own doors."

Malik's fist struck the table. "We act because it is our duty to protect all people."

The tall man in the navy suit rose and smoothed his sleeves. "I, for one," he said, savoring the phrase, "refuse to jeopardize our stability for a few hundred dead outsiders. Mr. Kol has given us security. Why risk that for people who were never meant to sit at this table?"

Malik's vision blurred. Heat burned behind his eyes, a mix of anger and disbelief that crawled up from his gut like sickness. "Do none of you have compassion? We should open an investigation into TerraLux Minerals immediately."

"Chairman Sahar," the man in the navy suit said, "with all due respect, if there's nothing else, I'd appreciate dismissal. I have more pressing matters."

One by one, they stood and drifted out. By the time Malik found more words, the chamber was empty.

Maybe they're right. Maybe I'm only a polished, compliant mouthpiece for a system rotten to its core. He slid the gavel into the drawer and shut it, the soft click louder than any vote.

Malik left the chamber and stepped into the main corridor leading to his public office. The change in light hit first. Marble stretched ahead in a polished ribbon, so clean it almost refused to remember footsteps. Chandeliers hung at measured intervals, their crystal drops scattering light in fractured shapes across the floor.

It should have felt grand.

Along the walls, there were murals of workers and councilors side by side, faces lifted toward a shining dome. *Unity.*

Progress. The words were not written, but he could feel them pressed into every color. Lies, every stroke.

"Father."

Malik stopped mid-stride.

The voice pulled him back more effectively than any gavel. At the far end of the corridor stood his son, Eren, leaning against the wall beneath a chandelier. His school blazer hung half-open, buttons mismatched. His tie drooped in a loose knot he clearly hadn't bothered to tighten. Dark hair stuck out at uneven angles, the result of anxious fingers raking through it again and again. A sixteen-year-old trying very hard not to look sixteen.

Malik's chest tightened. He saw himself at that age—restless, mischievous, allergic to decorum—and the resemblance hit him with quiet force.

"Shouldn't you be putting together care packages for Nova Angeles?" Malik asked, attempting sternness but hearing the softness underneath.

Eren shrugged, eyes flicking away, guilt or defiance or both in the gesture.

Shame burned through Malik. "Outsiders didn't choose their circumstances," he said, barely above a whisper. Victor Kol had ears everywhere. "This dome was built on their labor. We owe them compassion. We owe them memory."

"I don't have the passion to serve others," Eren said. "That's your path, not mine."

"You need to see the larger picture, son. Kol's influence is strong. Don't let it make you forget who you are."

They walked a few steps in silence until the corridor ended at a floor to ceiling window. Beyond the glass, the city spread out in careful lines, towers glowing under the dome's false sky.

Eren drifted toward it, tilting his head as his eyes moved over the view below, all polished glass and ordered streets. "I get it," he said. "I do. But Mr. Kol has built a lot for us."

Malik set a hand on Eren's shoulder. "For someone who doesn't want my path, you do love a debate. Come. Let's go home."

They neared the elevator when a janitor rounded the corner too quickly. The metal bucket clipped Eren's knee. He recoiled as if struck.

"Watch it!"

"Eren," Malik said. "Be polite."

Eren wiped at his spotless trousers. "I know who he is. An outsider."

Malik recognized him as one of the newer staff on this floor, part of a recent rotation Kol's office approved. The man still carried the stiffness of someone not yet used to the building.

The janitor bowed his head. "My apologies, sir."

Malik returned the gesture with a weary nod and remembered the outsider's name. "It's all right, Jude. Thank you."

Jude's eyes flicked up once, meeting Malik's. A quiet understanding passed between them—shared exhaustion, shared awareness of everything Eren did not yet understand.

Malik stepped into the elevator and let the doors slide shut. He didn't correct Eren again. Not tonight. The committee had worn him down, scraped him thin.

Still, the boy's demeanor remained with him, sharp as grit in a wound, made worse by the brief look Jude had given him before the elevator sealed them apart.

11

ARAYA

Hours crawled in the vast, silence of space before the light cruiser shuddered awake.

Insiders were impatient about everything under the sun, so they made outsiders build beefier engines to hit Mars in record time. Araya found that hilarious in the bleakest possible way, because insiders avoided sunlight like it was contagious. Which was extra funny, considering Nova Angeles hosted three real plagues in Araya's lifetime—and none of them came from the sun.

A hundred thousand pounds of red lustronium ore powered Los Angeles, and that meant the cruisers ran from planet to planet nonstop. All that progress rode on outsiders' backs. For their trouble, outsiders didn't get raises or medals. They got "recruited"—bagged, tagged, and shipped off-world, away from Earth and anyone who might notice they'd vanished—then worked until their grit ran out.

Insiders got warm showers and a universe accompanied by unlimited customer service, and they were premium members.

Zero gravity shot Araya off her chair, but the safety strap yanked her down. The buckle cracked. The back of her head kissed the headrest, and the impact rang through her teeth like she'd bitten a wrench.

She inhaled. Coolant stink and recycled air made it halfway in and stalled out. Nova Angeles smog went down easier.

Cruisers peeled off toward Earth or settled into Mars approach lanes as the planet filled the window.

The ship tipped nose-down into Mars's rusty haze. The cabin jolted, and the restraints cinched across her chest and shoulders, coiling like a horned viper. A bite from one of those put many outsiders six feet under sand. Same energy here.

The facility rose out of the red murk. The dome, same size as Los Angeles, squatted on a wide plateau.

Araya rubbed her chin, and her brain finally bothered to connect the dots.

Olympus Mons!

She knew that name because she read it in a textbook an insider had tossed. Anything insiders didn't want—outdated technology, torn clothes, food scraps, plastic film, and the occasional "why would anyone need this?" book—went by train to Nova Angeles and got dumped.

Most people scavenged for tools, filters, or anything that sustained life.

Araya usually went for books. That ticked Zaheen off. And honestly, Araya couldn't blame her. When they had room for two bags of loot, and half the town elbowed each other for the good supplies, hauling around books was a questionable life choice.

As a dreamer, Araya read everything on Los Angeles and Mars. She wanted a shot at the inside, and when that day came, she planned to walk in informed, savvy enough to poke at the systems that sunk her people and, if she was lucky, fix a few of the rules that caused injustice.

Propaganda was a word Araya learned recently. Zaheen returned home after a scavenge run with an old dictionary that still had the F–S pages intact. The rest had... alternate careers. A–E became kindling. T–Z became toilet paper. Literacy was a luxury, so Araya read every word before Zaheen had better uses.

Araya read the long-worded book about Mars front to back and back to front, and that's when she noticed propaganda.

Victor Kol—at the bright, punchable age of fourteen— ventured to Mars and decided the highest point on the planet would make a perfect nest for his corporation.

Araya called bullshit. The man couldn't even stomach a stroll in Nova Angeles. Propaganda at its finest.

The Mars book laid out the truth in quiet little facts. Olympus Mons. Biggest volcano in the solar system. Tall enough to make Earth mountains look like bad posture. And right on top of it, Victor planted his shiny dome and slapped a name on it: Perihelion—the point in an orbit when a planet is closest to the sun.

He sold it like destiny. Mars leaned in for him. The sun welcomed his approach and said, *Finally, the center of the universe has arrived.*

The ship lurched. Yelps rippled through the cabin as bodies hit restraints. Araya squeezed her eyes shut.

Don't look at Dante. Don't look at Skye. They'll see it. Fear rising.

Araya had practiced hiding it most of her life. It made everything easier. Still, their presence grounded her. If this was hell, at least she wasn't diving into it alone.

Across the cabin, someone gagged. Barf bags crinkled in sympathy, a sad little orchestra of people losing arguments with their angry stomachs.

The cruiser drifted into the hangar and glided past rows of parked vehicles. Sparking wires flickered like weak lightning under cracked panels. Along the bay wall, cargo containers were stacked in neat, sealed columns, uniform as gravestones and about as welcoming.

The cruiser landed. Vents kicked on and pumped a blast of sterile air into the cabin with a hiss. Araya waved a hand in front of her face. It didn't help.

She flinched a half-second too late when the lights snapped on. Her vision blew out to white. When it cleared, guards filled the aisle. Their crimson armor caught light and threw it back in glares.

Matching the planet. Nice touch if I wasn't worried about a baton to the gut.

At the front, a guard tapped her baton against a gloved palm. "Prepare for offboarding," she said. "Line up, outsiders."

Araya stepped behind Skye and pressed her fingers into the tense muscles at the back of her neck, working out the knots. It helped. She'd gotten good at it.

Zaheen came home from scavenger runs folded up like a bad chair, and Araya learned exactly where to press to turn groans into sighs.

Hiking dunes was like climbing a staircase made of flour. Steps slid, muscles overcorrected, and micro-panics traveled straight to the spine.

Dante groaned, fist clamped over his mouth, and slid in behind Araya. "I lost everything. Worse than drinking a gallon of sand water."

"Don't lose anything else on me," Araya said.

"Face front." The guard lifted the baton and gave it a lazy flick down the aisle. "March."

Araya shuffled. Head bowed. Arms wrapped tight across her torso. Goosebumps crawled up her skin. She once read that outside Perihelion the temperature hit negative one hundred. That was two hundred degrees colder than her accustomed winters.

The jet bridge funneled them into a steel corridor. Windows ran along one side, and they hijacked everyone's attention, Araya's included.

Mars filled the frame in all its violent colors. Blood-orange skies bruised darker at the horizon. Ridges scarred in the distance. Dunes tangled with rock. The surface looked scraped raw, like the world had been dragged across concrete.

"Not good," Dante said, and pointed.

Workers in sterile suits march by, rolling carts stacked with body bags. Araya's brain did that fun trick where it tried to turn looking into meaning and meaning into prophecy. *That's you next. That's Skye. That's Dante.* Like the universe was taking requests.

Nope. No thanks. She yanked her gaze away so hard it felt like a muscle strain. She focused on Skye's back and kept walking.

Ten minutes of silent footsteps later, they crossed into a second hangar bay.

This one swallowed sound. The room was enormous and empty, a hollow box that climbed so high the overhead lights stopped being lights and turned into a harsh white smear. The far wall might as well have been on another continent. Three doors waited there, evenly spaced and identical beside a bad paint job that read: *Tunnel 1, Tunnel 2,* and *Tunnel 3.*

The group of around one hundred outsiders sank to the floor like someone cut their strings.

Araya lowered herself and folded inward—arms tucked, shoulders rounded, knees close—trying to become less of a target. The concrete bled cold through fabric, her skin, and seeped straight into her bones.

Skye hugged her knees, and teeth chattered. "Mars is cruel."

The speaker overhead crackled. Every head tipped up.

"Welcome to Perihelion, a TerraLux Minerals mining facility. I'm Victor Kol. I'm honored to have you join our operation. Your service marks a new chapter in human progress. Work with discipline and pride. Together, we power the future for the good of humankind."

Araya scoffed. Her breath fogged into a faint cloud and drifted away.

"Here, you will be working with red lustronium, the most energy-dense mineral ever discovered. Capable of powering entire domes, stabilizing failing grids, and keeping what remains of civilization alive. Without red lustronium, Los Angeles goes dark. The world outside swallows what's left of the inside. That is how valuable your work is."

Araya wanted to scream at the ceiling. She wanted to untangle the logic and throw it piece by piece.

"Be respectful to staff and follow orders. Your bodies will adjust to the cold. These are not the one hundred degree winters you're accustomed to. And yes, your stomachs will settle. High-speed interplanetary travel is jarring. Like every new cohort, you are in transition. It will pass. Please be aware, our facility has state of the art gravity stabilizers so it will be like walking on Earth, for the utmost productivity."

The silence afterward lingered just long enough for Araya to roll her eyes.

"You will now receive your assignments. Review the numerical code on your vest. It's your new identification. When a guard calls your number, answer 'present' to confirm. The people of Earth thank you. Los Angeles thanks you. I thank you."

Numbers barked across the hangar. Outsiders stepped forward on cue. Bodies were redirected into three lanes like livestock. Left. Center. Right.

"Worker 48-43-02-40, report."

Skye rose. "Present."

"Report to tunnel three." The guard shouting identifications scanned the list. "Worker 58-10-68-50."

The color left Dante's face. "Present."

"Report to tunnel three."

He turned to meet Araya's eyes and gave a small nod, like they were confirming a plan. Araya returned it, fists clenched in her pockets.

The one other remaining outsider trembled beside her. Sweat ran down his arms and back in panicked rivers. Araya looked down at her own clothes. Dry.

The guard scrolled her tablet. "My final two workers. Worker 65-81-90-80, report to tunnel three."

The man stumbled to the guard. "P-present."

The guard's eyes flicked to Araya's vest. "Worker 95-71-90-80. Report to tunnel two."

Her stomach dropped so hard it felt like the floor had vanished. The room tilted. That invisible cord tying her to Skye and Dante snapped in one clean cut.

She stole a look at them—at Skye's hunched shoulders, at Dante's puppy eyes—and forced her attention forward before her face betrayed her.

The other outsider folded in on himself, hands clasped so tight his knuckles bleached. "Please send me home. My family needs me. I'll do anything."

The guard crossed her arms and scoffed. "Not my concern."

Araya lowered her head and started toward tunnel two. Each step felt like walking away from the only lifeboat on a sinking ship. The other outsider screamed and pleaded behind her.

"Worker 95-71-90-80," the guard shouted, and Araya froze mid-stride. "Switch to tunnel three. He won't last a day."

Relief hit Araya so fast it almost buckled her knees. Tunnel three, tunnel two, she didn't care which was worse. Worse was alone. She ran—too fast, but she couldn't help it. She reached Dante and Skye and gave them a quick smile.

The door at the end of tunnel three rose with a hydraulic whine. The line shuffled. Boots scuffed across the cold floor. Araya went last. And as the door consumed her, one thought pressed itself into her mind: *Will I ever see Earth again?*

12

ZAHEEN

Zaheen pushed into the crush and felt the plaza close around her. Bodies shoved and slid, a tide with elbows and sharp shoulders. Each breath cost. Heat pressed down from above while warmth rolled off the crowd from all sides.

Stalls sagged under rusted tin and splintered wood, their canopies patched with whatever people could find. Strips of faded cloth. Plastic sheeting gone cloudy with age.

Vendors shouted for coins. Spices burned the air. Char and grease and something sweet that might once have been fruit. Smoke from seared skewers curled upward and smeared itself across the sunlight, turning the sky into a cloud of yellow and gray. Somewhere close, a child cried. Somewhere else, someone laughed too loudly.

She caught a thread of music, refusing to die in the noise. Two musicians hunched over battered instruments, one with a bow worn to near nothing, the other plucking strings that had been knotted back together. Their baskets sat bone-empty, woven reeds fraying apart.

Dancers glided in slow arcs nearby, palms raised. Dust

clung to their hems and ankles as the crowd streamed past without seeing, the same blindness she knew too well. Bright scraps of fabric flickered at their waists.

Zaheen hauled her scarf up until it covered her nose, the material rough against her skin, and drew in a breath laced with smoke, the taste of Nova Angeles on her tongue.

She flicked sand from her robe and began to pace. The crowd flowed past like water around stone.

After their conversation with Jude, Holly had told her, "Go home. Rest. Come back ready for what's to come."

Zaheen needed a breath, but whatever came next would demand quick action and a speech learned by heart. She didn't know why yet, only that she committed every word Holly gave her.

Through the blur, she found her old friend.

Holly sat on a sun-bleached bench, her canteen cupped in both hands.

Zaheen steadied her breath and went to her. "Are you sure whatever you're planning will work?"

Holly lowered the canteen. A pale wisp of steam rose, twisted once, and disappeared into the haze. "There's always a chance of failure," she said. "But what if it's a chance at success, too?"

Zaheen offered a hand. "You're not worried at all?"

Holly took it, rose, and surged into the crowd. "Why should I be? Now, come."

"Not even a little?"

Holly glanced back with a quick smile. "Not even a grain of sand."

Zaheen hurried to her side. "So, where are you taking me now?"

Holly stopped before a shack on the outskirts of the plaza, so warped it barely counted as shelter. The door hung crooked—one hinge clinging by rust, the other whining at every shift of wind. She spread her arms as if unveiling a cathedral. "Here we are. Take it in. This is where it starts."

Zaheen frowned. "You're not serious."

"Oh, but I am, Zee."

The shack looked ready to fold in on itself. Planks bowed and split from years of heat. Seams gaped like wounds left open too long. The tin roof sagged under its own decay, rust flaking in brittle scales. A gust set the place clattering like a rack of bones, as if the next breath might peel it loose and send it tumbling into the sky.

"What have you gotten us into?"

Holly laughed. "This place holds more than it shows."

"It better. Because I'm not seeing much to like."

Zaheen ducked through the doorway. The space was so tight she had to turn sideways. Holly slipped in behind her, and the door settled shut with a soft, weary groan.

The air inside was somehow worse than outside. Stale and dry, with dust pressed deep into the wood. Paint peeled from the patchwork walls in brittle curls. No furniture waited for them. Only a threadbare rug sprawled across the floorboards. Three cloaked men stood in the gloom; shapes knotted together in low conversation.

"Stay here," Holly said. "I'm going to have a word."

Holly crossed the room in quick strides and joined them. A few exchanged words, and their voices broke into laughter. All three of them glanced over at Zaheen.

Holly peeled away from the cluster and started back. The trio fell in step behind her.

"You're speaking at their event," Holly said.

"What event?" Zaheen asked and glanced around. "To an audience of sand fleas?"

"Best step off the rug," one of the men said.

As Zaheen stepped off, the trio slid their hands under the rug and, with one practiced pull, peeled it back to reveal a hatch.

One of them crouched and knocked a code. Three quick knocks. A pause. Two more. A pause. And three more.

"Who are they?" Zaheen asked Holly. "What is this place?"

The hatch answered first. It creaked, hinges shrieking as it lifted. Gold light surged up from below, washing their faces in a molten glow.

Holly rested a hand on Zaheen's shoulder. "Welcome to more than rumors," she said. "You're standing on the Sand Alliance's safe house."

Zaheen's mouth went dry. "I thought the Sand Alliance was just smugglers and message runners like Jude."

"It is," Holly said. "We have people in desert towns to agents poised as employees for political offices in Los Angeles. These men are part of it. Jude is. I am. And now you're proving your worth to our kin. Consider this initiation to revolution."

Zaheen went still. *Revolution means sacrifice. And sacrifice means loss. Araya cannot be a loss.*

"I met Jude at one of these rallies long ago," Holly said. "They're closed-door for a reason. Outsiders have betrayed us. They've sold names, safehouses, coordinates for resources. Only trusted and brave outsiders are welcome. This is the heart of the rebellion."

Holly's hand sank a little firmer on Zaheen's shoulder. "And your pulse is already part of it."

Zaheen stared down into the stairwell. "I don't know about this."

"You don't have to. None of us did when we officially joined. If you want to build coalitions and drive action that dismantles Victor Kol's empire, this is the place to do it."

Zaheen bit her tongue. *I only want Araya.*

"We need organizers," Holly said as if hearing Zaheen's thoughts. "We need leaders. We need you."

"I know the Sand Alliance has a history of violence. That's not who I am. Are you going to expect me to spill blood for this?"

Holly's expression softened, but it didn't soothe. "You're a gentle soul, Zee. I wouldn't ask you to betray that."

Not an answer. She crossed her arms. "Yes or no?"

Holly dipped her chin. "Those are the only doors that lead to Araya."

Zaheen knew there was no other path. If reaching Araya meant stepping into danger, that's what she would do. "I choose to join."

"You're making the right choice," Holly said. She took her hand and squeezed. She let go and headed down the stairwell, beckoning Zaheen to follow.

Zaheen did, and the three men locked the hatch from the other side. Shadows thinned and gold light gathered as the steps opened into a cavernous chamber. Heads turned, curious and guarded.

Holly guided Zaheen past rusted tables leaned on splintered legs. Crooked chairs groaned under strangers with folded arms and rigid backs, their eyes tracking every step.

Candles set in iron brackets threw restless shadows across faces worn by weather and worry.

Holly stopped at the foot of a low stage and touched Zaheen's arm. "Just say what you rehearsed."

Zaheen focused on the stage. The boards sagged. Velvet curtains hung in tatters and swayed with the faint draft that bled through the room.

She met the stares. Knives for eyes. Whispers floating like dust on the wind. Candles hissed and popped. Wax hit stone with a dry tap.

A tall woman with shoulders broad enough to part a crowd rose as Zaheen stepped onto the stage. "Holly, who is this?"

"A diamond in the rough," Holly said.

"My name is Zaheen Mandisa," she said. "Like you, Nova Angeles is my home. Like you, someone I love has been taken by Victor Kol. We've watched our people disappear to Mars and his city while he calls it progress. Los Angeles calls it necessary, but accountability is long overdue."

Chatter caught like fire in dry brush. Small sparks at first, then flares racing wall to wall, until the chamber hummed with restless energy. Zaheen saw her own ache reflected at her.

"And what do you propose we do?" Holly asked from the floor.

"Protest," Zaheen said. "Refuse to disappear quietly. Demand a voice. Demand change. Each week, the cargo train rips past Nova Angeles on its way to Los Angeles. Victor Kol rides it and takes credit for work that is not his. Tomorrow, it returns. I will stand at the tracks, and I refuse to move. I'll lead anyone willing to stand with me. Victor Kol must answer to us."

Outsiders rose as one. Some shouted for the end of Victor, others applauded. Others lifted their fists. Zaheen stepped down from the stage and into waiting hands that caught her, clapped her back, and gripped her arms as if anchoring her to them.

Holly joined her side, smile bright, eyes blazing with something fierce and proud. She leaned in so only Zaheen could hear.

"You hear that?" she said. "That is what it sounds like when they decide you're worth following. We haven't had anyone be brave enough to bring protest to the fold in many, many years. Welcome to the Sand Alliance."

Zaheen gave a short nod. In the quiet corner of her mind, one thought held fast.

Will this path bring Araya home? I don't know. But there is no other path, and momentum is already hurling me down a road I can't retrace.

13

JUDE

At the fringes of the Los Angeles bazaar, Jude shadowed the chairman and his son, just another cloaked figure flowing with the tide. To the untrained eye, he was nobody.

Minutes earlier, he watched them exit the elevator from the narrow sliver of shadow outside Malik's office window. As the doors hissed shut, Jude slipped out the side entrance and into the winding corridors, then the street—always a few strides behind, and stalked where their attention wasn't, guided by instinct more than sight.

He saw the bazaar for what it was: theater.

Shoppers fanned themselves beneath a synthetic sun and pretended it could burn. Silk whispered. Coins clinked. Laughter floated like perfume—fragrant, and masking odor. It was all part of a careful score. A choreography of selective blindness.

Jude brushed the inside of his cloak where the forged identification cards lay stiff against the lining—his ticket in, and out. A gift from the Sand Alliance.

The mission was simple: get close to Chairman Sahar,

infiltrate his office, and copy the credentials that would grant their agents access to the forbidden inner zones where supply storage was kept—the places no one from Nova Angeles was ever meant to see.

He'd done it. Every piece had clicked into place.

Jude wandered past merchant tables and examined trinkets to textiles. *Pretend you care. Play the part. The cause matters more than your anger.*

His targets never left sightline. Framed between striped canopies, their silhouettes stood out against the rising steam from the food grills. He watched them the way a hunter watches prey, reading the cadence of their steps, the flick of a glance, the slight, unconscious tilt of a shoulder. Every twitch and hesitation was catalogued and stored.

And he had more on Eren than Eren would ever guess.

The Sand Alliance kept records—stacks of notes written by hands like Jude's. They painted a clear picture: a rebellious sixteen-year-old desperate for Victor Kol's approval. A boy who picked fights for sport. Who treated cruelty as amusement.

Jude hadn't forgotten the scandal. Eren and five friends snuck onto a passenger train bound for Nova Angeles. They hurled rotten food at outsiders and shouted insults.

It nearly cost Chairman Sahar his post. Insiders refused sympathy for outsiders, but the optics of it all nearly led to catastrophe for the Sahar family.

Jude doubted Eren forgot, either.

The damage control had been neat: Malik pledged that his son would spend the rest of his youth assembling care packages for the same people he humiliated, until the day he left his father's home.

"Anything catch your eye, honey?" The vendor stood in a crisp brown suit with star-stitches flashing like cheap constellations.

Jude said nothing. He skimmed the delicate filigree of a gold necklace, its pendant a shard of desert glass. The motion steadied him, gave his hands something to do while his mind spun backward. The metalwork was impossibly fine, almost unreal, like it had slipped through from another era.

He wanted to climb a rooftop and scream that this place was a lie. A stage set over a mass grave.

"You like that one?" the vendor asked. "Fresh off an outsider. So, I'm told."

Jude dragged his glare down and replaced it with curiosity. "What was the outsider's name?"

"Does it matter? An item like that," he said, smug, "was made for the inside. Splendor like this doesn't belong in sand."

Jude angled his body to move on.

"Wait."

Jude rolled his eyes. "I'm not interested in your trinkets."

"What I'm about to show you," the vendor said, and ducked beneath the table, "isn't a trinket."

With a theatrical flourish, the vendor reemerged, cradling a small metal box. It was no larger than a loaf of bread. He set it down, flipped the latch, and hinges creaked.

"A one-of-a-kind find," the vendor said. His grin stretched too wide. "Not something you stumble on twice."

The object was sleek and obsidian, a ribbon of crimson flickered on its blade. He hovered a hand over the dagger.

"Ah-ah." The vendor yanked the box to his chest and

wagged a finger. "No touching without payment. No fingerprints on her shine."

"What's the material?"

"Forged from Mars rock. I'll throw in the necklace too."

"I'll take both."

"That easy?" he said. "Stars above! I'm better than I thought."

Jude reached in and closed his hand around the hilt. An insider would call it art—a collector's piece meant for glass and climate control, its history scrubbed clean and framed as triumph. A trophy without blood.

Jude knew better.

This was Mars. Grit and ruin forged into a single blade. Made from the same red world that killed his people, the same world he'd spent his life trying to pull them back from. The reason he joined the Sand Alliance in the first place.

The weight of it dragged his mind elsewhere. Back to the plaza in Nova Angeles. To the tin shack he once called home.

He was back on the day everything changed.

The red hair struck him first. Skin sickly pale. The name surfaced like a bruise pressed too hard: Mr. Kurier. The messenger arrived at his door, stole his daughter, and shot his wife when she chased after them.

Jude could still hear his daughter's voice. *"Stay back... I need a father to come back to."*

And he had let her go.

He told himself he had no choice. That resistance would have only gotten them all killed. He regretted that decision every day of his life.

Twenty years passed. The labor terms on Mars were fifteen. On the fifteenth anniversary, a letter arrived from

TerraLux Minerals. There had been a tunnel collapse. Seven died. Her name was third on the list.

The blade in his hand held all of that. A history. A promise to the shackled he would personally see them free.

He slipped the blade and necklace into his cloak and tossed coins onto the table in return.

The vendor swept them up. "Have yourself a splendid evening."

Enjoy these evenings while they last. My people are coming for you. Jude gave a silent nod and turned, vanishing back into the crowd.

14

JUDE

Jude caught his targets breaking from the crowd. The duo peeled off like a dust devil spun loose from sunbaked concrete. They didn't so much as glance at the public platforms. They moved straight for a reinforced metal door tucked beside a bank of sleeping sensors.

Relief loosened something tight in his chest. He was tired of pretending to browse, of the bright stalls and the false laughter and the eyes that might look too long his way. Finally, he could act without half the city watching.

Chairman Sahar lifted his keycard. Blue light rippled across the panel, and the door exhaled open. Both disappeared inside.

Jude let everything else smear into background. The shuffle of bodies, the antiseptic bite of recycled air, and the steady blink of cameras. He fixed on the clock tower above the platform. 6:43 p.m. Two minutes until the next train.

The station spread out around him like a miniature city. High curved ceiling. Steel ribs and glass panels. Rows of platforms. Information boards flickering over the main concourse.

Commuters pooled in loose lines, drifting between kiosks and benches the way a delta broke into an ocean. This was where all of Los Angeles funneled through when it needed to go anywhere.

Rule one: don't stare. Rule two: move like you belong. Rule three: we risk all.

He repeated the Sand Alliance creed under his breath and slipped along the station's fringe. Eyes to tile. Sliding through gaps in the crowd before they closed. He folded himself into the rhythm around him, the slow shuffle and soft sigh of people already done with the day.

Two metro officers glanced up, and marched right past him.

Good. Invisible is safe. To anyone watching, he was nobody. To Jude, every step was a countdown, one stride closer to the door and the asset that waited behind it.

He reached into his pocket and brushed the forged identification of Chairman Sahar. Cold edges. Cheap laminate. The Sand Alliance techs had worked through three nights to finish it, hunched over scanners and cracked screens, stitching stolen data from Sahar's office into something that might pass a quick check.

Jude smuggled out those fragments one by one. Every risk, every near-miss in those halls, sat now in the weight of that card. All of it was worth it. If the card worked.

Jude stepped up to the scanner, pulse ticking in his throat. He raised the card, careful not to let his hand shake. *If it fails, you run. No hesitation. No turning back. And you pray the officers don't put a round in your back.*

The panel flickered once. Twice. And washed blue. Playing pretend janitor for a couple weeks had been worth the reward.

The door opened, and he stepped inside.

Lemon cleaner rushed up and stung his nose. The carpet cushioned each footfall so deeply it felt wrong under him, plush enough to trip him if he wasn't careful. Everything in here whispered money and distance from the world he came from.

Jude inhaled, steadying himself, and slid into the mask he'd practiced—loose shoulders, neutral eyes, bored half-focus, a body belonging to someone who had nothing to sweat about.

His anxiety bled off, drop by drop, melting into the blandness around him.

Small. Unremarkable. Invisible. The rhetoric insiders used to diminish outsiders. He turned those words into armor. Sharpened them into the one advantage that let him ghost through their world and steal whatever truths they guarded.

Up front, Malik and Eren settled into high-backed leather seats. Their heads angled together, their voices lost under the private line's low, steady thrum.

Jude didn't bother trying to listen.

The intercom crackled. *"Metro approaching. Please mind the gap."*

Chairs scraped back in perfect unison. Two dozen insiders rose together. Jude rose with them, matching their cadence, keeping his breath steady.

Light burst through the tunnel. The approaching train screamed, metal howling as it tore down the track. He stepped forward with the crowd as the metro car came to a stop.

One hand drifted in his pocket and found the Mars-forged hilt. It grounded him. Reminded him why he was here. *Get the kid. Get my people home. Then all of this goes away.*

Three guards stormed in from the same entrance Jude entered, batons raised, eyes sweeping the platform. "Chairman Sahar, you called for help?"

Malik shoved Eren toward the idling car. "Get in!" The chairman pivoted, stabbing a finger at Jude. "This person has been tailing us. I suspect foul play. Arrest him."

Jude rushed—one step, two—angling for the open doors, for Eren.

A baton slashed across his path, halting him cold. "Drop the knife!"

Jude drove a clean, brutal punch into the first guard, dropping him to his knees. The second swung wide. Jude ducked, and the baton smashed into another guard's face. He crumpled, blood spattering across the tiles.

Shouts rose. Crowds scattered. Jude slipped through the gap.

The last guard charged. Jude slid past him and locked an arm around his neck. They hit the floor together. The man gasped and folded in on himself.

Jude pushed to his feet as the next metro screamed into the station. He slipped through the narrow gap and into the car as it surged away. The doors sealed with a soft metallic sigh.

Jude slammed his fist into the wall. Eren was gone. And with it, the plan, everything Jude had been gripping, slipped clean through his fingers.

Holly's going to kill me. He could hear her frustration already, could see the look she would give him if he came back empty-handed. A scolding was in order. More importantly, the sinking realization that Victor Kol was still out of his reach.

ARAYA

A rail-born shriek tore through the metro carriage.

The lights snapped awake. Araya flinched and raised a hand to block the glare. Dust drifted through the beams in slow curls. A few glowing grains brushed her cheek and caught in her throat. She coughed once and tried to steady her breathing. The grit settled deeper, thickening in her chest until it felt like her body was tightening around it.

Skye and Dante sat on either side of her with their heads tipped back into the haze. For a moment, the drifting dust made them look suspended in a red constellation. Araya blinked hard. She felt too tired for wonder today.

The metro car lurched and screeched to a halt, the sudden stop nearly sending Araya airborne. Fellow outsiders were thrown from their seats, bodies colliding with the floor and each other as shouts and clatter filled the car.

The ceiling speaker crackled to life. *"Tunnel three barracks. Disembark."*

The doors opened, and the loss of home hit Araya immediately. The sandy expanse was gone. In its place stretched a narrow, blinding corridor. White walls. White ceiling. White floor. Buzzing lights stung her eyes until they watered.

Everything funneled forward in a single direction. No side paths. No escape hatches. Just a straight chute, like the kind a butcher uses to line up cattle for slaughter. Araya felt like something marked and numbered, pushed along to wherever the insiders wanted her to go.

She kept her head down and fixed her gaze on the tiles. She reached around until her arms brushed Dante's and Skye's.

She wanted to tell them, *I'm here. I'm not going anywhere.* But she knew this would have to do. They had no idea she needed the touch just as badly.

Like a riptide, guards in red armor appeared from the far end of the corridor. Araya watched the wave roll closer, boots striking the floor in hard, even beats that bounced off the walls. The line of outsiders tightened on instinct. The space seemed to shrink with every step the guards took.

When the guards reached them, they split into two lines and moved along the edges of the crowd. Outsiders funneled down the middle toward the end of the hall, where a vault door waited. Two steel beams clamped across its frame, metal sunk deep to keep it sealed. The door looked thick enough to stop anything.

In front of it stood a man in a silver suit.

The fabric caught every strip of light, loud against his waxy skin and close-cropped, lacquered hair. The shine wasn't flattering. It made him look cheaper, like someone trying too hard to look important. His face was long and angular, each line held tight with control. His eyes were dark as space, taking everything in without giving anything back.

"Tell me he doesn't look like a walking vendor cart," Skye said, just for Araya. "All he's missing is a swinging pan set."

Araya almost laughed—almost. One slip, one laugh, and she pictured herself beaten by batons.

The man in silver lifted a hand. A small gesture, but the guards reacted instantly. They peeled off toward narrow side doors recessed along the walls. Metal panels slid open to swallow them, their boots still hitting in perfect time until the doors shut and the sound thinned out and vanished.

He let the silence settle, heavy as static before a storm. It was now Araya, the crowd, and this absurd looking insider.

"Welcome to your new home," he said. "I'm Director Sorev. Supervisor of Perihelion."

It must be the worst post of all time if you're this far from Victor Kol. Araya pressed her tongue to her teeth, damming words that would cost too much.

Director Sorev gestured to the door. "We operate as a team on Perihelion. Accountability is crucial. Without it, the excavation of red lustronium descends into chaos."

A slow curl touched his lips, a smile that never reached his eyes. Something in it made Araya's skin prickle. It was the same kind of smile Carmine Kurier wore when he gave her the news she'd been selected for Mars.

Araya felt the old truth rise in her chest. People like this always found their way to the top. Men who hid cruelty behind calm voices, and treated authority like a weapon they were entitled to swing. Different face, different suit, same rot underneath. The system built itself around and through them.

Director Sorev slid his keycard over the glass panel. It gave a sharp beep. Inside the door, heavy locks thudded as the crossbars pulled back. A strip of green light washed across the ceiling.

The vault opened. Metal scraped against metal in a long, low groan, as if the whole frame hated the process.

"Please, find your new beds. Your identification codes are stamped along the floor," Director Sorev said. "Get some rest. Perihelion demands a great deal."

Araya lowered her head as she passed the insider. She stepped into a chamber of beds arranged in rigid rows, each one another slot in a human filing system. Beige sheets wore a rust-red film, the outsiders on them frail and weathered.

She walked down the central aisle, eyes tracing the faces of those who had come before her. Wrinkled. Skin to bone. Dust-stained. Frail.

A hard truth settled. No one at home spoke of these people. Outsiders missed their loved ones, but life slid back into its channels. No action. No change. No voice was brave enough to step out of the quicksand that the insiders kept them in.

"My bed's this way," Dante said. The sound of his voice pulled Araya out of the pit of despair she fell into. "We're going to get through this."

Araya pulled her face into something that passed for a smile. "I know."

Dante watched her a beat longer. He was already learning her tells. That should have annoyed her. Instead, it felt like a hand on the back of her neck, keeping her upright. "I promise, Araya."

"Don't keep promises here." Araya scanned the rows. "Where's Skye?"

"Front corner."

Skye sat curled in on herself, knees pinned to her chest, chin tucked down. A fortress made of elbows and shins.

"We'll talk soon," Araya said. She gave him a quick nod and peeled away.

Each bed was the same. One thin sheet, a narrow pillow, and a rectangle of floor with a black-stamped code. Araya slid her foot over the numbers beneath her: 95-71-90-80. The same sequence was stitched over her heart on the vest.

The mattress dipped under her palm. At first it felt soft, almost welcoming. But the bar underneath, a hard line pushing up through the padding, reminded her nothing on Mars would hold comfort.

She lowered herself anyway. The metal bit through the thin mattress into her muscles, but she stayed there and told herself it counted as rest. There was nowhere else to go.

On the bed beside Araya, a woman about a decade older sat cross-legged, posture straight as a soldier. Her head was shaved to the scalp, stubble dusted red from tunnel grime. A faint scar cut across one eyebrow. Her eyes—sharp, steady— tracked Araya with the calm awareness of someone who had survived more than she'd let on.

Araya offered a wave.

The stranger's face softened instantly. "Iman Kalima."

"Araya Santera. From Nova Angeles."

Iman swung her legs over the side of the cot, her bare feet hovering just above the grimy floor. "Nova Angeles," she said. "You've already endured a lot if you're from there. I hear messengers hunt in Nova Angeles more than other spots. It's the closest place to take from."

"I'm sure we've all endured greatly to end up here. Where are you from?"

Iman paused. Not for long, but long enough for Araya to see her mouth tighten and her mind drift somewhere far away.

"A small town about an hour south of Nova Angeles," she said at last. "Barely a dot on a map. Just desert and wind and houses that never quite stay standing. I miss it. The dry air. That ridiculous sun that felt like it wanted to melt you alive."

Memory tugged at Araya. She kept her voice light, stepping sideways from the pull. She knew how quickly memory could drain her into despair. "How's the food here?"

Iman wrinkled her nose as if a rotten smell had drifted past. "A bowl of sand would taste better."

A laugh slipped out of Araya before she could stop it. "I miss the sand."

"Me too. Who would've thought, right? Nothing's better than grabbing a handful and watching it fall through your fingers. Sand has cadence."

"Therapeutic," Araya said.

"I've met others who have been up here many, many years, you know."

Araya's breath caught. *That's a lifetime. That's forever.*

"If you want, I'll mentor you. Show you how not to get noticed. How to stay out of trouble."

Araya's heart kicked faster. Her gaze swept the room. Bunk after bunk. Bent backs. Hacking coughs. Faces that never lifted. Eyes already emptied out.

"I didn't mean to scare you, Araya."

Araya dragged her focus back to her. "Why so many years?"

Iman leaned closer, as if the walls might be listening. "A long time ago, someone tried to escape. The insiders caught him. They executed him in the mess hall. Made everyone watch." She went quiet for a breath. "After that, they added years to the rest of our terms. Guilty by association."

Iman straightened. "They want you to slip, Araya. Break a rule. Step out of line. One mistake, and they have a reason to keep you here forever. They don't care what it costs you. Insiders only serve six-month rotations. They'll go home and touch real earth while your senses roughen and forget the planet altogether."

Her mouth twisted, something like a tired smile with no humor in it. "Some days I don't even think about home anymore."

Araya pulled her blanket up and held it close. "I'd appreciate your help. I have someone I need to get back to."

Iman reached across and touched her arm. "It'll be nice to have a new friend."

"Friends," Araya said and smiled.

"You should get some sleep. Iman laid down and rolled the other way. "They'll wake us before you even feel the chance to find your dreams. Goodnight."

Araya eased back on the bed. The mattress nudged her spine, blanket scratching skin, and the smell of sweat clung to her nose. She closed her eyes. The dark was no more comforting than the light.

16

JUDE

Jude stepped off the metro into Midtown West, Los Angeles' luxury quarter. He'd never belonged here, not for a single breath, but he knew the place all the same from the traces insiders left behind.

Mopping floors and wiping windows in public offices had their uses. Officials talked when they thought no one important was listening. They left doors unlocked while they bragged about promotions. They dropped addresses and menus on desks and forgot about them. Jude picked all of it up. Passed pieces of it along.

He funneled what he learned to the Sand Alliance. Supply routes. Storage hubs. Locations that made for clean raids. He slipped forged IDs into the right hands so others could move through velvet checkpoints.

He even suffered through the smug tours officials loved to give to their high donors, mopping in the background while they boasted about the newest restaurants and polished storefronts in their perfect little corners of Midtown West.

So, when he lost his targets, he didn't have to guess where

they went. He already knew where men like Chairman Sahar would go. To Midtown West.

The station's clock tower glared down over the platform. 7:32 p.m.

Midtown West's metro hub looked nothing like the degraded train stations Jude knew near Nova Angeles. The glass ceiling arched high overhead. Screens scrolled departure times in neat lines. The floor gleamed, too clean to feel honest. Everything was smooth. Controlled. Designed to move people without letting them think.

The crowd ebbed and flowed as one train emptied and another filled. Bodies pressed in from every side. Shoulders bumped his, elbows brushed his ribs, and he suddenly missed the sandy expanses back home.

Out there, at least the world had room. Wind and sky and his shipping crate on the outskirts of Nova Angeles where he hid after everything was taken from him.

His wife killed. His daughter shipped to Mars. He swore to one purpose ever since. Victor Kol would fall, no matter how long it took. He'd be sure of it.

He sat alone in that crate, scheming while the Sand Alliance existed in scattered pockets that never seemed able to pull together long enough to force real change.

Zaheen arrived, a nobody who lost someone, just like him. Just like all outsiders. Somehow, that made her different. Her grief felt like a story people could follow. It gave shape to his anger and turned it into something that almost looked like hope. And Jude was not a man who trusted hope. If it could move him, it could move others. Maybe enough to end Victor Kol for good.

Ten feet ahead, near the base of the escalator, a guard stood planted by a marble column holding a tablet.

Jude caught a glimpse of the screen. His own face stared back at him from the glow. It read: *WANTED: Treason, Class 5.*

Adrenaline surged, but he forced his breath steady. His hood hung low, a strip of shadow draped across the upper half of his face. He counted twelve guards spaced along the platform. One more waited at the top of the main escalator, where the station funneled into the streets of Midtown West.

Jude adjusted his stride. Smoothed out the urgency. Slowed his steps a fraction and let his arms swing like he had somewhere ordinary to be.

Just another belt-and-button insider. Tired from the grind. Heading home to a dinner that didn't exist. *Be ordinary. Ordinary is invisible.*

The escalator rose in front of him, a slow-moving river of metal steps carrying people toward the street. At the top, the guard blocked the exit. The crowd funneled past him one by one. Guards stopped one person here, another there, peeling back hoods and tugging off hats, exposing faces to the station's bright light.

One curt nod, and each cleared commuter vanished into the artificial sunset.

Jude brushed the knife hilt hidden deep in his pocket as his turn crept closer.

"Lift your head," the guard said as Jude reached the top. "Hood off."

Jude drove his fist into the guard's nose. Bone met cartilage. Cartilage lost. The guard didn't even have time to swear before Jude hit him again. The man toppled backward onto the escalator. Gravity took over from there.

He rolled, bounced, and slid down the metal steps, limbs tangling the wrong way, until he hit the grate at the bottom in a heap that looked less like a person and more like a broken toy.

The crowd shattered. People shoved and stumbled, scrambling away from the escalator, from Jude, from the idea that violence could spill into their perfectly curated commute.

Jude surged forward, forcing himself through the press of bodies. He used elbows. Forearms. Whatever allowed. The tunnel spat him out into a courtyard.

Midtown West greeted him with stone paths traced in perfect geometric patterns. Tower gardens climbed the walls; every leaf trimmed into obedience. Water shimmered in narrow channels that cut through the square, not for drinking or survival, just decoration. None of it matched the world Jude came from.

Time to disappear.

He ducked into an alley and dropped behind a dumpster, one hand locking around the knife hilt at his waist. His pulse thrashed in his ears, fast and angry.

Footsteps pounded past the alley mouth. Voices barked clipped commands. The sound chased itself away down the corridor until it dissolved into the district's clean stone and curated silence.

For now, Jude escaped.

He tugged his hood tight and stepped out from behind the dumpster. Puddles shivered beneath the fairy lights strung overhead, their reflections breaking into shards of false stars. The polished chemical smell faltered here—sweet perfumes thinning into the sour reek of food waste and wet stone, a hint of something left to die beyond the glow.

His boots clicked against the alleyway's slick pavement, the sound too loud in a place meant to be forgotten. It echoed off stucco walls and bounced back to him like a warning.

A woman sat slumped between two mounds of trash. Tattered cloth hung off limbs pared down to bone. Her skin looked brittle enough to tear. Patches of hair were missing. When her mouth fell open, Jude saw gaps where teeth should have been.

"How much for your cloak?" he asked.

She stirred and lifted her head. The light caught her face —deep lines carved by sun, wind, and time. She was a map of survival, badly worn.

"You're an outsider," she said.

"What makes you so sure?"

"Your skin's burned. Your body says you don't eat five meals a day."

"Or maybe I'm a dangerous insider having a bad night."

She barked a laugh. "Insiders beg. They don't run. And no one in here calls themselves insiders."

Jude pulled out a protein bar he'd been saving for emergencies and set it in her hand. "I'm that obvious."

She tore it open and bit down like it had been years since her last meal. "Thank you, outsider."

Jude crouched so they were eye level. "If you hate it here so much, why not go to the sand? My people would take you in."

"Rot is rot," she said. "Doesn't matter where you're buried. But at least here the sun can't peel me like fruit."

Jude saw the mirror in her. The version of himself waiting if he failed.

"Things will change," he said. Mostly to convince himself. "For people like us."

"Perhaps." She tugged at the cloak on her shoulders. The fabric resisted. Her arms trembled as she worked it free. She pressed her rags into his hands. "Take it. You need a new look. They won't stop hunting you."

He draped his own cloak over her shoulders. "Trade," he said.

She studied him through rimmed eyes, and for the first time, he thought he saw something like faith stir there. "You're a kind soul. I hope luck follows you."

"Maybe you're my four-leaf clover," Jude said. He tugged the borrowed sleeves down, hiding the knife at his waist.

Jude stood. "What do you know about Chairman Sahar? Midtown West. Where he hides."

Her smile thinned, brittle as old paint. "Ah. I see. Just know this—what you're trying has been attempted more times than you can count."

"Yeah," Jude said, the rough fabric itching his wrists. "I'm stubborn."

She flicked a bony hand toward a pile of old tabloids at her feet. "Ivory Row. That's where they live. That's where gossip breathes. Sahar drinks at the Dome Pub. Everyone knows."

Jude scanned the pages. Landmarks. Names. "Stay safe. Liberation's coming." He ran back into the glittering lie of the city.

17

ARAYA

Araya slept for a couple of hours. Maybe. Sleep came in fragments, broken every few minutes by a hacking cough or whimper from nearby beds.

There were no clocks. Time was measured by discomfort. When the lights snapped on, her first instinct was to burrow under the covers and pretend the world had made a mistake. She squeezed her eyes shut and reopened. After the third try, it was very clear Mars wanted her here.

She got up. So did everyone else. Seasoned outsiders knew better than to argue with light.

Crimson guards collected Araya, marched her and the others down the corridor, and planted her on the metro beside Iman. Minutes later she was dumped into tunnel three.

The outsiders marched single file. Collars yanked up over mouths and noses. Her breathing went ragged. Every inhale scraped. Martian air had a way of announcing itself. The taste hit first—red lustronium dust coating her tongue, fine as flour and smelly as rotten eggs.

She glanced over her shoulder. Dante stood farther back. Skye even farther. The identification sequencing had done its job in keeping them separate. A few digits on fabric, and suddenly they were strangers again.

The machinery droned. Every so often, a distant blast rolled through the rock. The ground shuddered. Fine debris sifted down from the ceiling and drifted like bloody snow.

Araya grazed the tunnel wall. Crimson ore filmed her skin —thick, tacky, and warm. It smeared across her fingertips and seeped in slow lines like a cut that refused to seal. She wiped her hand on her pants. The red left dark, sticky streaks in the black fabric and dulled the silver safety stripes.

Iman handed Araya a mask and put her own on. "Here. Now you."

A shelf was carved straight out of the rock, jammed with rows of masks like a supply closet that had given up. Rubber straps hung limp. The frames were dull and scratched, the edges worn smooth by years of breath, sweat, and grit.

Araya blinked, disoriented by the endless butterscotch walls, and realized she drifted all the way to the front of the line.

"Thank you." Araya hooked the strap over her head and tugged it down. The fabric rasped against her cheeks like burlap. The rigid frame bit into the bridge of her nose and pressed hard against her mouth.

She inhaled, and tasted dust. The seal wasn't a seal so much as a polite suggestion. Haze slipped in at the corners and settled in her throat.

"You'll get used to it." Iman wiped her sleeve across her sweaty forehead.

Araya coughed and nearly spat the muck out but forced it down instead.

"Fumes from the core," Iman said. "They leak up and cling to everything."

Iman led Araya deeper into the tunnel's belly.

Ooze seeped out of the rock and slicked the stone. Overhead, yellow bulbs flickered in weak, uneven bursts. Araya stared up at one, hoping for warmth and brightness. Some fake version of the sun.

The bulb gave her a dull glow and faint buzzing, dying out of spite.

At the tunnel's center, a conveyor belt crawled along the rock like a chained animal. The gears whined. Vents coughed up fumes. Steam curled and clung to rust-eaten barricades before drifting off, bored and poisonous. Red-streaked ore clattered past in a steady rattle and vanished into the dark, headed somewhere important. Not for her.

Outsiders worked in tight rows, one station a few meters from the next. Masks erased faces. Every outsider was an anonymous body. Interchangeable by design. People reduced to moving parts. Anything that made them individuals had been rubbed off, same as the paint on the safety stripes of her mining uniform.

"I hope Dante and Skye are okay."

"Friends of yours?" Iman asked.

Araya nodded. "New. Like me. Friends. Like you."

They reached their station. Two hooks had been hammered into the rock at shoulder height, each holding a red helmet stamped with an identification number. One for Iman. One for Araya.

Araya lifted her helmet and turned it in her hands. The plastic was scuffed. The inside smelled like old sweat. "How do I tighten it?"

Iman slid on her own. It sat crooked as if designed for someone else. "You don't. One size fits all."

At the base of the hooks, two tools waited like they'd been left there fifty years ago and everyone agreed not to talk about it. A pickaxe with a head dulled to a rusty copper. A shovel with a metal handle wrapped in peeling tape curled away in strips like dead skin.

Araya picked them up and tested the weight. "Do you have a preference?"

"I'll take the pickaxe." Iman gave it a quick bob. "Shoveling's easier."

"That's kind of you."

Iman smiled. "Mars needs a little kindness."

Araya drove the shovel into the ground. The blade bit into rock and she leaned on it. "Okay. How does this work?"

"The one with the pickaxe breaks the wall." Iman demonstrated with a swing. "You wear it down until it gives."

She hit the wall again. "The shoveler piles the rubble onto the conveyer belt. That feeds tunnel two. Processing's there. Packaging is Tunnel One."

"Sounds simple enough." Araya stabbed the blade into the rubble by Iman's boots and learned something immediately: Martian rock had zero interest in cooperating.

The shovel bit, the pile resisted, and the impact snapped a clean line of pain up her wrists like the handle was plugged straight into her bones. "I take it back. Far from easy."

She pried up a load. Her arms flared like someone had

swapped her muscles for wet rope. She shuffled to the conveyor. Araya tipped the shovel. Debris spilled out and clattered onto metal with a sharp, ugly rattle that bounced down the tunnel.

This was the job.

Scoop, carry, dump. Again. Again. Again.

Araya shoveled for hours before the first incident occurred.

The ache in her arms settled into a steady throb, blending with the drone of the machines, the rhythm of strike and scrape, dump and return.

Two stations down, an older man buckled. His knees gave out. His mask slipped free, torn loose as he hit the ground. He gasped once, twice, hacking so hard the sound dragged a knife down Araya's spine. Red dust burst from his mouth, spattering his uniform, hands, and the floor. He writhed, clawing at the air, and seized.

Guards stormed in. New outsiders like Araya froze mid-swing, shovels half-raised, pickaxes hanging useless in the air.

But the veterans, Iman included, didn't falter.

They didn't even look up. Arms rose, fell, rose again, steady as clockwork. Chipping. Lifting. Feeding the belt. A man dying at their feet was no more remarkable than a cloud passing overhead.

Araya recast the man on the ground as herself. She pictured her own body coming home in a metal box. On the other side,

Zaheen waited, tears carving tracks through her dusty face, as officials handed over a sealed casket and a list of meaningless causes. None of it changed the truth. Araya would still be dead.

Is this what I'm meant to become?

"Ignore it, Araya," Iman said. "Keep working."

Araya dumped the rocks onto the belt and staggered back to Iman's side. "We have to help him," she said. She drove her shovel into the dirt so hard the impact rattled up her arms.

"No." Iman said. "Focus on yourself."

Araya looked past her.

The guards formed a tight ring around the fallen man. One dropped to his knees and pressed his hands against the outsider's chest.

Once. Twice. The motion was stiff and hurried, more habit than care. His gloves slipped on the mix of red lustronium dust and spit and blood smeared across the man's shirt. After a few pushes, he pulled back, already done trying.

The outsider's mask lay crooked beside him. His mouth hung open, lips crusted red. Grime clung to his teeth. Each failed breath sounded like it was being dragged through wet gravel.

"What's wrong with him?" Araya asked.

"Red Lung. Red lustronium coats your respiratory tract until you can't breathe."

Araya could almost feel the dust inside her own chest, settling into every crevasse until she too would perish of the same fate.

By the time she was back to work, one of the guards had slung the limp body over his shoulder. The man dangled there, arms hanging loose, boots knocking against the guard's back with each step. He looked less like a person and more like a sack of spoiled grain being hauled away.

"Casualty in tunnel three," the guard said into his walkie-talkie. "Notify Los Angeles. We need another body."

She turned to Iman, heart rattling against her ribs. "The body bags. It must have been Red Lung."

Iman's eyes flicked sideways, quick as a gust, and back to the wall. "No, Araya. That wasn't it."

Not Red Lung. Then what? What's worse than drowning in dust? The question swelled. She swallowed it back down where it belonged, into the cracks of a whisper. "I need to know."

Iman struck the wall. "No. You don't."

Araya dropped her shovel and crossed her arms tight across her chest. The clang echoed down the tunnel. "I need to know," she said again, louder this time, daring trouble to come.

"Pick up your shovel."

Araya hesitated, heat rising under her mask. Then she unclenched her arms and reached down. She closed around the handle, the wood biting into her palms as she lifted.

Iman hit the wall with her pickaxe. "There was a rebellion," she said. "A movement. Nothing huge. Just people trying to go home. Small things—skipped shifts, broken tools, resistance in quiet places. It spread like fire."

She swung again. "Director Sorev put it out a couple of days before you showed up."

Araya drove her shovel into the rubble at Iman's feet. "Put it out?"

Iman's head dropped, chin pressed to her chest, as if she

could make herself smaller. "Firing squad," she said. "So much blood."

When she finally looked up, tears tracked down her cheeks. She wiped them away fast, like she was afraid someone might see.

"Did... did anyone survive?" Araya asked.

"Not a single soul. You're the replacement crew. They needed experienced workers from other tunnels. That's why I'm here."

Araya's heart seemed to stop at the shout of a guard heading their way.

Iman's grief vanished. Her face smoothed over, every line of despair sealed. She went back to work as if nothing had been said.

How do you do that?

"Stay polite and quiet," Iman said, eyes fixed on the wall. "No matter how ruthless they get."

Araya's pulse hammered in her ears. Pain throbbed at her temples. She forced her arms to keep moving and drove the shovel into the rubble.

Lift. Heave. Stagger to the conveyor. Dump it. Watch it slide into the dark. Do the job. Follow orders.

The guard loomed over Iman. "Drop the pickaxe and face front!"

She obeyed. Iman let the pickaxe go. It hit the ground with a dull thud, kicking up a puff of red dust that curled around her legs like smoke from an unseen blast.

"What makes you think talking on shift is acceptable?"

His hand snapped out. The slap cracked like thunder. Iman's head whipped sideways. Her helmet skittered across the gravel. Her mask slipped askew, exposing her mouth to the poisoned air. Red dust clung to her lips.

Iman's eyes darted everywhere but at him—down to the floor, to the dust, briefly on Araya—anywhere but his face.

"I asked you a question."

"I was helping a newcomer with training," Iman said. "I take full responsibility."

The guard laughed and shoved her.

Iman slammed against the wall. Her knees hit the gravel, and her palms skidded across it, skin peeling as she caught herself. She hunched in, shoulders drawn tight, as if trying to fold her whole body into the smallest space possible.

"Please," Iman said. Her voice was barely more than breath. She stayed down, forehead close to the rock, asking the planet for mercy.

Araya clenched her fists. Every instinct begged to spring forward and drag her friend to safety. More importantly, to drag her fist to the guard's face.

She hid the urge. Helping meant punishment. Punishment meant distance. Distance meant losing Zaheen forever. She hated her logic, hated herself for agreeing to it, but it was true. Zaheen came first. No matter what.

The guard circled Iman, savoring every second. "You don't get to make rookie mistakes. That's not how this works."

If this is what obedience buys, what will defiance cost me?

"Get up. Get working. Your record makes me feel generous." His mouth twisted into a smirk. "Don't waste it."

Iman lurched to her feet. She snatched her helmet and jammed it on without checking the straps. The mask hung wrong, mouth exposed. She didn't fix it. She reclaimed her pickaxe and swung. The wall spat red dust. She swung again. Again. And again.

"And you." The guard's eyes cut to Araya.

She froze beside the conveyor, shovel clutched so tight her knuckles ached. Not even when the messenger had pressed that cursed envelope into her hand back on Earth did fear hit this hard or this fast.

The shove came as expected, and she caught herself.

He chuckled, a sound with no real humor in it. "Sturdy," he said, stepping back. His gaze dragged over her like a butcher choosing his cut. "Stay that way. Outsider filth"

He walked away.

Araya stood there, heartbeat thudding in her throat, shovel still locked in her grip. Her muscles screamed for her to fight back. Her mind screamed to run. Instead, she forced her legs to carry her to Iman.

She dropped to a crouch beside her. "I'm so sorry."

"Stop," Iman said. She slapped away Araya's reach.

"Iman, I'm—"

"Don't say you're sorry again." Iman pushed herself up, arms trembling before she forced them still. The pickaxe rose and crashed into the rock. Shards rained down. Red dust misted the air between them. "I'm not mad at you. I'm mad I'm still here. I just want to go home."

Home. Araya saw Zaheen's face, the tiny room, her wash bucket, and the sandy streets outside their tin door. Her life felt small at the time. Now that version of herself felt impossibly far away.

She drove her shovel into the pile, letting the force of red lustronium carry some of the panic out through her exertion.

I have to get home. I have to get Iman home, too.

"There's more," Iman said after a moment. "Things you need to know. But not now."

19

JUDE

Jude slipped in, more shadow than man, peeling himself off the wall as he passed through the arch into Dome Pub.

The stench was nauseating. Perfume, smoke, and forced laughter collided into dizziness meant to overwhelm the senses.

He dragged his hood lower and lengthened his stride, letting the folds of fabric hide him as much as they could in a place like this. His body knew how to vanish, years of practice, even in a room determined to blind him in light.

He reached the bar and slid onto a stool, back angled just enough to keep the door in sight.

His gaze swept upward. The ceiling—a white-stone dome laced with restless laser lines—shifted in patterns that never stilled. To insiders, it probably looked elegant. To Jude, it seemed like a cage pretending to be a sky.

Golden beams bent in impossible angles, falling like broken sunlight caught behind glass. The walls shimmered maroon beneath copper-framed mirrors, each one polished to perfection.

Jude felt a quiet, aching pity for the insiders. They never stood beneath the real sun. The sun was cruel, yes, but it was honest. It stripped away comfort and illusion, left nothing to hide behind. Even on the worst days, when it blistered his skin, it belonged to him in a way the dome never could.

Patrons admired themselves as if their reflections held secrets worth worshipping. Lips glossy. Teeth white as limestone. People posing in front of mirrors. Jude couldn't tell whether it was vanity or loneliness that drove them.

Their clothes clung like wet skin, translucent fabric hugging ribs and hips until modesty was nothing more than an old rumor. Bodies pressed close, brushing without apology.

He shifted on the stool, fighting the irritation crawling across his skin. All of it—the shine, the noise—felt like an assault. Places like this weren't built for people like him.

Give him rust and grit. Give him the scrape of wind against tin walls, the groan of his container in the desert night. That was honest. This was not.

Insiders cradled glasses, swirling jewel-bright liquids Jude couldn't name. He watched mouths open, lips curling around words that never reached the eyes above them. Masks talking to masks.

The music thudded, rattling the space and knocking around his skull until thought splintered.

Everyone glowed. Faces painted gold, sharp cheekbones carved by artificial light. Hair rose and curled and twisted, sculpted into impossible shapes like artifacts stolen from an ancient gallery. They waved to servers without looking, and the servers came.

That kind of ease... what would my people give for it?

Behind the bar, the mixologist worked her stage. Dry ice hissed smoke, and neon bloomed in cups too bright for nature. She poured molten reds and bright blues into a shaker and let the music carry her wrist and hips until even the bottles seemed to dance.

A snap, a twist, and she set a drink beside him, the color of amethyst fire. The crowd gasped, applauded, and dazzled. Jude was a statue.

The music changed, and the crowd spilled toward the dance floor. Bodies rushed in a single, pulsing tide. Jude remained where he was at the bar, a fixed point in the flow, hood shadowing his eyes.

"Anything to drink?" the bartender asked. She motioned to the arsenal of bottles gleaming like jewels behind her.

"Nothing too strong," Jude said. "I've got business later."

"One of my specials, then. Coming up."

She salted a glass and dropped four ice cubes. Blue and yellow streamed together like fractured light through a prism.

"This one's a secret," she said. The insider stirred with a tiny whisk, a playful smile tugging at her mouth. She winked. "Preserves the flavor. Try it, you'll like it."

He lifted the glass. A punch of sweetness snapped his senses awake. He licked the salted rim.

"Very nice," Jude said, surprised, and took another sip. "What do you call it?"

"Old L.A.," she said. "I wish I could've seen it."

She chuckled and leaned in, tucking back strands of hair that gleamed like an oil slick under the bar lights. "Before the sand swallowed the coast. And the fires turned green to ash. I've always wondered what it'd be like to see an ocean."

Jude folded his arms, gaze drifting upward, but he didn't

see the ceiling or the lasers. He saw sand and fire. Burned towns. Scorched dunes. Families torn apart. His own life reduced to ash the moment they took his daughter and killed his wife.

Everything after that had been desert: dry, brutal, endless. Of course, that was all he saw when he looked ahead.

"I've never cared for the heat," he said. "Snow... that's where I'd rather be. A mountain peak, and the hush of winter." His voice softened, almost wistful. "To see snow, that would be enough."

The mixologist raised a finger, almost poking his chest. "At least we've got this dome over our heads. A society worth living in."

Jude let out a humorless laugh. "More like a fake reality. A blindness that leaves everyone in here floating in their own bubble."

Her brow arched. "Maybe that's what keeps people going. A skewed perception. If they saw the world as it is, maybe they'd break. Hell, I know I would."

"Or maybe they'd do something about it."

She shrugged him off. "Insiders aren't the charity type."

That tracks. They'll drink their Old L.A.s and dance until the desert catches up to them. "You know Chairman Sahar?" Jude asked casually. "Crazy what happened to him earlier."

"That man tips well," she said.

Jude spun his glass and took another sip. "You know him then?"

"Between you and me," she said, and nudged her chin toward a deliveryman slipping out the exit, "his residence put in a massive order tonight. That means an even bigger tip."

Her eyes flicked to Jude's receipt. "Speaking of..."

Jude dug into his pockets, past lint and worn fabric, brushing the familiar outline of his knife before closing around coins. He set them on the bar. "Keep the change," he said, standing. "I'm the charity type."

Without another word, he slipped into the stream of dancers, shadow folding into shadow. The crowd swallowed the space he left, music and light rushing in to erase him as if he'd never been there at all.

Outside the pub, Jude crept past a row of gleaming electric sports cars.

The deliveryman hefted several bags into a black sedan, slammed the door, and bass thundered as the engine growled to life.

Jude rolled under the sedan before anyone could glance his way. Heat swarmed. The undercarriage toasted his palms. Oil and exhaust clawed at his nose. He locked his fingers around the frame, every muscle rigid to hold his weight.

The car lurched forward. The first burst of acceleration punched the breath out of him.

The world narrowed to metal under his hands and strain in his joints. His body begged for relief, but he held on. Let go, and he was back in Midtown West with guards on every corner and his face on every screen.

Jude tilted his head, peering past the spinning tires, and ignoring the roaring road inches from his back. Wind knifed at his face, and he pretended it was no different than the sandstorms he faced outside. Though it was. Under the car, he had no control of where to hide and had to take the pain for what it was.

When the car slowed, ivory walls rose, smooth as elephant tusks and tall as towers. At their center, a gate with gold-tipped bars shimmered in quiet insult to everyone outside. The gilded beauty and décor were unseen where he came from. Through the gate, the artificial moon lay soft lines on perfectly manicured trees.

The deliveryman leaned out the driver's window. "Order from Dome Pub."

"Got it," said the security officer at the gatehouse. His posture was loose, almost bored, but his eyes were alert, scanning every item in the bag with the lazy precision of someone who trusted the system to back him up.

"Head straight down the road," the officer said, and returned the food to the driver.

With a low groan, the gates began to part, and Jude held on tight.

20

JUDE

Jude never saw anything like it. The road forward didn't look real. It gleamed with no cracks or stains, like someone had unrolled it fresh that morning.

Trees lined both sides, standing at attention. They weren't twisted by wind or dried by drought. They stood in perfect intervals. Each crown was clipped so precisely it looked more decoration than living thing.

He watched fountains shoot water into shallow pools, spilling in clear, glittering sheets. Plump koi drifted beneath the surface, lazy and full, waiting for their next meal.

In Nova Angeles, he was accustomed to stretching a single bucket of water across three days. A few swallows to drink. A handful to rinse sand from his face. Whatever was left to wash scrapes after the desert tore at him from supply runs deep in the desolate wastes.

Jude never saw this much green. Beyond the fountains, roads, and trees, unrolled endless hills as far as the eye could see. The Sahar residence looked like the planet chose one place to save and left everything else to rot.

By the time he dragged his eyes away, the van was already braking. It eased to a stop at the base of the estate's wide steps.

Jude slipped free from beneath the chassis, hit the ground with a muted thud, and ducked behind the rear tire.

"Sir, stop," a voice barked.

He drew his blade, pulse spiking. *Was that for me? Did I slip?*

Guards poured out from the mansion doors. Their suits were pressed, every crease perfect. Rifles hung across their chests, polished so bright they looked more like jewelry than weapons.

"We need to inspect the bag."

Jude exhaled, relief loosening his chest by a fraction.

The driver handed over the bags. Guards opened them and skimmed the contents with bored efficiency.

Jude risked a look past the tire.

The mansion rose from the hill in one unbroken sweep of pale stone. Ivory walls glowed under estate lights. Tall columns marched across the front, four stories high, their shadows stretching long over the perfect stone steps. Balconies jutted from the upper floors, trimmed with wrought-iron railings that curled like vines.

Jude spotted her before he registered the opening doors.

Her face held a warm sheen, accentuating cheekbones sharpened by years of standing beside power. Dark curls fell, pinned back just enough to flash the turquoise at her ears. Her gaze swept over the guards, the driver, the bags, taking inventory without a flicker of worry.

She stood at the top of the steps in a flowing floral dress. It was not an accident. She chose the one spot that made every eye land on her.

Jude knew that posture. He saw it before in political broadcasts, in glossy stills on Nova Angeles billboards. Leila Sahar. Los Angeles' sweetheart.

Jude hated her.

Every year or so, she swept into Nova Angeles with Chairman Sahar for a town hall. Curated questions. Limited seating. No real conversation. On the way out, she tossed petals over the children, all smiles and soft words about *their bright future.* She left crates of fresh fruit behind to remind people what they didn't have, packaged as a reward for hard work.

Leila Sahar cradled newborns, kissed their foreheads, and assigned them an identity number. Locations logged. Futures recorded for messengers to retrieve at age twenty for those with their numbers drawn.

All wrapped in what Leila liked to call *kissing every baby with hope and prosperity.*

What made it worse was knowing she grew up in Nova Angeles. She fought thirst, grit, and empty cupboards. Instead of joining the fight, she found a way out for herself— into Los Angeles. Her life was built on the backs of people she left behind.

There you are. Jude smiled at his target.

Eren hurried down the steps and hooked his arm around Leila.

"We've had quite the day," Leila said as she reached the car.

The driver bowed. "An honor, as always, to serve you, madam."

"The honor is mine. Thank you for all the hard work you do to keep our people fed." The words flowed easily, the kind that sounded good to voters. She took one of the bags herself and turned away. "Eren, pay him please."

"How much?" Eren asked.

"Four hundred, sir."

Leila and her guards slid into the mansion.

The instant Eren was alone, Jude sprang from behind the tire, red blade pressing to the driver's neck. "You scream, you run, you cry," Jude said, eyes on Eren, "he dies."

Eren shot his arms skyward. "I can give you money."

"Money isn't what I want."

"If you want to talk to my father... he'll listen. I can go get him."

Jude shook his head. "The circumstances aren't right. I don't want to hurt you."

His eyes flicked past Eren, scanning the mansion's entry, no guards for now. Relief would be temporary. They'd come. They always did.

"Please," the driver said. "Just do what he says."

Jude didn't spare him a glance. His focus stayed fixed on Eren. "Get in the car."

Eren's voice cracked. "Can we just talk?"

"Another step," Jude said, and pressed the blade harder, "and he bleeds."

Eren walked toward the car and opened the back door. Jude shoved him inside and released the driver. The man bolted for the mansion and didn't look back once.

"He's getting help. You're not getting away with this."

Jude wanted to laugh. *Of course, I am.*

Eren lunged—messy, frantic, all instinct and no thought —reaching for Jude's knife like courage could outpace years of combat training.

Jude's fist met his nose with a sharp crack. Eren dropped instantly, limbs loose, consciousness torn away before he hit the seat.

Jude caught him. Eren's head lolled against his shoulder. He lowered Eren carefully, easing him onto the leather. The boy's arm slipped loose and fell to the side.

Jude lifted his arm, tucked it back in, arranging him with the quiet care of a parent settling a child who fell asleep somewhere they weren't meant to.

"Believe it or not," Jude said under his breath. "I didn't want to do that."

He shut the back door and circled to the front, hands shaking as he dropped into the driver's seat. The engine roared to life. He slammed the gas and the car lurched forward, tearing past the mansion steps, glittering fountains, manicured trees, and green hills.

In the rearview mirror, the estate shrank to a clean little lie of perfection in a world littered in desolation.

He'd taken a boy. Someone's son. Eren grew up cushioned from real hardship, and for one sick heartbeat Jude envied that kind of safety. He thought of his own daughter and felt something twist. Guilt ran under his skin like a second pulse. He was doing exactly what the outsiders had done to him. Reaching into a home and tearing a family apart.

If this works, millions of kids never go to Mars. No more caskets. No more numbers. One boy for millions of lives. One boy of a corrupt politician.

The thought tasted foul, but he held onto it anyway.

He saw flashes—his wife's body in the doorway, his daughter's face as they dragged her away, Holly and Zaheen knocking on his door decades later. All of it stacked up behind the choice he had just made.

"I'm not doing this for myself. This is leverage. This is how things change."

But another voice rose inside him. The one that sounded like every monster who ever said the same. "I'm not a killer. I'm not like them."

The sentiment provided no comfort. He drove out of Midtown West with an unconscious boy in the backseat and a thin, fraying belief that this one wrong might be the only way to stop a thousand others.

21

ZAHEEN

Tranquil mornings greeted Zaheen with a soft brush of gold, though sunlight bled through smog thick enough to choke a small creature. She stepped into it anyway, letting the warmth cling to her weathered skin.

Before her, dunes unfurled in rippling waves of ochre and ash. The horizon was smudged with a faint gray of smoke. Thin clouds sagged across the sky. Shadows crawled like weary beasts over the sand.

On the front patio of Holly's bar, she let her body sink into an old wooden chair. It groaned, a brittle sound, but held. She curled her fingers around a chipped mug and lifted it close, steam brushing her lips. The tea was bitter, dense with desert herbs, but comfort spread through her like a secret flame.

Her gaze caught on the pale outline of the moon clinging to the smudged heavens, as if it, too, refused to leave.

I'll get you back. No matter what it takes. It's my promise to you.

The door creaked open behind her, a slap of wood on wood as the screen fell back into its frame.

Holly settled beside her, cupping her own mug. "Tea in the morning can mend what the night tried to ruin."

Zaheen lifted the mug again, steam curling up in frail ribbons. She sipped—sweet, floral, with a bitterness at the back of her tongue. Soothing, yes, but only on the surface, like a bandage laid over a wound that still bled beneath.

She set the cup on the side table, fighting the dull throb gathering behind her eyes. She let her lids fall, willing herself into stillness.

But silence betrayed her. The messenger's smug smile stamped behind her eyes. And always, the question, hammering until she felt split in two. *Is Araya still alive? Or ash, scattered on a foreign wind?*

Her hands balled into fists in her lap. She opened her eyes to the haze, to the ghost of the moon still clinging to daylight. "I don't sleep anymore," she said. "I just lie there and think."

"Tell me, dear, what do you think about?"

"The messenger. Victor Kol. Chairman Sahar. Jude. Los Angeles. Mars. Araya. All of it. My eyes lock on the stars. It's the only time I feel close to her...like she's still out there, somewhere above. And I'm stuck down here. In this... this... wasteland."

Holly exhaled. Her eyes lifted to the low ceiling of haze that smudged out the sun. "I understand your pain." Her words trembled and broke. A tear traced a shining path down her weathered cheek before she wiped it away.

"The stars..." Her breath hitched. "They remind me of my son. A tease I can never escape." Holly paused, steadying herself with the practiced dignity of someone who'd spent years hiding grief. "We're both haunted. Misery recognizes its kin."

Holly set a weathered hand on Zaheen's knee. "We focus on what we can control. Every single step forward. That's how we win. Don't stare at the sky anymore, Zee. It'll only hurt you."

Zaheen forced herself to nod, though part of her bristled at the command. How could she look away from the sole source of connection to her other half?

Holly rose and pressed her weight into Zaheen's leg before she withdrew. "They'll be here soon. I'll brew more tea."

The door swung shut behind her, and the sound thinned into the scorched air, leaving Zaheen alone beneath the muted sky. She kept her gaze from the vanishing moon and let it settle on the road that cut toward the horizon, a thin promise of somewhere else.

As she watched, morning began to rouse the streets from their fitful sleep. Doors rasped open on crooked hinges. Outsiders shuffled from rusted tin huts, clutching baskets, shaking dust from cloaks that snapped in the gritty breeze like faded banners from forgotten wars.

Two boys wrestled a wheelbarrow up the slope, its wooden joints shrieking, piled with stale bread and sacks of sun-bleached spice. Beyond them, others trudged toward the dry sea, faces swaddled against the grit, shoulders bowed beneath empty burlap bags.

If luck didn't desert them, they'd return with fragments of the drowned towns—copper wire, intact cans, splinters of once-fine wood. Ghosts of a world that sank and left its corpse behind.

At the far end of the street, a crowd was forming, hoods drawn low, cloaks the color of storm-smeared haze. They moved as one. Sand eddied at their ankles, spinning into tiny devils that danced and died with each step.

When the crowd reached the warped boards of the patio, one figure eased free of the mass. She was tall and sinewed with long pale hair that fell in loose waves over her shoulders. Sun had kissed it the color of desert straw.

Up close, Zaheen saw the years written on her the way the wind carved stories into rock. Fine lines fanned from the corners of her eyes; deep creases bracketed her mouth. A few threads of silver brightened the hair at her temples. It reminded Zaheen of Holly, the same worn-in steadiness, and burden of having seen too much and kept going anyway.

The woman climbed the steps and stopped so close that Zaheen caught the faint salt composites on her skin.

"We are here for the demonstration," she said. "We are people of the Sand Alliance."

Zaheen stood. "Thank you for coming. I mean that deeply." Her gaze moved from their leader to the masses behind—survivors, every one of them. Survivors like her.

"I thank you all," Zaheen said, and bowed.

Without even a nod, the woman pushed past, fabric whispering over wood. "Let's discuss logistics inside. I'm parched."

The Sand Alliance trickled in. They didn't speak much, just low murmurs, scraping chairs, the sounds of contemplation before confrontation.

Zaheen watched from the corner, unsure she belonged.

Holly poured the last cup and clapped, the sound bright

against the hush. "Welcome, my friends! Please, make your-selves at home."

Holly spotted the woman in charge. "Is that Vivian Hale?"

Vivian pushed back her hood. To Zaheen's surprise, the hard lines of her face loosened into a smile that glowed like a flare. Holly had always been able to pull light from people, but this was as if a piece of history had stepped through the door.

"Holly Rowan," Vivian said, and placed a hand dramatically over her heart. "Do my eyes deceive me, or has the universe finally granted me a kindness?"

Holly covered her mouth as if swallowing a sob and rushed forward and hugged.

Vivian gripped the back of Holly's coat. "It's been far, *far* too long. I wondered if I would ever see this stubborn face again."

"You look—" Holly's laugh wavered and cracked.

"Like I clawed my way out of an art museum after refusing to die beautifully?" Vivian flicked her wrist with theatrical disdain. "Please. You should see the desert. It tried to age me out of spite."

Holly let out a watery laugh, tears still clinging to her lashes. "You haven't changed."

Vivian arched a brow. "You're no spring chicken either, my dear. But look at us. Still standing and raising trouble."

They hugged again, longer this time.

When they finally parted, Vivian let out a sigh. "Forty-five years," she said. "Do you realize I've spent more of my life away from Nova Angeles than within it?"

Zaheen heard stories of the Sand Alliance's builders, the

ones who left the city for entire lifetimes to strengthen outlying towns and knit fractured communities back together so the next generation might inherit something steadier. But she never imagined meeting one.

Vivian brushed grime from her cloak with a flourish. "I suppose you could say I have been busy. Rebuilding one community at a time, laying stones where hope used to be. Exhausting work, truly. My knees protest daily."

"Your timing could not be more perfect," Holly said. "We need your hands. Your history."

Vivian nodded, a slow, regal dip of the chin. "Well. If the world insists on falling apart, someone must hold the seams."

Holly beckoned with a small wave. Zaheen hesitated and stepped into the circle of warmth the two older women had formed.

"Look at this," Holly said, her breath catching. "My first firebrand and my protégé. Side by side. I've waited so long for this."

Zaheen felt that pride settle over her, heavy as a mantle she had not asked for.

"Zaheen, meet Vivian. Vivian, meet Zaheen." Holly's smile deepened. "Zaheen, the story I always tell you about the freight train we tipped during the ration riots—the one from my reckless youth? Vivian was right beside me that day."

"Right beside you and cursing your name the entire time," Vivian said. "You nearly got us flattened. I say that with great affection."

Vivian clasped Zaheen's hand in both of hers. "The movement has waited for this moment far too long. At last, a new flame."

Zaheen tilted her head. "The moment for what?"

"Do not be naïve, child." Vivian's lips twitched, the expression hovering somewhere between fondness and caution. She traded a look with Holly. Zaheen felt it sweep over her like a draft through open doors, leaving her exposed, as if the two women spoke in a language carved by decades she had not lived.

Vivian's stare returned, cool and sure, pinning her in place. "Rebellion, of course. Why else come back to this forsaken place? I've wandered across more towns than I can name, built half of them back up, and word still travels faster than a sandstorm. They say you are the voice of a movement too stubborn to die. And everyone outside"—she flicked her fingers toward the door as if gesturing to an entire world—"is waiting for you."

Child. Zaheen bristled. She wouldn't let Vivian's age or edge fold her small. They wanted the same things. Their battles raged in the same direction. But one word, *rebellion,* hit her like a gust that scoured skin raw, stripping her thoughts down to bone.

She dropped her gaze to the dust-caked boards beneath her boots and forced herself to look up again. "I don't want this protest to become a bloodbath," she said, and looked to Holly. "I only want to bring Araya and the others home. After that, we can negotiate with the insiders."

Holly reached for her. Her callused fingers curled around Zaheen's fist with a gentleness that broke something open. "We agree," she said. "Vivian and I both. No violence. Not today."

"Not today. But what about tomorrow?" Zaheen said. "When Kol bares his teeth again? How many tomorrows can I buy without paying in blood."

"Let's worry about today and see what we can accomplish," Holly said, and Zaheen hated how simple she tried to make things sometimes.

Vivian inclined her head. "Holly speaks truth. Today is about presence and making Victor Kol feel every life he has ignored. We stand tall. We remain composed. We let him see that the ground beneath him is shifting." Her pale eyes sharpened. "But remember this. Power is an illusion. And when a man realizes his illusion has shattered, he does not go quietly."

"I won't let it," Zaheen said.

"Oh, I do hope you're right, Zaheen," Vivian said. "My people are ready for peace today. But they are not strangers to the storm."

"Then now's the time," Zaheen said.

Vivan nodded, shouting to the crowd. "We move to the tracks. This will be peaceful. Zaheen leads us."

The crowd surged like a shifting tide. Zaheen found herself carried to the front, Holly at her right, Vivian a few steps behind. Together, fractured in idea, but moving in the same direction, they stepped into the rising day—song and silence, peace and fury—each conviction discordant on its own yet bound by one pulse, one refusal to surrender the future.

22

ARAYA

A sour, rotten breath wafted up from the tray in Araya's hands.

The food sloshed in the bowl. Brown sludge sat in uneven coils and smears, shiny on top, dull underneath. She saw residue in Nova Angeles landfills that looked more appetizing.

She and Iman took their seats in the cafeteria's gloom.

Sweaty pipes ran overhead in neat, parallel lines, beaded with condensation that occasionally dripped on random outsiders. Lights bathed everyone in jaundice. Long metal tables stretched out in rigid rows, bolted to the floor.

Outsiders packed the benches shoulder to shoulder. Uniforms were all stained the same dull red brown. Everyone wore the tunnel—on their clothes, in their hair, in the tired way they sauntered.

Araya scanned the walls. They sagged under layers of patchwork: plates screwed over cracks, repairs stacked on repairs until she couldn't tell what was original and what was emergency improv.

She poked the sludge with her spoon. The surface shivered, and she leaned back a few inches. She didn't get this far by trusting suspicious puddles.

Iman saw her face and let out an exhausted laugh.

Araya eyed the bowl. "Just making sure it doesn't sprout legs."

Iman stabbed her spoon into the muck, lifted it dripping, and shoveled the whole wobbling mass into her mouth.

Araya gagged on principle. "It smells like an insider squatted over my tray and left this behind."

Iman swallowed. "You'll get used to it."

"No... I won't."

Iman's spoon paused halfway to her lips. "You need the energy."

"What I need is a new set of tastebuds. I can't do this."

"Eat." Iman shoveled more sludge.

Araya lifted her spoon, and the sludge quivered. She brought it closer. Closer. One bad decision away from her mouth.

"Is this seat taken?" Dante slid onto the bench across from her, looking like he'd been stored in a dustbin.

"Dante!" In Araya's excitement the sludge fell off her spoon and back on the tray. "I'm so glad you're alive."

"Likewise, my friend." He scooped a mouthful of gunk in his mouth. Araya fought the urge to gag again.

Skye dropped onto the bench beside Araya and hooked an arm around her shoulder. "Good to see you buddy. You're looking redder than a sunburned insider." Skye slid a finger down Araya's cheek. Red lustronium residue coated it.

Araya slid her finger down Skye's and revealed the same. "Takes one to know one."

Skye ate up a mouthful of sludge. "This tastes like it was scraped off a horse's ass."

Araya laughed. "Well, it is jackass-made," she said, and peered over to the cafeteria workers yelling for outsiders to move down the line faster than they could scoop gunk on their trays.

Dante tipped his head toward Iman. "And who's this?"

"My station partner and friend. Her name's Iman."

"A friend of Araya's is a friend of ours. I'm Dante." He nudged his chin across the table. "That's Skye."

Skye nodded at Iman and pointed her spoon at Araya's untouched tray. "If you're not eating that, I will. I'm starving."

"Didn't take you for a fan of horse shit," Araya said.

Skye lifted her pinky as she prepared another bite. "It's of the finest delicacies an insider can make."

Everyone laughed but Iman.

Araya turned toward her. "Iman... you alright?"

Iman forced a smile. "Just tired."

Araya glanced around the cafeteria. Guards loitered at a comfortable distance, close enough to intimidate, far enough to pretend they weren't listening.

"In the tunnel," she said, "you told me there was more you needed to reveal to us."

Iman went still. "I'm not sure I should. I never said *us*. I said *you*."

"You can trust us too," Dante said. "We want out. Anything you know could help our..." His eyes darted toward the guards. "...escape."

Araya gulped and decided to betray Iman's trust. "The body bags weren't from an accident."

Iman glared, but Araya didn't care. If there was more to say, she needed the information to get back to Zaheen.

Skye's spoon slipped from her fingers and clattered against the tray. "What do you mean?"

"They were murdered," Iman said. "All of them. Every worker from tunnel three." She looked at each of them in turn. "That's why you're here. You're the replacements. I was transferred here because they needed some veteran workers to keep quotas on track."

Skye's mouth opened a fraction. For a second she looked stunned, but the shock burned off. "That's an even better reason to get out."

Dante raised a finger to his lips. "Keep your voice down."

"Easy for you to say. I've tried more times than you can count," Iman said to Skye. Any softness in her face had vanished. "You need to meet someone. That's what I wanted to share with Araya."

She tipped her chin toward a table farther down the row.

Araya followed the gesture and found a man sitting alone, folded over his tray like gravity had been turned up just for him. He was wiry, not big, but tightened by necessity. His face was all angles, as if someone had carved it fast and quit halfway. Hair too long, dust caught at his temples.

When his gaze finally caught Iman's, something passed between them without words. Recognition. Warning. Agreement. He carried his tray over and slid onto the bench beside Iman like he'd been there the whole time.

"This is Bren," Iman said. "Tunnel three transfer like me. Farther in than the rest of us."

Up close, Araya caught the details Bren didn't bother advertising.

His shoulders sat too high, like he was perpetually braced for a hit that might come any second. His fingers trembled when he set the tray down, just enough to notice if you were looking for it.

"Bren, I've found three suitable choices."

Araya looked to Dante and Skye, and back to Iman. "Suitable? You've been testing me?"

"I wouldn't call it a test," Iman said. "I've been watching who you back, and how you carry yourself when it costs you."

Araya didn't care anymore. She needed answers. She leaned past Iman, and locked eyes on Bren. "Tell us what you know."

Bren wiped brown sludge with the back of his sleeve. "I've been here long enough to observe what most people stop noticing," he said. "Camera sweeps. Guard rotations. Blind spots. Supply restocks."

His eyes flicked up. "That camera's about to turn."

Araya tracked it. Sure enough, the lens glided across the room on its little programmed patrol, drifted over their table, and moved on like it had better things to do.

"We have a plan," Bren said. "Iman and me. We've tried to run it six times. Every time we get close, the recruits back out."

Skye leaned in, impatience vibrating off her. "Spill it."

"How do I know you won't fold the second things get messy? Are you prepared to kill if necessary? How many helpless outsiders will you leave here to get back home?"

Dante scraped the last smear of paste from his tray and set the spoon down. "I'd rather die trying than rot here."

Araya nodded. "Same for all of us."

Iman reached out and put a hand on Bren's arm. "We can't be picky."

Bren held her stare for a long beat. "Fine."

He lifted both hands, curled his fingers inward, then snapped them open like something invisible had just detonated between them. "Loud and coordinated. Get the gist?"

"How?" Skye said, already halfway out of her seat.

Bren rested his chin on his knuckles and rolled his eyes. "Red lustronium, obviously. We punch a hole out of here. Split the guards. Break to the upper tunnels. Secure a ship." He paused, eyes scanning the room out of habit. "That's all I'm sharing for now. The more we all know, the easier it is for them to sniff us out."

His gaze cut around the table. "You're in or you're out. If you're out, you never get back in."

Araya looked at Dante. Then Skye. Both were wound tight, ready to leap. Her mind supplied its own montage: bodies crushed under a collapse. Guards firing blind into smoke. Outsiders dying inside a plan that was supposed to save them.

"As long as we try to save everyone," Araya said, "we're no better than the table next to us."

Bren snorted. "The table next to you doesn't have a plan to get out."

"The table next to us deserves to go home as much as you or me."

"This isn't a casual invite," Bren said, shaking his head. "Someone vouches for you." He tipped his chin at Iman. "She trusts you. That's enough for me. But it also means we move fast. Trust is rare. And wasting it gets people killed. I've seen too many dead bodies."

The intercom crackled overhead. *"Break over. Report to your tunnels."*

The cafeteria shifted like a single organism responding to a stimulus. Chairs scraped. Voices died mid-breath. Fear slid back into place.

Bren stood and turned away from the table. "Sometimes protecting your own skin keeps you alive longer than protecting someone else's."

He walked off, tray in hand, blending into the crowd. "I'll be in touch," he said over his shoulder. "Decide fast, or we move without you."

PART TWO
SHIFTING SANDS

We'll rise like great dunes, resilient and formidable. Our collective is a sandstorm surging toward Los Angeles. Not even the cosmic void between here and Mars can break my spirit. My love knows no bounds. My pursuit knows no end. I will bring you home.

—ZAHEEN, CITIZEN OF NOVA ANGELES, RISING
LEADER OF THE SAND ALLIANCE

23

ZAHEEN

The sun beat down without mercy, a white-hot hammer striking a world already baked and broken. No cover. No shadow. Only dunes rolling out in every direction and heat waves writhing like restless spirits.

Zaheen stood at the center of it all.

The wind spat grit against her cheeks, each grain a tiny blade. She tasted dust, sharp as memory, and felt the desert reminding her—again—of everything it stole. This land held no grace. It had consumed her home, her certainty, and now it kept Araya somewhere she couldn't reach. *Come back to me.*

A tremor shivered through the rails beneath her feet. At first she mistook it for the desert settling, but the sound rose —low, heavy, and distant. A pulse. A warning. A train gathering speed far out on the horizon.

The vibration climbed her legs and set her spine humming like a bowstring pulled taut. She felt the force before she saw it. Felt the power barreling toward her, one mistake away from turning her body into debris on the tracks.

Her heartbeat matched the growl rolling across the plain.

Sweat stung her eyes. Sand needled her skin, burning hot, as her hair whipped across her face like a flag. Every instinct begged her to step back. She refused.

Around her, the others held their positions.

Holly grabbed her arm. The pressure was a wordless reminder not to break.

You don't have to tell me twice, Zaheen thought, tightening her jaw as the rails hummed beneath her boots. She looked past Holly to the outsiders gathered at the town's edge. A crowd pressed close, bodies wrapped in sun-bleached cloth, eyes fixed on the tracks with something caught between terror and hope.

Out on the rails with Zaheen and Holly, the Sand Alliance stood firm, boots rooted on steel and gravel.

Maybe the bystanders thought she was reckless. Maybe they thought she'd lost her mind, standing in the path of a train that could crush a line of people without slowing.

Fine. Let them think that. The only goal Zaheen was truly reaching for—what she ached to have back—was Araya.

"For our people on Mars!" Zaheen shouted.

Zaheen felt she had no right to be shaken. Her love, and so many across her community, faced worse. On Mars. In tunnels. In places where the sun couldn't reach them. In rooms where strangers controlled every action.

Zaheen, at least, had friends beside her. Mentors. Allies. She didn't know what Araya had. Maybe she had the same. Maybe she had nothing at all.

"Hold steady," Vivian said from Zaheen's other side. "If we falter now, we might as well offer the conductor our heads on a silver platter!"

The train's horn ripped through the dunes. A single

savage blast that shoved air into her chest and rattled her teeth. Another followed—shrill, brutal—echoing off the desert until the sound felt like it came from inside her bones. Its headlights strobed across the sand in violent bursts, each flash a command: scatter or be crushed.

Zaheen bared her teeth. "To cower is to tell our loved ones we gave up!"

The train thundered closer.

Zaheen closed her eyes and pulled in a long breath. The smoke coated her tongue, acrid and hot. *This is the ledge. One misstep and we all go over.*

Was any of this worth it? The meetings. The late-night maps on dirt floors. The promises whispered to strangers. The speeches about courage and unity. All of it pushed her to lead innocent people onto these tracks, under this merciless sun, as if her belief alone could shift the world.

Holly always said movements were stitched together with hope, maybes, what-ifs, the stubborn faith that enough people standing as one could force someone, somewhere, to listen. But now, with the train bearing down and the ground trembling like it was trying to warn her to run, doubt slid in.

If this is where it ends... Araya, I gave it everything. I didn't hold back. Not once.

Zaheen shut her eyes and focused on Araya's face—dark hair, soft grin, the way her eyes lit in the afternoon light— refusing to let it blur.

Metal screamed. A brutal, wrenching screech split the air.

Gasps erupted from the outsiders watching in Nova Angeles. Someone cried out. Another shouted a warning. Then came a deep, dragging huff, the unmistakable sound of a massive engine battling its own momentum.

Zaheen's breath caught. She opened her eyes.

The train screeched to a halt a meter away. Heat bled off its metal hull in thick waves. Steam curled from the vents in long, coiling strands, like the breath of some cornered beast trying to decide whether to maul or retreat.

The doors slid open with a hiss sharp enough to raise the hairs on Zaheen's arms.

Guards poured out in silver armor polished to a cruel gleam, boots striking in perfect unison.

"Clear the tracks," the captain said. "You're interfering with priority shipments to Los Angeles. Any defiance will be met with force."

Zaheen raised her chin. "We demand an audience with Victor Kol."

The captain stepped forward. His baton rose until it hovered between her brows. "Last warning. Step off the tracks or be removed."

Zaheen stepped into his threat. The baton pressed a circle on her forehead. "Victor Kol."

Applause drifted from the open doorway. "I must say... this is almost inspiring."

Victor Kol emerged, shadow first, then figure. He descended the steps with the smooth assurance of a man who never once feared consequence. The desert heat bent around him as if it knew better than to touch him. His navy robes were pristine, unmarked by dust or sweat, the fabric shifting with each step in quiet, controlled sways.

Behind him, guards adjusted their formation automatically and tightened until they formed a perfect wall to guard his every angle.

Zaheen felt the familiar burn in her chest. *This is the man who takes everything from me.*

Victor's gaze swept the Sand Alliance as though he were surveying a mildly interesting inconvenience rather than a blockade. "To stand here," he said, "in this heat, in my path—truly, it's a bold choice. Misguided, but bold."

Zaheen forced her voice steady, grounding herself in every face behind her, in every loved one shipped off to Mars. "Victor Kol. We're here for reclamation. I'm not leaving until you make this right."

24

ZAHEEN

Fear climbed Zaheen's spine and pooled between her shoulders. She locked her knees and forced herself to stay upright. This might be the only opening she ever got.

She held tight to the picture that had dragged her across miles of wasteland and kept her upright when her body begged to fold. Araya. Torn from her arms by the messenger. The feeling of her slipping away. The continual dread afterward.

Hold it together. Don't waste this.

Victor Kol adjusted his stance with a calm that drew every eye. A tilt of his head corrected a soldier's posture. A raised hand sent the rest falling into line. He didn't need to bark orders. His smallest movements were enough to make an army obey.

One by one, the guards stepped forward. Armor clicked. Boots struck sand in a steady rhythm. They split into two lines facing each other until a narrow corridor opened from Zaheen's position straight to Victor.

Every instinct begged her to attack, to kill him before he

gave the next order that would ruin another life. She kept her hands relaxed by her thighs. Violence would only prove him right about her people. And he was far from right.

He gestured for her approach, and the captain backed down.

As she stepped closer, Victor tipped his head, studying her with a birdlike focus.

"Reclamation," he said, savoring the word. "Is that the charm you've cast over these people? Whisper hope into their ears until they mistake it for truth?" His smile thinned. "What shall I call you."

"Zaheen Mandisa." The name left her mouth steady. "You took my land. My partner. My people. You call me a spellcaster, but you are the one on the stage, selling chains and calling them salvation."

Victor's mouth curved. He almost seemed pleased. "Zaheen Mandisa. Such fire."

"It grew from what you burned."

"May I ask your age, Ms. Mandisa?"

"You may not," she said.

"You don't look a day over twenty. Your grit could serve well on Perihelion. I'll make note."

Zaheen wrinkled her nose and glared. "You're a coward, forcing outsiders to do your dirty work."

"I believe what you meant to say is, *genius*." Victor lifted his hands in a gentle gesture. "I prefer solutions that don't involve bloodshed, Ms. Mandisa. Truly, I do. I was on my way to observe the latest haul of red lustronium. Your people were not taken. Your land was integrated. Outsider sacrifice maintains equilibrium. A small price for peace."

Zaheen's hands curled into fists before she forced them

open again. Her heartbeat climbed high in her throat. The guards sensed it. Their helmets shifted in unison. Their batons rose a fraction. The air felt one spark away from rupture.

"Integration without consent is only conquest with a different uniform," she said. "No more shipments or disappearances. I'm speaking for the people who stand with me. Release our families. Let outsiders return home. Sit with us. Speak with us. Start dialogue instead of demanding tribute."

Sweat slipped down her cheek. Victor watched its path with unsettling patience. "I'm afraid that request exceeds your authority," he said. "I don't take kindly to an outsider telling me how to run my business."

He took a step closer. His voice dropped to something coaxing, almost affectionate. "Perhaps we should continue this somewhere else. With less sand. Fewer eyes. The desert makes me cranky."

"Not happening," Zaheen said.

Victor shrugged and spun away. "Don't say you weren't offered the opportunity to talk."

Vivian's voice cut through the heat with perfect clarity. "You don't get to ignore the voice of the people!" She swept forward, robes flaring like a desert blossom caught in a storm. The guards blocked her path in a seamless wall of metal.

Vivian pressed against them. "Do you truly believe this is a performance? This is life and death, Victor Kol. These are human beings. Have you forgotten what a human looks like beneath all your machinery?"

Victor glanced over his shoulder. "Red lustronium powers your generators. It purifies your water. It keeps your markets from collapse. TerraLux Minerals does not exploit you. In return, I ask that you contribute. That you function as a part of the mechanism that keeps you alive."

"We never asked for your domes," Holly said, and rushed to the shield wall beside Vivian. "We never asked for your charity. You took our homes and families. Then rationed survival like scraps thrown to dogs. That's theft."

Victor paused. He turned just enough for sunlight to catch his face. "Why would I offer sanctuary to those who reject structure? You may despise the system, but it's the only thing standing between your communities and extinction."

Vivian shoved past Zaheen, but Zaheen caught her by the arm. "Don't," she said.

Vivian pulled free. Her eyes burned like twin embers. "Give us justice!" She lifted a rock from the sand and hurled it with every ounce of fury the desert had ever gifted her.

The rock struck the back of Victor's head. He dropped. The blow stopped him mid-stride, pitching him forward into the sand. A red bloom spread across the collar of his robes as he clutched at the wound, a strangled sound leaking through his teeth.

"Kill them," he said. "Kill these sand vermin."

The guards surged. Outsiders answered with a roar. Chaos erupted. Screams rose. Sand exploded upward in choking clouds. Limbs and batons collided. Helmets clanged. Bones gave. The world shrank to silhouettes thrashing in a storm of grit.

Zaheen dropped to her knees. "I wanted peace."

A body hit the ground beside her. A young man, no older than her, face frozen in shock, skull crushed, blood seeping into the sand until it turned a thick rusted red.

I don't even know his name.

"Zee!" Holly broke through the haze, arm outstretched, fingers searching for hers.

Zaheen's eyes snapped wide. A guard in full armor barreled toward them, massive and unyielding. "Holly, look out!"

Before he reached them, Vivian appeared like a streak of fire. She drove her fist straight into the guard's throat. The impact made a sickening, wet crack. He stumbled, choked, and she followed with an uppercut so sharp it snapped his head back, pressure buckling his spine. He collapsed into the sand and didn't rise.

Zaheen stared, stunned, pulse pounding. "This isn't what I wanted. Not like this."

Vivian wiped blood from her knuckles. "Are you hurt?"

Zaheen shook her head, unable to pull her eyes away from the bodies on the ground. "All those people... this is on us."

"Then let my hands stain," Vivian said. "Oppression struck first. I'm striking back." She turned and sprinted into the fray, robes snapping behind her.

White gas rolled in. It hugged the sand in a creeping sheet, and rose up legs and torsos, tightening its grip.

Screams gave way to coughing fits. Outsiders staggered, clutching at their throats, clawing at their eyes. Some tried to run. Most collapsed within seconds, limbs jerking as the gas tightened its hold. The battlefield dissolved into writhing shapes swallowed by pale vapor.

"Immobilization gas," Holly said.

Zaheen forced herself to turn, vision stinging. "Do you see Victor Kol?"

"Forget Victor," Holly said, grabbing her hand. "If we stay, we die."

Zaheen looked down. White vapor wrapped around her boots, climbing higher in thick coils. Her calves went numb. Her knees locked. Holly yanked harder, dragging her across the shifting sand.

They plunged into the dunes. Wind knifed across their faces. Some part of Zaheen fought to keep her eyes open, to keep running, to not give up—not when Araya was still out there—but the gas had won.

Her vision smeared. The dunes blurred into streaks of gold and white.

The last thing she saw was Holly's silhouette before everything collapsed into black.

25

ARAYA

Araya sat in the metro with her friends packed around her, but her attention snagged on the stranger across the aisle.

A dust-smeared, bruised woman stared back from the window's reflection. Fine, red-crusted lines webbed her face. She looked like every other Nova Angeles survivor—sunburned, underfed, and held together by stubbornness and bad luck—but the one thing that used to live behind her eyes had dimmed.

Nova Angeles had always been cruel in familiar ways. Wind scraped skin. Heat robbed sleep. Sand infested lungs and gave outsiders a perpetual cough as a souvenir. But she and Zaheen had learned the rules. They adapted and survived.

Mars didn't have those same rules.

Back home, on the western bank of town, there were cliffs that crumbled every summer. Heat cracked the rock until it gave up and fell, burying anyone walking beneath. Zaheen and Araya never scavenged there in summer. That was erosion in real time—gravity collecting its debt. Watching the land eat itself.

That same feeling lived here, in her chest. Not the physical danger. The *inevitable* danger. Like the planet had its hand around her throat, squeezing just slow enough to make her understand what was happening.

She let out a breath she didn't remember holding and looked away from the window.

"I know that look," Skye said from across the cabin. "The pause before the leap. Happens right before your brain tries to save you."

Araya swallowed. "What if the leap kills people who didn't choose to jump?"

"Hesitation is choosing to get left behind."

Dante, beside Skye, nodded with approval. "Loss is baked into the deal," he said. "At least with a plan... dying might mean something."

"We don't have to accept this deal. We can develop our own."

Iman nudged her shoulder into Araya's. "You know there's no other deal."

"I'm not talking about Iman or Bren or escape," Dante said. "I'm talking about all of us. The deal we're born into as outsiders. From our first breath to our last, death's already sitting at the table."

His gaze shifted, quick and automatic, to the cameras bolted into the corners. "Staying here isn't peace. It's surrender. They use us. Grind us down. Toss us when we're spent. And we pretend that's the only life we get."

He reached for her hands. "It doesn't have to be."

Dante's quiet conviction. Skye's sharp-edged fire. Iman's solid presence at her side. Araya hadn't meant to let any of them matter. That was rule one. Nova Angeles taught her the price tag on caring, and it was always higher than she could afford.

She loved one person. Zaheen. That was all she could handle.

And for one selfish second, she wished she'd never met them at all. No bonds. No losses. No new ways to be hurt. No constant, gnawing fear of watching them die because she chose wrong in the wrong moment.

Dante. Skye. Iman.

That was the truth, and it stung like a bruise. She cared. That was what terrified her most.

"They're both right," Iman said.

Araya looked at her.

"Doing nothing and hoping things change on their own isn't a strategy. I tried that." She nodded down the car, at the rows of exhausted faces and slumped shoulders. "I'm still here. So are they."

The carriage lights flickered. Once. Twice. The overhead strips stuttered and flared into a harsh white that shoved every shadow into the corners. Something clicked above them. A relay. A switch. A decision being made by a system that didn't care about people.

The speaker crackled. *"Exit single file and return to your designated stations."*

The train eased to a stop. The hum in the walls died, replaced by the tick-tick of cooling metal. A soft chime sounded, and the doors slid open.

Araya's pulse climbed the second she clocked the guards.

Not the usual handful. Dozens. Crimson-plated, shoulder to shoulder, lining the tunnel like someone had decided paranoia was a décor choice.

"This complicates things," Iman said.

"Break line! To your stations. Double the ore this shift. Move!" The guard yelled the same statement every couple of minutes.

The miners scattered like startled birds—heads down, tools clutched tight, bodies funneling into the frantic tempo the guards demanded. Fear did the organizing. No one needed a map. Everyone already knew where to run.

Araya reached her station with her lungs half-burned and her thoughts tripping over each other trying to find answers.

A guard stood at the tunnel mouth and lifted a megaphone. The feedback shrieked—one long, ugly wail that made every spine in the tunnel straighten on instinct.

"There's been an incident outside Los Angeles," he said. "Many died. Outsiders. Insiders. Survivors are now in the regional penitentiary. They'll be executed for their crimes."

Dizziness surged so hard she grabbed the edge of the station wall to keep herself upright. Her knees went soft. Her vision pulsed in and out like the lights were blinking behind her eyes. Panic dumped metal into her mouth, sharp and coppery, and suddenly every nameless outsider the guard mentioned had Zaheen's face.

Zaheen in a holding cell. Zaheen under a gun. Zaheen—

Stop.

"Let this be a warning. Anyone who challenges what Victor Kol has built will face consequences. If you're unclear on what that means, ask the veterans. They remember."

"You're murderers!" an outsider shouted from two stations down.

The tunnel stripped her down. Her skin matched the red-brown walls. Dust welded itself to her hair. Dark rings cratered beneath her eyes, like the rock branded her with exhaustion. She lifted her chin anyway. "All of you. Murderers."

A baton drove between the woman's shoulder blades and folded her to the ground. Another guard wrenched her arms back. There was a pop, and a sound that might've been a scream if the tunnel hadn't swallowed it. Gravel sprayed as her knees hit stone.

Something inside Araya snapped.

Rage and helplessness, every emotion she stacked in separate mental boxes crashed together. Before thought could get a vote, her body lunged, dragged toward the woman pinned to the floor.

"No!" Iman said. She grabbed Araya. "Get back to your station!"

Araya twisted free, but only for a single step. Something slammed into her side. The world tipped. Gravel tore her arms, and skin peeled open as rock ground against flesh. The impact punched the breath out of her in one violent burst.

Before she pulled air back in, a guard dropped his weight onto her back. Hands ripped her mask away. The first slap cracked across her cheek. Another strike followed. Another. Her head snapped left. Right.

The tunnel fractured into pieces—blur, focus, blur—each blow sewing pain deeper into her bones.

Stop. Please. Stop. The words never made it out.

Her throat closed like it had decided oxygen was a luxury she hadn't earned. She got her forearms up just in time to shield her face, but it barely mattered. The hits raged.

Fingers locked around her throat.

Her body panicked before her brain could even submit

the complaint. Her legs kicked, boots scraping on rock. She clawed at the guard's wrist. Nails skidded over armor, over nylon, over nothing she could hold.

Black crept in from the edges of her vision. Slow at first, curling inward like ink in water, swallowing detail and color and sound. *I'm sorry, Zaheen. I failed you. I failed us.*

She stopped fighting, and her eyes fell shut.

The pressure vanished.

Air slammed back into her lungs in a ragged gasp that tore all the way down to the bottom of her chest. She rolled onto her side and coughed until her body seized. Her palms slid over grit as she reached for something solid.

When the world finally snapped back into focus, she saw Dante. He stood over her, both hands locked around the guard's neck. Teeth clenched so hard his jaw trembled. His arms shook with effort, and his grip didn't ease. There was no debate on his face about what he wanted to do.

It lasted a second.

Two guards hit him from behind and ripped him off like he was a loose panel. They drove him into the wall. Fists flew. The sounds were ugly—bone on armor, flesh on stone, breath punched out of a body that refused to give it up. Dante stayed upright, taking hit after hit, refusing to curl, refusing to fold.

Araya forced herself up. Every joint screamed. Pain lit along her spine and ribs, but she staggered forward anyway. "Get off him."

A fist sank into Dante's gut. His body folded an inch and forced itself upright. Sheer stubbornness burdened his organs. Blood sprayed the floor and painted his chin.

One guard peeled away and sprinted for the control station.

Araya's eyes tracked her on reflex. The guard flipped up a cover and slammed her palm onto a red security button. No alarm. No flashing lights. No siren. Which meant it was worse. Araya understood. Reinforcements.

Two guards ripped Dante's mask off. Another punch drove straight into his mouth. Red bloomed across his lips and teeth like someone dumped paint where it didn't belong.

"Stop!" Araya screamed. "Please!"

She lurched forward.

Arms locked around her from behind. Iman.

A beat later, Skye's grip joined hers, solid and unyielding.

"Let them take it out on me," Araya said, voice cracking. "Not him. Me. Please."

No one listened.

Across the way, the woman who'd shouted the truth first —the one who'd cracked the tunnel's fragile lie—was dragged along the ground. She fought, kicked, twisted, dug her heels in. The guards barely adjusted their stride.

"Enough." Director Sorev stepped into the harsh white beam that usually analyzed mineral seams. Two officers in matte-black armor flanked him, rifles up. "Bring the perpetrators forward."

26

ARAYA

Araya didn't fight as the guards hauled her across the tunnel floor and dropped her at Director Sorev's feet.

The woman cuffed beside her sagged inward, head bowed as if someone had scooped out her fighting spirit and stomped on it.

On Araya's other side, Dante was slammed down so hard the sound cracked like a whip. He curled in on himself, breath wheezing, blood threading down his chin and dripping onto the red grit.

Director Sorev didn't look at any of them at first. He surveyed the scene the way a butcher might study a ledger—calculating yield, waste, profit. Only when silence settled heavy across the tunnel did he speak.

"Who activated the emergency beacon?"

A guard at the console stiffened. "Sir," she said with a salute, "there was an altercation between our unit and three outsiders. One verbal." She aimed her finger at the trembling woman. "One protective." Araya. "And one aggressive." Dante.

"I see," Director Sorev said. His tone was flat, bored. "Verbal and protective may return to their stations. We don't have the manpower for disciplinary theatrics today. Victor Kol wants more ore, and I intend to give him exactly that."

Araya's heart hammered. Dante lifted his head just enough to look at her—his face wrecked, one eye swelling shut—but something in that look cut deeper than any blow. She read it as clearly as words: *You're safe now.*

"Red lustronium is the only mineral powerful enough to keep Los Angeles fueled," Director Sorev said. "Only on this planet, on Perihelion, can we maintain Earth's infrastructure. That," he said, stepping closer until Araya could smell the sterile bite of his uniform, "is why you are still breathing. That is why your lives are tolerated. Why your mistakes are tolerated. But only once. Consider this"—his lips twitched in something that wasn't quite a smile—"your single free pass."

The guard yanked the cuffs off the woman. She bolted before the metal hit the floor, scrambling back to her station as if chased by fire.

When Araya pushed herself upright, her legs shook so hard she had to lock her knees to stay standing. She turned toward Dante, a thousand apologies burning behind her eyes, but he didn't look back. His focus was on Director Sorev.

"Get him upright," Director Sorev said with a flick of his hand. "I'd like to hear his version."

Two guards stepped in and hauled Dante up by the arms. From where Araya stood, he was almost unrecognizable. Blood masked half his face. The rest of him was bruising and split skin, everything blurred together until there was no space left for an expression at all.

Iman's fingers slipped into Araya's hand. The squeeze was small but steady.

"I..." The word scraped out of Dante's throat. His head tipped and jerked upright again as he fought to hold it there. "I was... protecting... my friend."

A cough ripped through him. His body folded forward, like something inside had landed a punch.

Araya flinched. Every part of her wanted to move, to stand between him and Director Sorev, but she knew if she took even one step, it would only add weight to the punishment already falling.

She could barely stand to watch, but she made herself. Looking away would not undo what was happening. It would only make her a coward on top of it.

Her hand drifted to her collarbone, searching for the necklace Zaheen pressed into her palm the day she was taken. Her fingers met bare skin, and something in her chest seemed to open and drop away.

"They beat her," Dante said. Blood pooled at the corners of his mouth. "They were going to kill me for it." He doubled over with another cough. A thin mist of red speckled the floor and Director Sorev's shoes.

He took one clean step back, arms folding as his gaze dropped to the blood that had flecked his uniform. "Tell me, was it what you deserved?"

Dante's head bowed. Tears slipped free and vanished into the dust clinging to his cheeks.

"I was..." He dragged in air that rattled like loose red lustronium on the conveyor belt. "I was protecting my friend. They were..."

"Yes, yes." Director Sorev flicked his fingers as if brushing away a fly. "You've made that clear. I asked if you deserved it."

"No," Dante said. His voice was barely more than a rasp. "I was protecting a friend."

"Your answer to violence was more violence?"

Dante's mouth opened again. This time no words came, only blood.

"I'm sure you believed you had a reason, but belief does not move deadlines. Red lustronium does not mine itself. We're already behind. I don't have the time or interest to referee emotional outbursts. Aggression is unacceptable."

Director Sorev inclined his head toward the nearest officer, and a single shot cracked down the tunnel, loud enough to tear the world in two.

Dante dropped.

Blood spread fast—too fast—blooming outward in a dark, widening flower until the ground could drink no more.

Araya's legs gave out. Her knees struck the rock, but she didn't feel a thing. The world shrieked through her—an animal sound, raw and primal—and she realized it was coming from her own throat, swallowed instantly by the screams crashing around her.

Iman knelt beside her, hands gripping Araya's shoulders. Her touch trembled. The silent plea in it—stay with me, don't shatter—barely reached Araya through the numb roar, succumbing her mind.

"Violence against my guards will never get a pass," Director Sorev said, spit flying from his lips. The veins stood out in his neck. "I have a reputation and a mandate, and every single one of you is going to serve them."

His words echoed louder than the gunshot still ringing in

her ears. "Anyone who obstructs production will be dealt with accordingly. Someone dispose of the body."

Director Sorev turned his back on Dante as if he was nothing more than debris.

One of the guards stepped forward and leveled a finger at Skye. "You. Pick him up dump him in the waste chute."

Araya choked on shock.

Skye stumbled forward on shaky legs, her face streaked with tears and snot, her breath hitching in short, ugly sobs. She didn't argue. She knelt beside Dante, lifted his limp hand with both of hers, and began dragging him across the rock.

For the first time since arriving on Mars, Araya felt something inside her go frighteningly, dangerously still.

27

ZAHEEN

When Zaheen woke, she was lying in someone else's bed.

The ceiling above her didn't belong to any place she knew. Aged wood, warped from years of sandstorms, crossed overhead in dark, uneven beams that looked like old scars. Light slipped through narrow slats and broke into fractured stripes across the room. A whisper of hot, sand-scraped air crept in through the cracks.

Nothing moved. No guards. No crowds. No roar of a train.

She shot upright. The room tilted and swung. Pain stabbed behind her eyes and drove her back toward the mattress. She grabbed her temples and held still until the world stopped shifting.

Where am I? How long was I out? Did anyone else make it? The last thing she remembered was white vapor coiling around her legs. Holly by her side. Bodies dropped in the dunes like flies.

Zaheen took in what she could. A single wooden door. A table crowded with cloths and vials. Walls patched over and patched again. It might have been a stranger's home or a hiding place, but it was nothing she recognized.

She blinked hard, trying to steady the blur that washed over everything. The world came back in slow pulses. First light. Then shape. Then Holly's silhouette sitting close enough for Zaheen to touch. Relief hit with such force it almost knocked the air from her lungs.

Holly was alive. She held a mug out with a tired half-smile that never reached her eyes. "Drink," she said. "Immobilization gas leaves a headache worse than a dozen ales on an empty stomach."

Zaheen grabbed the mug. Steam brushed her face and eased some of the pounding behind her eyes. The first sip stung her tongue, and a gentle sweetness followed and settled her stomach.

"I'm so glad you're alive," Zaheen said. She set the mug aside and pulled Holly into a shaky hug.

"Easy," Holly said. "You need your strength first. Drink."

Zaheen let go. She took another mouthful and held it there before swallowing. The sweetness dulled the ache in her skull.

"Is that honey?"

Holly smiled. "I keep some for healing. This seemed like the right time to use it."

Zaheen lowered the mug below her chin, cradled near her chest. "How did I get here?"

Holly nodded toward the corner. "He'll explain."

Jude sat half in shadow, a mug of his own cupped between both hands. "Not the reunion I pictured," he said. "We're in my safe house."

Zaheen pushed herself upright. Her muscles protested, but she refused to let Jude see the strain. "Is everyone okay?"

The look he shared with Holly told her enough. There was no relief in it, only the tight, careful dread people wore before they broke bad news.

"I got back to town just in time," Jude said. "Saw the mess at the train tracks and didn't wait for it to get worse. By the time I found Holly, you were already unconscious."

He paused and took another sip. "Not everyone was as fortunate."

"Then we go back," Zaheen said. "There could be survivors."

Jude frowned. "That's not an option. The insiders are searching. For us. For you."

Do nothing while they hunt us? While the dead lie uncounted?

"I won't sit here," Zaheen said. She pressed her fingertips to her temples, desperate to quiet its pulse. The pain flared hotter instead. "If we hide, we lose everything."

And I have lost enough already.

"Jude has the boy," Holly said. "Chairman Sahar's son is the only leverage left. If we push without a plan, we waste momentum. Every piece we have is fragile."

Guilt flared. Zaheen set this path herself, and the boy was part of that choice. Alone out here, torn from the world he knew. His fear echoed too close to Araya's. Maybe she misjudged. Maybe none of this was clean. But the road toward liberation was never going to be clean. She had chosen it, and there was no turning back.

"Where is he now?" Zaheen asked.

"Somewhere secure," Jude said, and looked toward the

window. "I'll take you there." He drained the last of his tea and set the cup aside with a quiet exhale. "Needed that."

Zaheen swung her legs over the side of the bed. The floor tipped. Vertigo raged. She blinked, trying to steady the room.

Holly stepped in beside her, one arm firm around Zaheen's back to keep her upright. "Easy," she said. "You've been unconscious for half a day."

Zaheen stopped midstep, eyes wide. "Hours?" She couldn't tell if the spinning came from the injury or from what Holly had just said. Maybe both.

"You're awake," Holly said with a pat. "That's what matters."

Zaheen disagreed, but she saved her words. She crossed the room in three steps and closed her hand around the door handle.

Jude jumped into her path. "Hold on. I need you to be prepared for what you're about to see."

"Someone say it," Zaheen said. "What're you keeping from me?"

Holly's expression crumpled, the effort to stay composed breaking all at once. Tears slid down her cheeks before she could swipe them away. "I'm so sorry, Zee."

She pulled Zaheen into a tight embrace and held on. "It's not your fault."

Zaheen forced herself to stand still in Holly's arms and let the blow land. She pictured the worst. The movement shattered. Everything they'd built scattered in the dust. The messenger's promise to return to her, becoming reality. Yet beneath all of that, one fear took priority.

"It's Araya, isn't it?"

Jude opened the door and didn't look back. "Not Araya. You should see for yourself."

They stepped into the open air. The wind rose and dragged ribbons of sand through the alleyways. Vendor stalls stood abandoned, their tarps sagging under layers of sand and sun-bleached grime. The usual clamor had vanished.

The few people still outside didn't linger. Faces were hidden behind hoods. Figures slipped into alleys between buildings and behind doorways. Eyes darted away from hers, afraid to meet anything head-on.

The air carried a sour mix she couldn't name. Smoke. Blood. Something spoiled beneath both.

She rounded the corner into the plaza's center and gasped. Her hand slipped from Holly's grasp, and she dropped to her knees. She shut her eyes and tried to pull herself into darkness.

Make it vanish. Make this hell disappear. She opened her eyes anew, and nothing changed.

A thick rope stretched between the tallest buildings in the plaza, two squat stone blocks that framed the sky like a trap. Bodies hung from it. Six of them. They swayed in the shifting wind. Vivian's body at the center, as if the rope had chosen her to anchor the rest.

Wire bindings bit deep into wrists and ankles, carving raw grooves where skin had torn. The nooses chewed into their necks until flesh bubbled and purpled. Their faces were swollen. Their limbs rigid in the heat.

A stronger gust pushed through the plaza, and the bodies rocked. Flies lifted in a cloud, circling their feast with a hungry buzz. Maggots spilled from open wounds and dropped to the ground.

Zaheen rose. Tears blurred her vision, but she refused to

let them fall. "They're dead," she said. "Because of my plan. Because I said we had a chance."

"Don't." Holly raised her hand as if she could block the words before they reached her. "We all made that call. Vivian made hers. I loved her like family, but she knew what this might cost."

Cost. As if any of us understand the price. We've built a war with our own hands. Her gaze drifted back to the hanging bodies. The wind rose again and pulled at the rope. Vivian swayed with it. Her blonde hair hung in strands across her face, matted with dust and dried blood. Pale skin split along the jaw, and maggots worked through the openings in soft, shifting clusters.

"I'm sorry about Vivian," Zaheen said at last. She stepped into Holly's arms and held her close. "She believed in what we were building."

"She screamed for me," Holly said. "I did nothing. The insiders killed her, and all I could do was watch from the shadows."

Zaheen drew her in tighter, hand moving in slow circles across Holly's back. "You didn't have a choice. If you stepped out, you'd be hanging beside her."

Holly pulled away and swiped her cheeks, though the tears kept coming. "There's always a choice. I made the wrong one. Just like I did when I stood there and let them take my son."

Zaheen caught her trembling hands and held them steady. "You're still here," she said. "That matters more than you know."

"This happened about an hour after the chaos ended," Jude said, stomping on maggots in sand. "The insiders dragged people into the plaza and forced the entire town to watch. Then they disappeared. No patrols. Nothing."

His gaze returned to Vivian and stayed there. "She was brave."

Zaheen nodded. "This wasn't how it was meant to happen."

"No," Jude said. "But it's what we have now."

He reached into his coat pocket. "For you," he said, and drew out a thin gold chain. The pendant caught a sliver of sun and flashed. "Thought you should have this. I believe in you. So do the others who keep fighting."

The world narrowed to the small circle of metal in Jude's hand.

"That's hers." Zaheen snatched it from his palm. "Where did you get this?"

"Los Angeles," Jude said. "An insider claimed it came from one of the new miners."

Zaheen turned the necklace in her hand. She pressed it to her chest. This was Araya's. It hadn't returned by accident. She clipped the clasp shut and let the pendant settle against her skin. Her fingertips lingered there, unwilling to let go.

A memory stirred. The messenger at her door. His cold certainty. The way he tore Araya from her life, as if neither of them had ever mattered.

Yet here she stood. And here was a piece of Araya that he couldn't erase. He had taken what he could reach, but something of Araya had found its way back to her anyway. The necklace felt like a quiet defiance, a reminder that she wasn't finished, that she was stronger than any man who tried to crush her spirit.

She tucked the pendant beneath her robes and lifted her

gaze. Past the rope. Past the bodies. Past the broken skyline. She couldn't see the stars through the haze, yet she searched for them anyway. Once, looking up had been its own kind of pain, because it reminded her how far away Araya truly was. Now the ache shifted. The necklace turned it into something else.

Hope.

A thin thread still tied them together. Not by distance, but by choice. By memory and the small circle of metal resting against her heartbeat. And by the strength that had carried her through everything since that night.

If Araya's necklace found its way back to her, then she wasn't done. Zaheen drew in a slow breath and faced Jude. "I want to see Eren Sahar."

28

VICTOR

Victor Kol let his voice roll across the chamber with the controlled force of a cannon. His fist came down once, flat against the obsidian conference table. The sound thudded through the room like distant artillery.

The chandelier swayed. Light fractured into splinters and skated across the glossy black surface of the table and leapt to the white walls. It caught on the shelves that lined them, on rows of bronze statues frozen in eternal strain, vague human figures bowed under slabs of ore and rock the way the miners on Mars did.

"Someone beyond my walls attacked me, believing she'd see another sunrise," Victor said.

His mouth curved at the memory of the woman who had dared strike him. The thought of her steadied him, almost like a quiet high. He could see it again with perfect clarity: the crowd jammed into the square, his guards forcing her up the steps while she kicked and cursed, the noose dropping around her neck as the noise rose. Restless, furious, and utterly helpless.

He had stood at the edge of the platform and watched her body jerk and twist against the rope, watched the fight drain from her limbs. Her desperation crashed against him and broke there, leaving him untouched as she finally went still.

"She's not the first to mistake defiance for survival."

He looked to newly appointed Officer Rin Nakamura, head of Los Angeles security. She sat with her back straight, dark hair swept into a knot at the nape of her neck. A fine web of lines at the corners of her eyes hinted at years spent reading reports with the same unblinking attention.

After the encounter with Zaheen, Victor saw no choice but to make a change. He sent the previous officer to security duty on Perihelion and hired the next in line. Nakamura met his stare without a flinch. Only the tight set of her posture hinted at strain.

"This breach falls under your purview, Officer Nakamura," he said. "I demand retribution. Now would be an excellent time to prove your worth."

Officer Nakamura laced her fingers together, a small fortress of flesh and bone atop the table. "We've already begun, sir," she said. "A funding requisition is with the Ministry of Insider Preservation to send more military into Nova Angeles. Deputy Durand is streamlining tactical logistics as we speak."

"See that Chairman Sahar signs the approval by sundown," Victor said. He flicked his hand as if nudging the day itself forward. "Inform our engineers that sundown is to be moved up an hour. We'll adjust the schedule to match. We need this done immediately."

"He'll agree," Officer Nakamura said. "Chairman Sahar knows exactly what's at stake for him."

Victor held his silence. He wasn't so sure.

Chairman Sahar had the makings of a pest, the kind that should have been easy to crush yet somehow kept slipping through gaps. Victor spent his life in those same gaps, learning how to survive in the cracks and feed on other people's mistakes.

It was the only reason he hadn't dismissed Chairman Sahar entirely. The chairman clung to power with a familiar sort of desperation. In that tenacity, Victor saw an echo of himself, and the quiet realization unsettled him more than he cared to admit.

He shifted his attention to Deputy Julien Durand.

The younger man met his stare with a smile, one of those bureaucratic masks that never lit his coffee-colored eyes. Yet beneath the polished veneer, Victor recognized something familiar. Hunger. Ambition. A mirror of his own rise.

"Your strategy, Deputy?"

Deputy Durand angled his tablet forward, its pale glow washing over the lower half of his face. "Energy-grid stabilization, sir."

Victor waited for more.

"Our dome infrastructure rests on two levers," Deputy Durand said. "TerraLux Mineral resource flows and Chairman Sahar's committee. If we want to increase our security presence without stirring civilian dissent, we pull both at the same time."

"Tell me something I don't know," Victor said.

Deputy Durand inclined his head, unbothered. "Then here is what you have not heard, sir. We frame new guard deployments in Nova Angeles as a technical necessity built around energy conservation, grid integrity, and environmental control. The public believes we're protecting their breathable air and stable temperatures. The committee gets a crisis they can champion. No one protests."

"I would say this plan benefits all sides," Victor said.

Officer Nakamura watched the exchange in silence. "What of the insiders who sympathize with Nova Angeles? There are more than a few."

"Stories, Officer Nakamura," Victor said.

Her brow shifted a fraction. "Excuse me, sir?"

"You hear me right. Stories," he said. "People cling to them. Give them something that feels true from a certain angle, and they will hold it tighter than fact. We give them a story about order, about safety, about a fragile grid only we can protect."

He let the words settle, and added, softer, "Sometimes the truth has to be tailored for the good of society."

Victor thought of the stories that carried him to this room. Not lies, exactly, but stories shaped to match the fears of whoever was paying to listen. He stood in marble halls and shuttered boardrooms, offering salvation to private donors terrified of the ecological collapse their old-era trillionaires set in motion. He took their fear and molded it into seed capital, enough to raise the Los Angeles dome and crown himself the architect of hope.

Out of their panic for a place on the inside, and his own hunger to control what remained of the world's wealth, the Messenger Program took shape. A lottery on paper, it promised fairness while quietly sorting people by usefulness and obedience, by who the new world could afford to keep. The rest became outsiders, exported by their twentieth birthdays. Victor wrote the criteria. He decided who stayed and who vanished.

That was why he sat at the head of this table now. That was why no one else in the room ever would.

"Humanitarian outreach," Victor said. "More troops mean more assistance. More presence means more protection. Los Angeles is the last bastion of indoor civilization, so TerraLux Minerals will underwrite the expansion as a gesture of goodwill to both zones. It'll also support enforcement in Nova Angeles. Symmetry for appearances."

The door hissed open. Chairman Sahar stepped inside. The usual polish on his features, the careful statesman's composure he wore for cameras and councils, had dulled to a weary tarnish. Faint shadows pooled beneath his eyes.

"My apologies for the delay," he said, and settled into the chair beside Victor.

Victor angled toward him, studying the tightness around his mouth. "What weighs on you, Malik?" he asked, and let his hand rest the back of his seat in a practiced gesture of concern.

Malik exhaled and lowered his head. "My son has been kidnapped."

"Oh, Malik," Victor said. "I can't begin to imagine what you're feeling. You have my deepest sympathies."

Malik ignored him and turned to Officer Nakamura. "A full deployment mandate from the top would significantly expedite the search for my son."

"Chairman," Officer Nakamura said, her tone even, "you recognize this emergency session has broader implications than your son alone. Nova Angeles is destabilizing and radicalizing. We can't afford to let emotion override systemic integrity."

"This is systemic. This is as urgent as it gets."

Across the table, Deputy Durand had a faint sardonic smile tugging at one corner of his mouth. "Is it?" he asked, the word more challenge than question.

"This room is for solutions," Victor said, and swept the table, "not sentiment."

His attention settled on Malik. "Your son will be returned. Of that, I have no doubt. Officer Nakamura will see that every necessary resource is deployed."

And in that assurance, Chairman, you will owe me, whether you see it yet or not.

"Now," Victor said, and faced Deputy Durand, "back to the pressing matter of troop deployment into Nova Angeles. Rebellion spreads. One unattended spark becomes a blaze. It corrodes cohesion, shatters hierarchy, strips away the illusion of control."

Malik scoffed. "You're gambling with proximity and pride, Victor. Do you truly believe columns of armored men marching through neighborhoods will pacify anyone? You're feeding tension."

Victor studied him for a long beat. He wasn't wrong, but anger swelled. "Chairman," he said, "this is your moment to decide how cooperative you intend to be." His tone cooled, all pretense of warmth gone. "Consider this your only warning."

His next words dropped nearly a register. "Deputy Durand's proposal is to be approved in full at your next committee meeting in the Ministry of Insider Preservation. I trust you understand what is being asked."

Deputy Durand typed on his tablet. "Uploading documentation now," he said. "Your office should have it by the time you return, Chairman Sahar."

Malik pushed his chair back and rose. "Are we finished?"

Victor stood as well. He allowed no one to stand above him. His officers followed a heartbeat later, rising in unison like a single, trained tide.

"For Officer Nakamura and Deputy Durand, yes."

The doors hissed open, and the two officers departed in synchronized silence.

Victor lowered himself back into his seat. He extended his hand toward the opposite side of the table. "Sit, Chairman Sahar."

The chairman hesitated, caught between instinct and duty, and lowered himself into the chair.

"I understand how this looks. You're being asked to shelve your son's life for bureaucratic optics. But as Officer Nakamura stated, Eren will return. You must hold perspective, Chairman. Duty. Home. Continuity. These are what anchor us."

"This isn't politics for me, Victor. I have a child to protect."

Victor wanted to laugh. *Of course, it's politics. Your whole existence is because of my politics.*

"So, you intend to resign? Withdraw from committee responsibilities? Perhaps test your odds in Nova Angeles instead? I will ask very plainly," Victor said. "Would you negotiate with radicals for your son even if it places Los Angeles at risk?"

Chairman Sahar bowed his head. "I remain loyal to TerraLux Minerals. To our structure. And you."

"If I find even the stench of betrayal," Victor said, "your existence will become exemplary. A reminder to others." He rose and crossed the chamber with the unhurried grace of a man whose path had already been decided three steps ahead. When the door panel chimed, Carmine Kurier stood where Victor had instructed him to be.

Victor's expression shifted at once, warmth sliding over his features like sunlight on a summer's day. "Mr. Kurier," he said. "A welcome sight."

The messenger bowed as Chairman Sahar hurried past without a word.

"I have an assignment for you, Mr. Kurier. A high-value target. Succeed, and I will see you rewarded with property and status."

"Of course, sir. Just give the word."

Victor's smile held. The warmth did not. He felt the absence of it, a hollow at the center of his calm. "Her name is Zaheen Mandisa. She is a traitor, a desert rat, a terrorist. I want her found. You will bring her to me."

29

ZAHEEN

Zaheen stood just beyond the lantern's reach, arms crossed tight against her chest, her back pressed to the bunker's rust-pocked wall as if she could sink into it and vanish.

Distance was intentional. If she stood too close, Eren Sahar might hear the shake in her breathing, catch the quiver in her voice, feel her fear in the air between them.

A kidnapped boy tied to a chair, and she pretended this was something she knew how to handle.

Every road that brought her here carried Araya's name. If this was the way back to her, Zaheen would take it, even with trembling hands.

Let the dark do the work my heart can't, Zaheen repeated to herself. *This is all for her.*

Eren Sahar sat at the center of the room, bound to a metal chair bolted into the floor, fabric pulled tight over his head. He sunk lower with time, shoulders dipped, spine curved as though he were trying to disappear into himself.

The rope marks around his wrists were noticeable, red ridges stamped into his skin, darker where the bindings bit deepest. She made herself look past them. Pain was everywhere in this world, always trying to take center stage. If she let it, she would never move.

Araya was the point. Getting her back was the point. Anything that didn't carry her toward Araya had to fade.

The bunker sat a half hour's hike from the outskirts of Nova Angeles, buried under dunes polished flat by years of wind. Out here, footprints blurred fast, wiped clean before anyone could follow them. Once, the Sand Alliance used this place as a fallback post, a blank spot on the map to slip into when insider patrols drew too close.

At least, that was what Jude told her.

Below the sand line, the ceiling groaned each time wind pushed overhead. The metal walls picked up the sound and passed it along, turning the bunker into a constant echo chamber.

Holly stood beside Zaheen, but there was a sag in her posture, a tired bend that had never been there before. One hand pressed into her hip while the other dragged across her temple, smearing sweat into grime. She barely said a word since their arrival.

Zaheen's heart nearly crumpled when she looked at Holly. Whatever this was for Zaheen, it was worse for her mentor. She tried to picture standing in that plaza, watching Araya on that rope, and her mind refused to go there.

Jude closed the space between him and Eren. He stopped behind the chair, hooked his fingers into the head cover, and ripped it upward in one sharp motion.

Eren jolted. The ropes snapped tight, holding him fast as the chair rattled against the floor. His eyes opened wide, skimming the room in quick, panicked passes until they locked on the dark shape of Zaheen pressed to the wall.

"You'll get used to the haze," Jude said. He folded the bag with care. "Burns at first. Your lungs catch on."

Jude brushed sand from his sleeves, eyes never leaving Eren. "Your nose all right?" The bridge was swollen and off-center, skin puffed and darkening to a deep purple.

"Don't hurt me," Eren said.

Zaheen told herself this wasn't cruelty. Still, seeing it up close hurt more than giving the order and walking away. She told herself this was mercy for her people. Out here, justice kept slipping into shapes she didn't want to name.

Guilt rose. She pushed it down. He was here for a reason.

Jude exhaled and scrubbed a hand over his face. "I knocked you out because you took a swing at me first," he said. He shifted his coat, revealing the Mars-red knife. "That was me being generous. If I'd really wanted to hurt you, I had sharper options."

Eren's bottom lip trembled. "Take me home."

Jude let out a short laugh. "Not happening. Not yet at least."

"I know people," Eren said. He grasped for leverage. "Powerful ones. You bring me home, and they'll make it worth your time. Money. Access. I can get you whatever."

Zaheen left the shadows and crouched in front of Eren. "They won't give my people what we want," she said. "I already asked."

Vulnerability slid over his features like a mask he had practiced in a mirror. "I'm just a kid."

"You think that works on me?" Zaheen said and scoffed. "You think I don't recognize it?"

Eren's eyes dropped.

"You ever haul water from a community well," she said, "and pass children crying for a sip, knowing you can't spare it if you want to live through the next couple of days?"

She paused, breath measured, anger kept on a short leash. "You ever get shipped off world to serve a corporation?"

Zaheen leaned in, close enough that he felt the truth in it. "Your father lives in comfort. So do you. Cocooned inside privilege. I live in the wreckage he calls order."

Eren's mouth twisted. "My father would never help you."

"We don't want to hurt you." Zaheen said and glanced at Jude. "But he has less patience than I do."

She hated using a threat. Hated seeing Eren flinch like that. Somewhere under the fear and conditioning, there was still a boy.

"I can't help you," Eren said.

Zaheen lifted his chin, firm but careful. "Someone was taken from me. She wants to go home. Just like you. Your father can make that happen. For both of you."

"She wasn't taken," Eren said, and wrenched free from her hold. "She was offered a future. That's different."

Zaheen felt the lie for what it was. There was no time to dismantle it piece by piece.

Before Zaheen could tell Eren he was only repeating Victor Kol's lines, that none of this could truly be what he believed, Holly stepped in, catching the heat before it boiled over.

"What's your dream?" Holly asked.

Zaheen almost scoffed. *Dream*. As if the word still meant something out here. As if wanting had ever kept anyone alive.

For the first time since the hood came off, he didn't scramble for an answer. "To be a pilot."

Eren lifted his head a little like he was looking past the bunker walls to the sky. "To fly beyond the dome. Across the wastelands. Over what's left. I want to see if the world really is all sand. Or if there are places they don't show us."

Holly shook her head. "There are no other places."

"I'll grow up, take a position, sit in the same rooms my father does." His mouth pulled tight. "I'll never know anything else. I don't want to be my father."

Holly's expression shifted. She stepped closer, slow and careful, as if she were approaching something fragile. Her voice lowered, roughened by years and loss. "That's what frightens you," she said. "Not being trapped. Becoming him."

Eren lifted his eyes to hers. "I don't want to be my father," he said again, and this time there was no tremor. "He's too kind. More of you should be shipped to Perihelion."

Jude stepped in and swung the hood back down over Eren's head, cutting off the boy's stare.

Holly remained calm. "You'll stay down here as long as it takes."

Eren thrashed against the restraints, words muffled beneath the bag, the anger suddenly loud but useless.

Holly turned away. "When that attitude breaks, we'll talk again."

Zaheen followed them toward the exit. Each step felt heavier than the last. Not victorious. Not righteous. Just worn through. They hadn't won anything here.

She glanced back at him thrashing in his chair. They gambled on empathy and lost.

The bunker door groaned shut behind them, sealing the

sound away, but it did nothing to lift the weight that followed Zaheen back into the open air.

When they reached the surface, Zaheen pulled her hood up against the wind and looked out toward the dome crouched on the horizon. Heat shimmered above the sand, blurring everything, until it looked less like a metal orb and more like a mirage.

"What now?" she asked.

"We keep trying to break him," Jude said. "Otherwise, this was a pointless exercise."

Zaheen turned to Holly, searching for the steady answer she had always given, the one that made chaos feel survivable. The wind tugged at Holly's robes and snapped the fabric against her legs. She stood silent, eyes fixed on the desert ground.

She had nothing.

Somewhere beneath the glare and the wind, reality settled in like grit between her teeth. Araya felt farther away than ever.

30

ARAYA

A touch landed on Araya's shoulder, light as sand, steady as a handrail in rough passage.

Iman, of course.

Araya remained frozen since the return to the barracks. Her eyes fixed on the floor beneath her boots, the one solid thing in a world that would not stop tilting. Not even Iman's constant companionship broke the curse she was under.

Zaheen waits for your return. Snap out of it. Anchor yourself. She repeated that phrase in her mind so many times that it no longer felt like a thought but programming.

Around that anchor, everything else churned. Every decision and hesitation. She replayed them with clinical precision, stripping the emotion aside the way analysts dissect a failed operation. Somewhere in that chain of choices, Dante died. She searched in every corner for a different conclusion.

"Araya," Iman said, nudging. "Talk to me."

"I keep seeing it," Araya said. "The bullet. The way his head snapped back."

Her breath hitched. The barracks seemed to contract

around her, walls inching closer. "He just fell. Like gravity remembered him all at once. And then Director Sorev walked off, like he wasn't—"

Her words broke. She folded forward, pressing her face into her palms. "All I wanted was to help," she said. "And now he's dead."

"Look at me," Iman said, with a fierceness Araya was not used to hearing from her.

Araya lifted her head, expecting comfort.

"It isn't your fault," Iman said, and placed her hand in Araya's. "But you must mourn later."

"Later?" Araya recoiled. *When did grief ever wait its turn?*

"We don't get the luxury to think of the past," Iman said. "If you fall apart, Director Sorev wins. You want Dante's death to mean nothing?"

"You make it sound simple."

"It is simple. If you don't want to see any more death, you hold yourself together."

Dante's face surfaced unbidden. "I won't let Director Sorev win," Araya said.

Her gaze drifted to the far beds. Skye sat hunched there, uniform streaked with dust, tears dried into pale tracks on her cheeks. She was a machine pushed past tolerance, and Araya had been the gear that seized.

"She hates me," Araya said.

"Then she'll hate you. Better that than death."

The intercom crackled, and Sorev's snaky voice led Araya's muscles to tense.

"Today has tested many of you. We have suffered a tragic loss. Violence will not become customary. Discipline will be restored."

The doors at the far end of the barracks groaned open. Four guards stepped inside. Conversation collapsed on itself, sound draining from the room as every head turned.

They split without a word. Two angled toward Araya's bed. The other pair veered toward the woman across the aisle —the one who had already been beaten nearly senseless.

"You," one guard said at Araya.

"On your feet," the other said.

Iman pushed up from her bunk. "Please. Araya didn't do anything."

A guard's hard shove sent Iman back onto the mattress. "This doesn't concern you."

Screams erupted near the other pair of guards. Araya turned just in time to see the woman lunge. Her hand shot to the nearest holster, fingers closing around the grip before the guard could react. She ripped the pistol free and staggered back, wild-eyed, swinging the barrel between them.

"Stay back," the woman said. "Don't—don't touch me."

The response was instant. The second guard drew and fired.

The shot tore through the barracks. The woman dropped where she stood, collapsing sideways against the bed. Blood struck the sheets and the stunned face of the woman lying beside her.

The guard snatched his pistol off the floor. Neither he nor his partner spared the woman a second glance. They each grabbed an arm and hauled her limp body toward the vault door, blood smearing a dark trail.

Araya shut her eyes. The screams clawing at her throat stayed there, trapped behind clenched teeth.

She didn't fight when the two guards seized her. Her arms

felt hollow, like they belonged to someone else. As they dragged her forward, she forced her head to turn, just once, catching Skye's stare across the room.

Skye's eyes were fire and ice at the same time. Hurt. Fury. Betrayal. Sorrow.

Araya's mouth moved, shaping a word she could not say out loud. *Sorry.*

Araya saw her future: a transport ship to the upper atmosphere of Mars, an open airlock, the endless dark, and Zaheen never seeing her face again.

31

MALIK

Malik eyed the plate in front of him, fork resting untouched beside his meal. The warm scent of spaghetti and garlic bread drifted up, mingling with the bitter tang of red wine.

The grand mahogany table beneath his hands gleamed in the low light, its surface smooth and dark, carved from one of the last old-growth trees—cut, shipped, and hoarded in Los Angeles for people like him.

Burgundy walls closed around the dining room. Rich paint swallowed the edges of the light and threw their shadows long across the floor. Beyond the shuttered blinds, the faint outlines of patrolling guards slipped past in regular intervals.

By every measure, it was a perfect dinner. And by every measure that mattered, it meant nothing without Eren.

He couldn't bring himself to meet his wife's gaze. Her disappointment sat between them like a third presence at the family dinner table. She waited for him to speak. To say anything. The silence only sharpened the memory of all the reassurances he used to give.

"What if he's dead, Malik?" she asked at last.

Don't say it. Don't speak such things into existence. Yet even as Malik drew breath, he knew the question could not be avoided. No parent ever outran that fear, no matter how carefully it was buried under hope.

"Our son is out there, Leila."

Her fork slipped from her fingers and struck the porcelain bowl with a bright, brittle ring. "I was stupid. Why would I leave him?"

"Because home is supposed to be safe."

Leila rubbed her temples, fingers moving in small, tight circles. "Did anything come of your meeting this morning? Is Officer Nakamura preparing a search?"

"They're pouring everything into an outsider uprising in Nova Angeles," Malik said. "We aren't the priority. Some woman named Zaheen Mandisa has their focus."

She sank in her chair. "So even our own security forces, charged with protecting the people of Los Angeles, won't bring Eren home?"

Leila's laugh came out sharp and humorless. "The son of a sworn-in public official? Malik, we must go around your committee and TerraLux Minerals. Victor has never cared about us. Can't you see that? He's using you."

Deep down, he always understood he was a piece on Victor's board. The difference was, until now, the position had kept his family safe. "It should be a last resort," he said.

Leila rolled her eyes. "Stop it."

"Stop what?"

He wanted to tell her that everything they had built— their family, their work, this thin, fragile version of stability—

could collapse if they pushed too hard. One wrong move was all it would take to tip the scales out of their favor.

"Wake up from this illusion," Leila said.

"We follow orders." The words tasted foreign, drilled into him through years of briefings and sealed rooms. He knew the system hollowed him out, bent him to its needs. Still, he clung to its rules, because letting go meant admitting his entire life had been a lie.

"You think I don't know that?" she said. She pressed two fingers to her chest, punctuating each word. "I know what happens if we don't obey better than you. I lived through it. I know what real suffering looks like. My first family is buried under the dunes."

He married that grief. Brought her into his home, given her his name. He asked Leila to trust the same system that wiped out her first family, and a quiet part of him worried she might let him disappear the same way one day, if only in her heart.

"I'm glad you escaped and found peace," he said. Malik reached across the table. She hesitated, just for a breath and let her fingers settle into his. "When I married you, I promised you would never have to go back out there. I'm keeping my word."

She slipped her hand from his. The loss of her touch sliced through him, cold as open space. When she lifted her eyes, the look she gave him burned straight through what little resolve he had left.

"A promise to me is a promise to *him*."

Leila's gaze drifted up to the glass chandelier. Its crystals caught the light and scattered it in soft fragments across the room, her hands, and face.

Malik followed her look.

The same chandelier had hung above them on their wedding night, one of hundreds glowing like suspended stars. He remembered her standing beside him in silk, wrapped in ceremony but carved out by loss, her family killed only months earlier for refusing the lottery orders.

He had felt the slight tremor in her shoulders, seen grief tug at the corners of her smile, and tipped her chin toward the lights, trying to give her something else to hold on to.

"Look at them," he had said then. "Let the reflections hold you."

She had nodded and, for a brief moment, he'd watched the shimmer in the crystals soften the pain she could not yet bring herself to name.

She cleared her throat and pulled Malik back to the present.

"You and I are not bad people. Just scared people," Leila said. She rose from her chair. "Fear is a sickness. It spreads. It's time we heal from it."

She walked around the table and stood behind him. Malik felt her presence at his back, then her hand settled on his chest. He caught it and held on, using the contact to steady himself as she leaned over his shoulder. Anger and exhaustion churned, but her touch narrowed his world to what mattered most.

"All I want is to protect our son," he said. "To protect you. You deserve better than an insider like me."

"Don't talk like that," she whispered in his ear.

"It's hard not to."

"When I first saw you, you were like my own mirage. You gave me a chance at life. I gave you proof that outsiders are worth saving. Remember that now. They took Eren because they're desperate. We get him back by helping. Stop letting Victor Kol keep you quiet in the very committee you chair."

The desert had never left her. It only learned to wear silk and shift through the steel world around them. In some ways, Malik knew she would always be stronger than he was.

She turned to face him, resolve settling over her features in a way he recognized too well. "A private investigator is our best chance," Leila said. "We look for our son in secret, or I go to the dunes myself."

He couldn't lose her to sand and haze. The image alone—Leila swarmed by heat and wind, hiking back into a world that had already taken too much from her—tightened something in his chest.

"I know someone who can help," he said.

Regret followed close behind. The man he was thinking of belonged to an earlier version of Malik's life, from long before titles and armed escorts, back when committee work still felt like service instead of strategy. They grew up together and sat side by side in those early meetings, before Victor's shadow stretched over every decision. Malik had no way of knowing who that man was now, or what the years had carved out of him. Power changed people. So did survival.

But the alternative was unthinkable.

He said it anyway because Leila stood in front of him, ready to walk back into the dunes if he didn't act. Because if this was the price of keeping her here, of bringing their son home, he would pay it. Over and over again.

"The less I know, the safer we are." Leila lifted her bowl and turned away from the table. She paused only long enough to look back at him. "Meet with whoever you have in mind tomorrow. If you don't—" she didn't finish the thought.

She left him to eat alone.

32

ARAYA

The guards hurled Araya into the cell like she was a sack of spare parts.

She hit the floor hard. Her boots skated on smooth stone, and pain fired up her legs, and settled into her hips with a hot, mean persistence. Her body folded on instinct. Arms up. Head tucked. She waited for the rest of it.

A kick. A baton. A bullet. That was the usual sequence.

But nothing came.

The door sealed with a hiss, and darkness closed in. The cell wasn't a room so much as a vertical mistake: a narrow stone cylinder that climbed upward into black until her eyes gave up trying to find an end.

Cold seeped out of the floor and into her bones. Araya wrapped her arms around herself blocking heat loss through stubbornness alone. Her muscles remembered other nights— half-collapsed shelters along the dunes, sand in everything, sleep that came in short, cheap bursts. That was her child-hood. Darting from one desert town to the next, sleeping wherever there was space, eating whatever she could trade for, never staying long enough to belong.

Not until Zaheen.

Zaheen had shown her a life that was more than surviving the next hour.

Araya shut her eyes and rebuilt the world in pieces that made sense. Heat. Sand. Haze. Places she knew. She would take sunburned skin and cracked lips under an open sky over this cage designed to break people from the inside out.

Even here—locked away on a world where people disappeared faster than rumors could spread—the thought of Zaheen still managed to tug a small, stupid smile out of her.

Her mind drifted back to the day they met.

The water ration line. Heat hammered the back of her neck. The sun had a personal grudge that day. Everyone stood too thirsty for small talk. Zaheen was one space ahead, the last person served before the vendor's tank coughed, sputtered, and died.

Araya knew that walk home. She'd done it too many times. Empty cup and dry throat. The constant, grinding awareness that thirst sits on top of every thought and refuses to budge.

But not that day.

Zaheen studied Araya like she was an actual person and not just another body in the line. She tipped half her share into Araya's battered tin cup. Quiet kindness. In a place that didn't budget for it.

Araya's voice came out rough, barely more than air. "Zaheen," she said. "Zee... help me."

Only the hum of the walls answered.

Araya knew memory wasn't a place. It had no coordinates

or gravity. It was a trick the brain pulled when reality became unbearable. She reached for it anyway, and grasped for familiar faces, for the outline of safety.

"I'm here, Araya." Zaheen's voice formed in the dark behind her eyelids, steady and warm. "I've always been right here."

The world assembled itself in stages. First sound—not the sterile whisper of vents, but wind, real wind, moving freely across open ground. Warmth followed, seeping into her skin until the cell's cold thinned, loosened, and let go.

The desert rose around her.

Dunes rolled outward in every direction, red-gold under a sky streaked with fire. Haze skimmed the sand and brushed her robes, familiar as a guiding hand at her back. She breathed in sunbaked earth and dry sage and felt her chest loosen for the first time since the door sealed.

Zaheen's fingers slid into hers. "Destruction has its beauty."

Araya didn't question how Zaheen was here. That wasn't how memory worked. She leaned in until her lips brushed the familiar curve of Zaheen's cheek. "The desert landscape is no match for your own," she said. "The best part is having you beside me. In this life and whatever comes after."

Zaheen lifted a hand and curled two fingers beneath Araya's chin, tipping her gaze upward. "Our realities are tied," Zaheen said. "As long as we're together, we don't break. But we can't forget the people caught in between."

"We help them by staying one," Araya said.

Zaheen's eyes widened. Urgency flared there now, sharp enough to cut through the dream. "Then you need to go back."

The dunes thinned into dust. When Araya opened her eyes again, she was standing on dry, fissured ground under an ash-gray sky. Vendor carts lay overturned around her, their frames picked clean like bones. Tin roofs sagged inward. Wooden beams splintered and leaned at bad angles, pointing at nothing.

Nova Angeles.

Bodies carpeted the plaza. Dozens. Maybe more. Limbs tangled. Faces slack. Eyes wide and fixed on the cloud-choked sky.

Araya took a step and nearly tripped over her own denial. This wasn't real. It couldn't be. It was just her brain doing what brains did when locked in a concrete tube: making up movies to keep itself entertained.

Her heartbeat disagreed.

A cloaked figure waited at the far edge of the square. Back turned. Staring past the ruins toward the endless dunes and the Los Angeles dome in the distance—its shell cracked open, exposed to the elements like a peeled fruit.

"Show yourself!"

The figure turned and walked toward her, and Araya's breath caught. "No. Don't take me—"

Her heel snagged on an outstretched arm. She pitched forward and landed hard in a field of the dead. The stench of rot surged up and grabbed her by the throat.

The figure stopped in front of her and lowered its hood. The messenger.

He didn't say a word. He just smiled—wide and wrong—eyes bright with delight, like every corpse in the plaza was part of a private performance he'd paid good money to see.

Araya shoved herself back, hands scraping through something wet. She froze and forced herself to look.

Dante's hand lay palm-up in the sand, slick with blood. A bullet chewed a brutal tunnel through his eye socket. The rest of his face was locked mid-scream, mouth open around a sound he never got to finish.

The scream came anyway. It tore out of Araya, ripping up from her chest like it had claws, carrying all the noise Dante didn't get to make.

The messenger laughed while she scanned the dead like a desperate accountant doing inventory.

Iman lay twisted nearby, limbs slack and bent at angles no living body should ever attempt. Deep gashes carved across her middle. Her mining uniform was torn and dark with blood. Her eyes stared up, empty of everything that had made her Iman.

Beyond her, Skye looked almost untouched. Sand dusted her cheeks like powder. Tears pooled and dried as if she'd curled up for a quick rest and simply forgotten to wake for a sunrise that would never come.

The messenger smiled. "Was it worth the price to return?"

Araya's gaze snapped past him. Framed against the ruined skyline, a body hung from a rope.

Zaheen's outline.

Araya refused to look straight at it. Because if she did—if she confirmed the shape, the hair, the curve of shoulders— then whatever was still holding her together would finally let go.

She clamped her hands over her ears and screamed. She poured everything into it, trying to drown out the messenger's laughter, the bodies, the rope, the broken bones of Nova Angeles.

The world tore away.

Araya snapped back into the cell. Darkness. Cold. The low, polite hum of the walls like they were proud of themselves. She stared into nothing, chest heaving, and counted each breath like it was a job she couldn't afford to screw up.

She didn't know how many more minutes she could endure before Mars decided it was finished with her.

33

MALIK

The upper tiers of Los Angeles thrummed with controlled chaos. Performers draped in exotic leathers and jeweled wire flipped and spun along the walkways, each acrobatic flourish a silent request for coins that rarely came. Malik kept his eyes forward. He learned long ago how to see without looking.

Mirrored pylons lined the perimeter of the walkways, tall and thin as metal trees. Their lenses lit the dome's ceiling with a pale, artificial sky. He voted for that blue.

Executives streamed through the canyon of glass and steel towers without pause or recognition, passing the performers the way data slips through a private channel—present for an instant, then gone. Malik flowed between spectacle and indifference, unnoticed, precisely as he intended.

The dome's weather program began its scheduled shift. Blue softened to gray, the transition so seamless most never registered it.

Malik did. He always did.

He could still hear the language of the bill as if it were yesterday: *optimization, efficiency, public morale.* The law tied the dome's climate controls to TerraLux Minerals' grid, turning every gentle sky into proof that the company kept their world running, and deserved their support.

He lifted his hood. *Mist next.*

The humidifiers would engage, a fine spray drifting over gardens. A manufactured downpour would follow. Then the dome would weep in earnest, on cue, at the exact hour he'd signed off on.

Laws I passed. Weather I authorized. The idea curdled in his gut. He imagined the outsiders beyond the dome, rationing water by the mouthful, watching real clouds pass without mercy. He pushed the image away before it could take root.

Malik reached a squat retro diner hunched between a glass med-lab annex and a drone-delivery storage unit. Grease-streaked windows reflected the dome's false sky in broken patches, while a buzzing strip of neon fought to stay lit above the door. He pushed through and let the heavy seal close behind him.

The hostess glanced up from her stack of menus. "Chairman Sahar," she said. "An unexpected pleasure. How may I help you?"

Malik offered a smile. The kind a boy wears when he's already stepped into a lie and is hoping it holds. His eyes swept the diner—chrome counters dulled with age, steel tables bolted to the floor, rows of black booths swallowed by shadow.

There. Back booth. Velvet-emerald suit.

"I'll be this way," he said. He dipped his head, a politician's courtesy, and threaded through the narrow aisle, past clinking cutlery and half-finished plates, toward the booth waiting at the rear.

Malik slid into the booth across from the man in the suit. Up close, time sat strangely on him. His hair had gone silver, the lines at the edges of his mouth cut deeper now, carved by choices rather than age. He looked like a man who outlived every version of himself.

"Dominic Dra—"

"I don't use that name," he said. "I'm a ghost now. That's what you'll call me."

Malik exhaled and sank back into the booth, the confidence he'd carried through the door bleeding away. This man was familiar and wrong all at once. Someone he had once trusted. Someone the world had reshaped while Malik had been busy reshaping it in return.

"All right," Malik said. "Ghost." The word sat strangely in his mouth, like borrowed code he did not fully understand.

Ghost leaned back, the vinyl cushion creaking beneath him. "The whole city feels like a pressure cooker. Lid's rattling, Malik. Surely you feel it."

"Pressure is part of leadership," Malik said. "Managing uprisings. Colleagues making backroom deals. Same song as always." He paused, thinking of the dunes beyond the dome. "People are running out of patience."

Ghost folded his arms across his chest, and Malik caught the familiar blend of affection and regret in his eyes. "You should've come with me when you had the chance. Disappearing is easier when you don't do it alone."

"Walking out is not an option," Malik said. "I don't get to slip away and rebrand. I have a family to protect."

The words landed harder than he intended. He knew it

was unfair. Ghost had sat beside him for years on the committee benches, sparring through midnight sessions and taking hits in hearings, absorbing the anger of lobbyists and councilors so the two of them could push through legislation that helped people, not the corporations they worked for.

Malik shifted in his seat, reining in his temper. "People need a voice," he said, quieter now, as if Victor Kol might be listening through the walls. "I know I'm not doing a stellar job. But someone must stand up to Victor in public."

Fondness flickered through Ghost's eyes. "I missed that conviction of yours," he said. He looked past Malik to the approaching waiter. "I leave the stage fights to you."

The waiter arrived with two dune-colored drinks on slim coasters, spherical ice clinking softly as it settled.

"Sand rum," he said, setting them down with a small bow. "Chairman Sahar. Always an honor. May I assist further?"

Malik shook his head. "That will be all."

"This goes on the Chairman Sahar's tab," Ghost said.

The waiter inclined his head once more and drifted away toward a couple just stepping into the diner.

Malik lifted his glass and gave the liquid a slow swirl. An acrid scent rose like a warning. He brought it to his lips, took a short swig, and winced. It might as well have been fuel. He set the glass down and narrowed his eyes across the table.

"Did you have to pick the most expensive item on the menu?"

Ghost smirked. "You don't want to treat an old friend?"

Malik chuckled and turned toward the window. Outside, the city lay under a manufactured shroud of cloud. Intercoms rumbled, their thunder sounds bleeding through the diner walls in low pulses. Simulated lightning flared, white bursts cutting the dark. A moment later, the sprinklers engaged, releasing rain in coordinated sheets.

"A miracle," Ghost said, lifting his glass. "One of our early victories. Moisture in a dome sealed by desert. Still proud of that piece of legislation."

"I wish we had more chances to do that kind of work," Malik said. "I miss having allies in halls owned by red-lustronium politics."

Ghost gave him a knowing look. "That time is gone. The system is going to crack, one way or another."

Malik raised his glass again, forced down another swallow, and grimaced at the burn, bitter as the times. "So," he said, choosing his words with care for whatever Ghost was running now, "business is steady, then?"

"Client base is rising faster than heat off the dunes. Support contracts with outsiders. Exit routes for anyone tagged for labor camps. Moving supplies to the people who need them."

Ghost leaned in, close enough that Malik could see the fine lines at the corners of his eyes. "Insiders are bleeding. You aren't exempt. When it's your turn to vanish, tell me. Don't make yourself a martyr. We could use your talents. Be smart about which side you end up on."

Malik eased back, Ghost's words thudded in his chest. Loss after loss rose in his mind, a cycle so deep he was no longer sure there was a way out. Even if there was, he knew he would not step off this track without both Eren and Leila beside him.

"You'll be the first to know when that day comes," Malik said. "For now, I would like to focus on the reason for this meeting. And I must question whether you will help, given your... increased contractual work with outsiders."

"Of course I'll take the job. You're still a friend, Malik. Even if your outward-facing politics align with Victor."

"Leila and I think he's outside. If he's alive, Nova Angeles is the only viable settlement within a hundred miles."

"What do you know so far?"

"I'm stranded inside the machine. Victor controls every channel. My son is not on his list of priorities. The only real lead I have is Dome Pub."

Ghost nodded. "Then that's where I go."

Malik lifted a brow. "Just like that? No contract. No angle?"

Ghost tipped back the last of his drink, set the empty glass down, and adjusted his collar as he slid toward the end of the booth. "The only reason I'm breathing," he said, "is because you covered up my death. If you hadn't, Victor would've shipped me to Perihelion for the rest of my days."

The memory rose uninvited. A vote held too early in the morning. Ghost standing in the chamber, threatening to break ranks, to side with the outsiders Victor was already writing off as expendable.

Then the purge. Anyone who agreed, anyone who hesitated, quietly reassigned off world.

Malik acted fast. Paperwork altered. A death certificate rerouted. A body that was never found. He pushed Ghost into the city's blind spots and gave him a life that existed between data entries, safe from the public eye and, more importantly, from Victor Kol's reach.

Malik reached out and clasped his hand. "We will find peace. In this life."

Ghost slipped his hand free, snatched Malik's untouched drink, and gulped it down in one smooth pull. "You weren't enjoying it anyway. Distinguished Chair," Ghost said, sweeping into an overly dramatic bow, "may that peace find the outsiders too. I'll call when I know more."

He walked out, vanishing into the rain-streaked glow of the diner's doorway before Malik could think of anything else to say.

34

ZAHEEN

The wind caught Zaheen's robes as she stepped into Holly's bar, the fabric snapping once like a warning bell. Old ale, smoke, and recycled heat clawed at her lungs.

Jude followed close behind, boots thudding softly against the worn floor.

Behind the counter, Holly did not look up. "Bar's closed," she said. "Sand Alliance business. Everyone out."

The remaining patrons left without protest. Scavenger runners, off-duty vendors, a few faces Zaheen recognized from her first days with the alliance. Holly had earned that kind of obedience over the years.

She should be leading this fight, Zaheen thought as they filtered toward the door.

Even the drunkest among them managed something close to a salute as they passed. Zaheen returned each with a slight nod, the gesture automatic now, heavier than it had been when she first learned it.

She wondered how many of them had lost someone on the train tracks because of her.

She believed in restraint. In presence. In standing in the way without becoming a mirror of Victor Kol. The uprising was supposed to slow the machine, not feed it.

Holly locked the door behind the last customer and dragged the shutters down. She returned behind the bar and slid two steins across the scarred counter, stopping them just short of Zaheen's hands. Condensation traced slow paths down the glass, winding like rivers.

"Any luck?" Holly asked.

If luck had ever found Zaheen, it lost the trail long ago. "Define luck," Zaheen said.

"You've never seen Perihelion with your own eyes. You've never touched Mars. You're not strung up on the wire. I would call that lucky."

Jude's shoulders sagged. "Three days, and Eren gives us nothing."

The strategic map Zaheen clung to felt like it was unraveling in her hands, thread by thread. Doubt crept in, quiet as fog. "We're sitting here waiting for a boy to decide what comes next. That feels wrong."

Her fingers closed around the golden chain at her neck. She pressed it against her sternum, grounding herself in the familiar weight. "I wish she knew."

"She does," Holly said without hesitation. "I would wager Araya asks the same of you when she speaks to her allies on Mars."

"I worry Araya would not recognize the person I'm becoming."

Jude took a slow sip from his stein. "I think a person can carry more than one version of themselves. I do it all the time," he said. "When this is over, you can choose who you're meant to be."

Zaheen shook her head. "You know better than that. There's no going back to before. This rebellion reshapes everything. We can't keep Eren. It undermines everything we claim to stand for. We're fighting to reunite families, not tear them apart."

Jude shoved his stein away. "Do you have any idea what I risked getting him here?"

"Everything," Zaheen said.

"And knowing that, you still want to cut him loose?"

"I let my misery blind me," Zaheen said, meeting his stare head-on.

Holly rubbed a hand over her face, slow and weary. "Zaheen, this kind of work, this kind of awakening, it's uncomfortable for a reason. I understand that. But I agree with Jude on this one."

A scream tore through the street outside. Zaheen was on her feet before she, crossing the room and wrenching the blinds apart.

The street was unraveling into chaos. Insiders marched in rigid formation, dragging bodies from doorways and shadowed alleys. Windows shattered. Doors burst inward. Outsiders—young, old, it didn't matter—were seized and hauled away like contraband.

Jude crossed to the window in three quick strides, took one look, and spun back toward Holly. "We can finish this later. Is there a way out?"

"Back door, through the kitchen. Both of you. Now." Holly's voice snapped with command as a heavy knock rattled the front door.

Jude slipped through the swinging door without another word.

Zaheen turned to follow.

The front door exploded inward, ripped clean off its hinges. Insiders flooded the bar in tight formation, weapons raised.

A hand clamped around her wrist—iron grip, tactical glove biting into her skin. Too late. Too slow. She didn't fight. Whatever chance she'd had to resist was back on the train tracks.

Another insider forced Holly forward by the arms. "Looks like it was just these two, sir," she called.

"Well done, Officer Nakamura," said a voice that sent Zaheen's heart into overdrive.

Her skin prickled. Heat flushed up her neck, shame and alarm rising in tandem, and the cold followed—a drop in her gut, an instinctual recoil like stepping barefoot onto something slick and alive in the dark. Her body knew before her mind did. She turned her head too quickly with the sick certainty of déjà vu.

Carmine Kurier strolled inside, hands clasped behind his back, as if the splintered door and broken glass were a mild inconvenience. His eyes found her immediately.

"Zaheen Mandisa," he said, smiling, polite as a chance meeting. "It's been far too long. A reunion, of sorts. Mr. Kol is most eager to—"

"Where is she?" The words tore out of Zaheen before she could stop them.

She lunged forward, rage cracking through the shock. The grip on her wrist tightened, another hand locking around her arm, yanking her back.

"Where is Araya?" she screamed. "What did you do to her?"

Zaheen twisted against the restraint, nails scraping uselessly against armor, the pressure crushing her chest.

"Ms. Mandisa," Carmine said, amused. "This kind of outburst only makes things harder."

Hatred surged through her, hot and nauseating, rising so fast it stole her breath. It burned through her chest and down her arms, drowning out every lesson she had ever clung to, every promise of restraint she had made to herself. She twisted against the grip on her wrists, lunging again.

"Zaheen," Holly said. "Zaheen, look at me."

The fury clawed at her insides, and this time she didn't try to push it down. She leaned into it, burning through every ounce of peace.

Carmine stepped inches from her face, close enough to feel like a deliberate taunt. "You will see Mr. Kol soon," he said. "And perhaps, if you behave, we can come to a solution."

She lurched forward as far as she could get and spat.

The glob struck Carmine's cheek with a sharp, wet smack. It slid down the edge of his jaw. His smile vanished and raised a gloved hand and dabbed at the spot with the tips of his fingers, and held them up to the light, inspecting them with scrutiny of a surgeon checking for contamination.

"Take them away."

Zaheen stopped thrashing. She stared at Carmine, her gaze nailed to his, hard as shrapnel, daring him to meet it, and hating him more for not needing to.

35

ZAHEEN

The sun bled along the horizon, its last light a thin smear of peach before the haze of Nova Angeles engulfed it whole. The city lay beneath its shroud, a husk of gray and smoke. For a moment, the moon pressed through, silvering the edges of cloud before sinking back into murk. The stars winked behind the haze, their signals broken, dulled by the gloom.

Zaheen sank to her knees in the sand-choked plaza. Grit chewed into her skin as the wind knifed across her face, stealing breath and heat in the same pull. She lifted her chin anyway and locked her glare on the six armored guards planted in front of her. Beyond them, four times that number formed a tightening ring—riot shields linked like a steel fence —corralling the citizens of Nova Angeles into a trembling pen.

Zaheen held her ground. She didn't flinch at the rifles or the shields. She couldn't. Her people were watching, and if she broke, they would too.

Train tracks. Screams. Blood. Bodies snagged on wire. The helplessness of seeing it happen and being unable to stop it. The memories came back so sharp they blurred the edge between what had been and what was coming.

Victor Kol stood atop the stage his guards had raised, the height handing him dominion over the circle below. His stare nailed Zaheen in place as his gloved hand swept outward, presenting the ring of onlookers—outsiders, every one of them—penned behind riot shields like livestock.

"My distinguished guest. Leader of anarchy," he said. "Zaheen Mandisa. Welcome."

She lifted her chin and squared her shoulders. Performance answering performance. "This is what passes for insider hospitality?"

"On the contrary." His smile didn't reach his eyes. "It's an honor to bring a little class to this miserable corner of the world."

He turned like a showman unveiling his cast—Officer Nakamura to his right, Deputy Durand to his left. Both wore polished silver armor, pistols riding their hips, crimson capes streaming in TerraLux pageantry.

At Victor's subtle nod, the front line pivoted as one. Riot shields swung and locked, piece by piece, until they became a single narrowing funnel.

Zaheen crouched and scooped a fistful of sand. She crushed it grain by grain, grinding her anger into the earth instead of flinging it at the men who'd caged her here.

Carmine Kurier's silhouette slid into view between the shields. Her body went taut on instinct, every nerve snapping awake. One strike. Just one. She could already feel the impact on her knuckles. She strangled the urge. She knew better. A punch would buy her nothing but blood, innocent blood.

Carmine strolled up and stopped in front of her. "The

star must take center stage," he said, flicking his scarf over one shoulder.

Hands clamped around Zaheen's arms. Guards yanked her upright and dragged her forward, placing her at Victor's feet like an offering.

Gasps rippled through the crowd.

Zaheen turned her head just enough to catch movement at the platform's edge. Officer Nakamura and Deputy Durand lifted a pole, angling it toward the center.

Carmine climbed the steps, whip coiled neat in his hand. "I hope I've made you proud, sir," he said, extending it toward Victor Kol.

Victor set a hand on his shoulder, heavy as a blessing. Almost fatherly. "You've done well, Mr. Kurier. As promised, promotion awaits when we return. One rung higher on the ladder."

He lifted his other hand toward the armored four-wheeler; its mottled plating dusted with sand. "Take a security escort and return to Los Angeles. Your services are not required here."

Carmine bowed. "As you wish."

He slipped back into the crowd, swallowed by shields and helmets. With him gone, the air loosened by a fraction. One less viper in the circle, for now.

The stage shrunk, resolving into a single point of focus: Victor Kol and the whip he now stroked, its leather coiled in his hand.

"Threats only work on those afraid to die," Zaheen said. She looked at the outsiders penned behind riot shields. "We will not submit. Even if you kill me."

"You think I'm here to kill you?"

Deputy Durand dragged his chosen victim up the steps and shoved Holly against the pole, binding her wrists tight.

"The movement never dies, Zee," Holly said, breath ragged. "We're invincible."

Victor smiled at Zaheen's dismay. "We'll see about that."

He lifted his arm. The whip unfurled in a cruel arc, leather shrieking through the air long before it struck.

36

ZAHEEN

Zaheen braced for the sound of Holly's scream. It never came.

Gunfire split the air with a vicious, tearing crack.

Zaheen dropped. Not from thought—instinct seized her spine and yanked her down. Her knees slammed into the boards with a force that lit up her nerves, pain flashed white and hot and sharp enough to steal her breath. She curled without meaning to, arms locked around her head, elbows tight to her ribs, chest pressed flat to the planks beneath her.

The plaza erupted.

Sound pounded the air—sharp, concussive blasts that came in stuttering bursts, close enough to shake the inside of her skull. The scent hit just as fast. Cordite, bitter and metallic, filled her lungs, clinging to the back of her throat. Heat rose from the ground in ripples and lifted a haze of dust and ash that blurred her vision.

A round cracked past her. Another struck the ground inches from her hip and kicked up splinters that bit into her arm. Return fire cut through the chaos.

Officer Nakamura's pistol barked. Muzzle flashes lit dusk

in brutal flickers, each one revealing a new fragment of hell: a man sprinted behind a toppled stall, a woman crouched with blood on her palms, insider guards attacked innocent outsiders in the fray.

On stage, Victor's entourage blanketed him in riot shields. A bullet found its mark into a guard, and his chest bloomed red. The remaining shoved the injured out of their shell and pushed Victor to safety.

"They must pay!" Victor shouted over bullets taking out the guards around him. "They must pay!"

Officer Nakamura locked her aim to the rooftops, and Zaheen launched herself at the insider.

The impact punched the air from her lungs. Armor slammed into bone. White pain burst behind her eyes. Boots slid on blood-slick boards. They went down hard, crashing onto the stage in a tangle of limbs, Zaheen's shoulder screaming as it struck the wood.

Her hand found Officer Nakamura's wrist, and she twisted, muscles bunching as she tried to tear free.

Zaheen yanked the pistol free. Fingers locked around the grip. Cold metal bit into her palm. She raised the gun, breath ragged, arms trembling as she leveled the barrel at Officer Nakamura.

Shame bloomed. Violence feeding violence, blood demanding more blood, a wheel that never stopped turning. Pulling the trigger would mean surrender. Not to Officer Nakamura. Not to Victor Kol. But to the rage and despair that built the cages, walls, and empire crushing her people in the first place.

Zaheen lowered the gun. "I don't quarrel with you. Only with Victor Kol. Return my mercy one day."

For a split second, something unreadable flickered in Nakamura's eyes. Not kindness. Not regret. A micro-hesitation, an error in timing so small it could be denied.

Zaheen named it anyway. She called it hope, because she needed something to call it.

Officer Nakamura sprinted after the retreating transports. Her boots hit the boards, found the edge, and dropped to the sand below.

The vehicles pulled away.

At the base of the pole, the fallen insider lay folded into himself, face turned down. His belt had ridden up in the fall. The key ring sat exposed against his hip.

Zaheen dropped to her knees beside him and yanked it free.

She crossed to Holly, careful where the stage had been painted slick by spilled red. She sorted through keys, found the right one, and twisted.

"Easy," Holly said.

"Just hold on Holly." Zaheen freed the restraints.

Holly folded forward. Zaheen caught her under the arms and pulled her close before her hands could hit the stage.

"Are you hurt?" Holly said, holding on.

"I was going to ask you the same thing." Zaheen tried to keep her voice level, to shape the words into something steady and reassuring. The effort failed. Her throat tightened, and the sound cracked anyway. Tears pushed out before she could stop them. "I'm so sorry."

"For what?"

"For nearly getting you killed."

Holly pulled back just enough to look at her. Up close,

the grime on her face cut sharp lines into her skin, dust and sweat streaked with dried blood.

Zaheen braced herself for anger.

Instead, Holly snorted and rolled her eyes, a spark of her old fire breaking through the wreckage. "Like I've always said, Zee. I know the risks."

Holly tipped her chin toward the empty outskirts of the plaza, where Victor Kol's convoy vanished into the dunes. "And watching Victor Kol scatter away like a desert rat?" A breathless laugh slipped out. "That was reward enough."

Something inside Zaheen finally gave way. She shook her head, tears still falling, relief swelled until it pressed hard against her ribs and felt unbearable to hold alone. The laughter came out of her without permission—sharp at first, almost hysterical, then softer, shaky, threaded through with sobs she didn't bother to hide.

"You're welcome," Jude said, slipping through the regrouping crowd, rifle slung loose over his shoulder.

"You missed," Holly said.

"I'm a little rusty."

Jude climbed onto the stage and pulled them both into a hug.

Zaheen stiffened on instinct, caught off guard by his closeness. This wasn't the Jude she'd come to expect—the distant strategist, the man who kept himself sealed behind purpose.

She didn't pull away.

When he finally stepped back, Zaheen faced the outsiders gathered below the stage. The plaza had gone quiet.

"Victor Kol built this stage to break us. To prove who holds power." Zaheen swept a hand over the boards beneath her feet. "But tonight, he revealed something else. Who he's afraid of. Who holds the power he tries to steal."

She let the silence stretch.

"If we want more than scraps. If we want a life beyond survival, a way home for our people, then we stand together. All of us. United. Under the same goal. I won't lie to you," she said. "It'll get worse before it gets better. But if you follow me—if we follow each other—the path to freedom comes closer every day, until we're standing on its doorstep."

She drew herself up, spine straight, the words landing firm and sure. "Now I ask... will you trust me?"

An arm lifted. And another. Then three, then dozens, until the entire plaza joined in.

"We stand with you, Zaheen! We are sand born!"

Zaheen lifted her face to the sky. In the thin, fragile strip between stars and smog, she saw Araya as clearly as if she stood beside her. The tide of the dune sea began to shift. Slow and inevitable, like pressure building beneath the surface before a storm breaks. She felt it under her feet, in the weight of the necklace resting against her heart, in the rigid structures of Nova Angeles itself.

A storm was brewing.

37

ARAYA

Light poured through the cell in narrow bands and laid pale lines across the floor. It didn't hurt her eyes, but it broke the dark Araya adjusted to, and by the time the door fully opened she had no sense of how long she'd been there.

Minutes and hours collapsed into the same dull stretch. Time no longer moved forward in any useful way. It stripped things down piece by piece, wearing away impatience first, until endurance became reflex rather than choice.

She raised an arm and turned her face aside as the light pushed deeper into the cell. Her body folded before her thoughts finished forming. Knees tucked in. Spine curved. Shoulders closed. The posture came from memory.

"Get up," the guard said. Her eyes adjusted in reluctant increments until the figure resolved out of the glare. "You've got a date with tunnel three."

Cold bled up from the floor into her legs and settled in her joints. It numbed everything except awareness. She pulled in a breath. Sweat dampened skin despite the chill, with adrenaline trapped behind a barrier she couldn't break.

"I said up. Or I'll drag you out."

Her head lifted first. She wedged an elbow under herself. Then her knees came in, joints screaming as she forced them to cooperate. She rose in slow, stubborn increments until she stood.

"File out," the guard said, close behind.

She complied.

Each step landed with a faint jolt that ran up her legs. Her body held together by intent alone. She shuffled out of the cell and into the corridor, and the warmer air brushed her skin.

Strange. When she first arrived on Perihelion, the cold shocked her, a clean, biting reminder that insiders controlled climate as casually as they controlled people. After the cell, the corridor's chill felt almost gentle.

The corridors turned without any sense of order. Left. Right. Downstairs when the guard snapped his baton. Araya stopped trying to track the route. There was no prize for knowing where she was.

Eventually, the barrack gates came into view.

The guard marched past her as if she wasn't there, lifted his keycard, and the lock chirped.

He shoved her forward. Araya stumbled, and gravity made its decision. Her hands shot out. Palms hit concrete. Pain ran up her arms like the body filing a damage report all at once. Behind her, the gate slammed shut with a heavy clang.

Iman reached her first. Hands already there, steady and sure.

Skye followed a breath later, face locked into that careful neutrality people adopted when caring was dangerous. But Skye's eyes betrayed her. She scanned Araya for damage.

"A little privacy," Skye said, pitching her voice toward the onlookers.

A few lingered. Curiosity had become a pastime in the barracks. When there was nothing to do but count hours, feel phlegm thicken in the chest, or cry in private for a reunion on Earth that might never come, Araya understood why they stayed to watch.

But they drifted off, one by one, until the room returned to its usual noise. Ventilation whispered overhead. Beds creaked. Someone coughed with the persistence of a body that refused to quit.

Skye dropped to a knee. "What did they do to you?" She pulled Araya into a hug.

That hurt. Why comfort her now. After Dante. Skye should hate her. Araya deserved that. Hate would have been clean. Easier to manage. Skye held on anyway, like pressure could force guilt into a smaller shape.

Iman crossed to Araya's bed, grabbed the blanket, and draped the scratchy wool over her frame. "Solitary confinement," she said. "You're safe now. You're with friends."

Skye reached back and closed her hand around Iman's wrist. "Can I have a moment?"

Iman hesitated. Her eyes flicked between them, weighing risk against need, but Araya's nod was enough to have her step away. "I'll be at my bed."

"Don't," Araya said to Skye. Her fingers worked the edge of the blanket, twisting the fabric tight and loose again. "Dante would still be alive if I hadn't made that call. People get hurt when they trust me."

That was the Nova Angeles way. Trust never stayed solid for long out in the desert; heat and hunger reshaped it, and leverage finished the job. Everyone had motives. Everyone kept score. Araya gave trust sparingly, and she gave it to exactly one person: Zaheen.

"Dante's death wasn't your fault. I wanted someone to blame. I chose you. That was wrong." Skye drew a careful breath. "The idea of losing you too..." Her voice dipped. "It broke something. Anger leaked out."

Skye met Araya's eyes and held them. "You're family, Araya."

Araya's eyes burned. Tears fell down her face before she could stop them. She bowed her head, shoulders curling inward, not in defense this time but collapse. Forgiveness did that. It pulled strength right out of her knees.

Araya pressed her face into Skye's shoulder and let herself cry, because for the first time since Dante died, she didn't feel alone.

38

VICTOR

Victor Kol stood in Chairman Malik Sahar's office and gestured for him to sit.

Malik obeyed, and lowered himself behind the wide, glass-topped desk. Behind him, floor-to-ceiling windows framed the spires of Los Angeles—needle-thin towers reaching for artificial moonlight.

Victor admired his creation before focusing his attention back on his colleague. The simple act of Malik sitting where Victor had indicated steadied him more than anything else had since the Nova Angeles attack.

Control, at last. Proof that the world still responded correctly when addressed with proper authority.

Victor allowed himself quiet satisfaction. Systems, people, spaces—everything belonged where he decided it would go. Order returned the moment others remembered that.

The journey home was spent in silence. Victor had held himself perfectly still in the transport, spine straight, hands folded, breath measured. He refused the smallest tell. Rage was inelegant. Panic was amateur. Even reflection was dangerous if left undisciplined. He controlled his body the way he controlled his empire, through restraint and denial.

And yet humiliation had found him anyway.

It settled beneath the skin like a slow-forming bruise. Deep enough to wound his ego. The knowledge that something had occurred beyond prediction—the world failing to respond as he designed—shattered him.

Victor despised the sensation because it resisted correction.

He built TerraLux Minerals on a single conviction. Human behavior was not natural chaos. It was architecture. It wants could be forecasted. Grievances redirected. Defiance softened and absorbed long before it ever reached the surface of his dominion. Give people structure, routine, and the correct incentives and they mistook compliance for choice.

Nova Angeles challenged that belief. Not with strategy or scale, but with something messier. Emotion through a figure who inspired action without permission. That possibility unsettled him more than gunfire. It suggested a crack in his design of society. Cracks could not be allowed to spread.

The fault would be isolated. Pressure rerouted. Behavior corrected until the system snapped back into alignment and rid itself of rot.

Rot started beneath the soil, where no one bothered to look. A root softened. A vein clogged. By the time the leaves browned, the plant was already lost. He didn't argue with rot. He cut around it and moved on.

Remove what was infected before it spread. Reroute nutrients. Starve the diseased parts so the rest could thrive.

Zaheen Mandisa had done him a favor, whether she meant to or not. She'd reminded him how delicate his order truly was. Not because she was powerful, but because she was *possible*. A flaw the system had allowed. A hairline crack that proved pressure could still find purchase.

And better yet, she'd made the rot visible.

Most decay didn't announce itself. It sank into the sand and worked in silence, eating at foundations from below until the first collapse looked like bad luck instead of negligence. But Zaheen had stepped into the light and festered for all to see.

She would make an easy enemy of the people.

"Leniency," Victor said, and placed his palm flat against the desk. "No more of it."

Malik adjusted the cuff of his sleeve and smoothed an invisible crease. Victor noticed the gesture. The pause carried numbers. Malik weighed costs, quietly sorting who he might protect and which reputations might endure the fire Victor planned to set.

Victor allowed Malik to question. Calculation always stripped people down to their true intentions.

"Your committee," Victor said, "will need preparation. Language. Framing. I'll handle the blade." His fingers flexed slightly on the desk. "You'll manage what comes after."

"Victor, I can't lead my committee down a path that escalates violence. That isn't governance. That's—"

"It would be unfortunate if the honorable Chairman Malik Sahar were suddenly absent."

Victor went on. "Think about the headlines. The speculation. The way it moves through your networks, into the institutions that trust you, into the lives you keep trying to protect."

Victor paced around the desk and came to a stop beside Malik. He studied him like a problem that refused to resolve. Men like Malik believed there was room between worlds. A space where morality and power could live side by side without consequence. Victor had watched belief collapse many times in previous subordinates.

Victor picked up a family photo off his desk and examined it. "What would I say to your wife? Or your son, when my investigators finally bring him home."

The boy meant nothing to him. He was a variable. A misplaced asset. A lever left unattended.

Victor understood Malik. He fractured when personal attachments went untested. Families softened hearts that should stay solid. Divided loyalties produced hesitation. Hesitation bred disorder. Loss corrected that.

Grief simplified priorities. It stripped men down to function. A dead child would not break Malik. It would focus him. It would burn away distraction and return him to purpose. Men worked best when the cost of failure became permanent.

He set the frame back on the desk and adjusted it until it sat perfectly square, exactly where it had been.

"Don't worry," Victor said. He resumed his slow walk across the office. "History treats insiders like you with kindness. I'll even see that your portrait hangs in a place of honor. Directly behind my desk."

He stopped and faced Malik. "A reminder for the man who replaces you of how the chain of command operates."

Victor watched the small signs. Sweat beaded his forehead. Malik's fingers pressed into the arm of the chair. Eye contact suddenly became difficult. Thread by thread, Malik was coming apart.

Victor sauntered to the window and folded his arms behind his back, the posture of a tutor preparing a final lesson. "When mercy turns into habit, systems forget who built them," he said. "Only clear and decisive power teaches people who holds command."

"What are you asking of me, Victor?"

"You are going to file as many violations as possible against the outsider Zaheen Mandisa."

Victor crossed back to the chair and lowered himself into it. "I had Mr. Kurier do some digging. An outsider called Araya Santera arrived on Mars three weeks ago. Close relation to Zaheen."

In Victor's mind, the list of betrayals formed itself. Enough to make anyone disappear. "Interference with the lottery. Subversion of repatriation policy. Intent to incite unrest for personal gain. Terrorism."

This was the language that mattered.

True power did not live in speeches or rallies. Those were for the restless, for people who believed volume could substitute for authority. Power lurked elsewhere—in forms, in charges, in quiet decisions rendered behind closed doors and stamped into permanence before anyone realized a choice had been taken from them.

A signature here. A sanction there.

It was a language most people never learned to speak. Administrative codes. Procedural phrasing. The kind of words that never raised alarms because they never sounded like violence. But people who spoke in plain grief, in anger, in slogans, never stood a chance against it. They could shout until their throats bled and still lose to a single clause buried on page fourteen.

"We file. We prosecute. We execute." Victor leaned forward a fraction. "What will it be, Malik?"

Checkmate. Victor trapped him back into a corner of loyalty tests.

"I'll do as you command," Malik said.

Victor rose and walked toward the door. "Don't test how far I'm willing to go," he said. "I'll tear lives apart by the millions to drag these two women down. I'll do whatever it takes to keep TerraLux Minerals at the forefront of society."

He looked over his shoulder. "Stand on the side that survives, Malik. History belongs to those who understand that."

Victor stepped into the corridor and closed the door behind him. Malik had agreed. The words were in place. The orders were in motion. Even so, unease trailed him.

Fear could drive obedience, yet it could also drive betrayal. Malik's answer came quickly, with no argument, no attempt at compromise. Victor logged it as data, another line in a growing file.

For now, he still had uses.

After Zaheen was secured, he would decide where Malik belonged. Inside the structure, obedient and useful, or beneath it, crushed quietly under the same weight that held everything else in place.

His thoughts returned to the boy.

If Eren was found, Victor had not yet chosen the most useful outcome.

Bringing the boy home might deepen Malik's attachment to the outside world. Losing him might fracture Malik first, then harden him into an obedient and emotionless subordinate. He would think about it, play his cards, and decide if Eren deserved a place in his manufactured world.

39

ZAHEEN

Zaheen yanked her scarf higher until it pinched the bridge of her nose and sealed her mouth. The desert didn't care. It exhaled anyway—wind thin as a razor and mean as a debt collector—dragging a red haze across the dunes until everything looked dipped in rust.

Sand hit her face in micro-needles. It found the tiny gaps: lashes, cheekbones, the soft spot under her eyes. The grit was annoyingly dedicated.

The desert likes to test you, Araya used to say before Zaheen went out on scavenging runs. *Learn its rhythm, or it will forget you were ever here.*

Zaheen hadn't understood what she meant at first. She'd thought Araya was being poetic. Turns out Araya was just being accurate. Out here, the dunes kept receipts. Miss a step, ignore a shift in wind, assume you're tougher than the terrain—*boom*. She was a cautionary tale for some future scavenger.

Araya always stood in the doorway when Zaheen left on her scavenging runs. She would watch Zaheen leave and track her down the alley until the corrugated walls stole her silhouette. If she watched long enough, the universe would be forced to return Zaheen in one piece.

Now Zaheen wished she could do the same—to catch a glimpse of Araya, if even through eyeing the hidden stars behind dense smog.

Zaheen and Jude trekked across the dunes for a half hour, cresting long sand-backs and dropping down the far sides like the planet had been built out of lazy waves. Every climb took something from her. Every slide gave it back as sand in her boots and debris in her teeth.

Heat hit from above and below. The sky hammered down. The sand reflected scorching temperatures right back up. It was like walking inside an oven while someone held a hair dryer to her face for fun.

The ground shifted. Each step sank, shifted, argued. One wrong angle and the sand tried to steal her footing.

She glanced over her shoulder. Nothing.

The wind already erased their trail, smoothing the surface behind them until it looked untouched. As if the desert could deny they'd ever existed. It was petty like that.

Jude hiked beside her without a word. He hadn't spoken since they'd passed the last boundary marker outside Nova Angeles, the final little sign that pretended the city had city limits, as if nature respected boundary lines.

She didn't push him. The quiet was...useful. Out here, words felt thin. Unprotected. Anything she said might be carried off before she was ready to own it.

And the silence did what silence always did. It gave her room to think.

Every step toward Eren Sahar dragged her deeper into a choice she'd never pictured herself making. She hated what they were about to do. Hate was supposed to be a big feeling. This made it feel like a toy word. A child's insult. Not large enough to cover the shape of what waited ahead.

Her throat went dry. "What if he doesn't buy the bluff?" Her voice was rough under the scarf.

"Who says we're bluffing?"

Zaheen glared his way. "The plan is to keep him alive."

She wasn't a killer. Not by training or instinct. If anything, her instincts pulled the opposite way. Fix what was broken, keep people intact, insist there was still a version of this world that didn't demand blood as an entry fee.

Bringing others into the fight had already forced compromises she could still taste like rust at the back of her tongue.

She understood violence, at least in theory. It was efficient. Violence narrowed the world to a single lane. It stripped away questions and replaced them with momentum—move, hit, survive—no pauses or looking back, no room left to ask what the motion was turning them into.

Survival demanded ugliness sometimes. She could live with that. She already had. What she refused was letting that ugliness dictate who she became.

Jude kept pace beside her, scarf pulled high, and his voice carried that loose, almost amused calm that scraped her nerves raw. "Tensions sit at a boil. Be glad this part fits what I'm good at. You lack the stomach for it."

Zaheen grabbed his arm and yanked him back harder than she meant to. "Do not mistake restraint for weakness. My convictions don't soften just because I refuse to burn everything down."

His eyes flicked over her and settled into an expression

that accepted only part of what she'd said. The rest he filed away as idealism.

Jude pulled his arm free. "If breaking morale inside shifts command for even a single day," he said, "method matters less than outcome. This stopped being a protest a long time ago."

He faced forward again, already walking, done with the argument. "It's a civil war now. Inside against out."

Civil war. Zaheen had always kept the phrase filed under *history* and *other people's disasters.* A case study. A headline. Something that happened in textbooks and archived footage.

Now it was her own future.

"The outside chose to follow me," she called after Jude. "I never promised them war."

"Victor Kol is already mobilizing," Jude said and halted. "We don't get the luxury of peace when armies are on the move."

Her options folded in on themselves until they were all corners: rescue or ruin, love or principle. Every path cut someone open. "I know why you push this hard," she said. "I want Victor Kol out of power just as bad as you."

He slid his rifle off his shoulder. "I'm willing to make sacrifices," Jude said. "If that's the cost of bringing thousands home and ending the mines for good, I'll pay it."

He tipped his head toward the hidden shaft, half-buried and invisible unless someone knew exactly where to look. "I'll get the kid."

Jude walked a few paces ahead and dropped to one knee. His fingers combed the sand with practiced efficiency until they struck metal. The latch surfaced under his hand and yielded without a fight, as if it remembered him.

Zaheen watched him vanish into the dark.

She turned to the horizon. The dune sea rolled outward, endless and indifferent. She pressed her scarf to her cheek and anchored herself to sensation. Rough fabric. Heat pooling beneath it. The steady drag of breath in and out of her lungs. Whatever waited back in Nova Angeles—mercy or catastrophe—she would walk into it for Araya. That part was still solid and held true.

Metal rang beneath the sand.

Jude emerged with Eren in front of him, one hand locked tight on the boy's arm, the other gripping his rifle. The barrel pressed between the boy's narrow shoulders, steering him forward.

Eren stumbled into the sunlight. Sweat darkened his collar. Dust clung to skin. The blindfold stayed cinched tight across his eyes.

"Welcome to the outside," Zaheen said as Jude tore the cloth away.

She studied him.

Eren's face was controlled—too controlled for someone his age. The flat focus of a kid trained to exist near violence without reacting to it. Not Victor Kol's cold certainty. Not Carmine Kurier's cultivated cruelty. There was no hunger here. No ambition. Just conditioning. A child taught that obedience was the same thing as virtue.

"You follow my orders," Zaheen said, "or you disappear under this dune."

A bitter curve tugged at her mouth. The performance cut both ways. Her voice carried a threat she had no intention of honoring.

Eren's knees hit the sand. "My allegiance is to Victor Kol."

"Give me that," Zaheen said to Jude, and he slid her the rifle.

She didn't want to fire. She prayed she wouldn't have to. She needed, desperately, for the threat to be enough. Violence was a door she refused to walk through. Bluffing meant standing in its frame and pretending she might.

"Comply," she said, injecting cruelty she didn't feel. "Or die."

40

ARAYA

When Iman delivered the news that her plan was going into motion today, Araya only saw Dante in her mind's eye.

The shovel chewed into her palms. Each scoop stripped away what little was left.

Dig. Lift. Toss. The rhythm carved itself into muscle, until old bruises blended into new pain and stopped bothering her. But behind all of that was the idea Dante would never get out of this tunnel.

She dumped the load into the conveyor and watched it disappear. The machine carried the rubble away, and she repeated.

Somewhere past the bend, Skye and Bren worked their own stations, too far away for coordination.

Araya looked Iman head on. "A signal? Anything?"

Iman shook her head. "We're at the mercy of Bren's sails now. All I was told is that you need to be ready. So do I."

Araya swallowed her groan and went back to work. Hours bled away: shovel, lift, dump, repeat. Every person and machine was a cog in a greater system.

The first blast hit like thunder trapped in a metal pipe. The floor jumped. The tunnel flexed and complained with a deep, ugly roar. Her body reacted before her brain got a vote.

She slammed a hand into the wall to keep from going airborne and immediately regretted it. The rock sanded her palm in one swipe. Red dust smeared her skin, thick and sticky.

Guards sprinted out of the tunnel's depths seconds later, red uniforms filmed in dust, boots slipping on loose grit. They didn't look like the usual strutting predators. They looked like people running from a fire.

One of them skidded to the emergency console and slapped the panel with a hand so dirty the screen smeared. The response was immediate. Alarms howled, harsh and constant, like Perihelion was trying to wake the dead.

A second blast hit. Then a third. The detonations rolled down the line in a nasty chain, each one punching through Araya's skull and rattling her teeth. She dropped hard to her knees. Pain shot up her legs.

Iman folded over her and wrapped around Araya's head. "Stay down!"

The conveyor groaned. Its metal frame shuddered, tried to keep working out of habit, but gave up. The endless crawl died, and Araya couldn't help but smile.

"Get up," Bren said. He was suddenly there, like he'd been printed into existence by the chaos. Rock dusted his hair and uniform. He was half crouched, bracing himself as gravel rained from the ceiling.

Skye dropped in on Iman's other side, grabbed her under the arm, and hauled. "Talk to me," she said. "Anyone hurt?"

"Just scratches," Iman said. "I'll live."

Bren was already clawing through loose rock near the wall, searching for something Araya couldn't see yet.

"Iman, Skye, take whoever can still walk to the hangar bay," he said. "Find a light cruiser. Get everyone onboard and wait for further instruction."

Iman sagged a fraction in Skye's hold, but her glare stayed locked on Bren. "Splitting up now is a death sentence."

"Someone has to pull the override codes," Bren said. "All ships auto-land in Los Angeles."

His eyes flicked to Araya. "That's where you come in."

Bren reached into the rubble, tore free a fallen stalactite, and weighed it in his hand like a weapon. "Go!" he said. "Araya, you're with me."

Medics rushed in the opposite direction; faces streaked with blood that wasn't all theirs. They hauled triage kits and ducked beneath sagging rock, shouting codes Araya didn't know and didn't need. Bodies lay where the tunnel buckled— some shifting, some immobile.

Araya tried to tell herself this was the cost of breaking something this large. Systems didn't collapse neatly. Perihelion was a behemoth that controlled the ebb and flow of goods between two planets, and Araya realized that destroying the facility would be harder than she thought.

"Wait," Araya said. She stepped into Bren's path. "I don't know what you want me to do."

Bren stopped just long enough to meet her eyes. "You keep me alive. Confirm I make it to the med bay."

"The med bay?"

"It's the only way we can get to the command center."

"Why would you—"

Bren raised the stalactite and drove it into his thigh. His

wail vanished into the tunnel's roar. Blood erupted through torn fabric in a surge.

A wave of dizziness slammed into Araya so hard her vision frayed at the edges. The air felt thinner, like the blast had stolen whatever oxygen was left. She locked her knees and dug in mentally. Folding under pressure wasn't an option.

Bren sagged and went down. "Medic," he rasped.

Araya waved down passing insiders. "Help! Medic!"

One broke from the cluster and sprinted toward them, skidding to a stop. "Don't move the spike," he said, already tearing open his kit. "If this rock shifts, he bleeds out."

Araya dropped to her knees and clamped both hands around the rock.

Warm blood slicked her fingers. Bren hovered somewhere between pain and consciousness, breath shallow, eyes unfocused. She tightened her grip until her knuckles burned, anchoring the spike.

"You're helping me carry him," the medic said as he slid a stretcher into place.

Araya looked down at Bren, limp and unconscious, and forced her mind onto the plan—get those override codes at all costs.

41

MALIK

Chairman Malik Sahar sat behind a desk that no longer felt like his own.

Economic projections crawled down his monitor. Growth curves. Mineral yields. Labor forecasts. Numbers dressed up as reassurance, as if a clean graph could make TerraLux Minerals look inevitable instead of a violent alternative to justice.

He reached the final page and slowed. The same requests were reshaped and renamed. Approval of land expansions. Output targets rose upward. Labor reallocation stamped necessary in language that pretended it carried no blood.

His cursor hovered over the authorization field and signed.

A green approval stamp flashed across the screen. Somewhere inside this warren of offices and committees, that single mark would trigger a chain.

A notification.

A runner.

A list pulled from a database. Messengers would then

knock on a door in Nova Angeles that would tear a family apart.

He told himself this was how he protected his own family. That staying inside, agreeing to compromises, kept Leila and Eren out of Victor Kol's direct line of fire. But every signature also lifted Victor higher, fed his empire, made the machine smoother for those already on top.

Malik pushed his chair back and turned to the windows. From this height, Los Angeles looked almost civilized. The city spread beneath the dome in tiers of light and shadow, engineered to look calm from above. Traffic lines glowed like veins. Towers rose in orderly columns. The sky overhead held its programmed blue.

That was the lie distance sold him. None of this existed without the labor of outsiders. He pressed his fingertips to the glass. *What have I become?*

His reflection stared back at him. He felt twice his age. His eyebags drooped, and for that matter, he couldn't remember the last time he slept for more than a couple of hours.

For years, he had convinced himself that signing approvals was the cost of proximity to power. Redirect. Delay. Bend morals for the sake of his name. He believed that until harm snuck up on one of his own. *Eren.*

It sickened him how long it had taken. How many signatures, meetings, and quiet nods across polished tables before the line finally crossed his own home. As if injustice only became real once it affected him.

Malik lent TerraLux Minerals legitimacy. Language. Process. He wrapped brutality in procedure and called it governance. He told himself the system could be steered. Instead, it learned how to steer him.

Ghost's words returned to him unbidden. *Being invisible has its advantages.*

Letting the machine grind on without his fingerprints registered as cowardice, but also relief. Malik could no longer tell the difference. If he stayed, he became complicit in whatever came next. If he left, he surrendered the last fragile influence he had, however illusory it now seemed. Either choice marked a betrayal. One of principle. One of people.

Malik pressed his forehead to the glass and closed his eyes. "I thought I was protecting you," he said, unsure whether he meant Eren, Leila, or the city below.

The phone rang, as if the system had been listening, and sensed his doubt. It reached into the room to correct it and drag him back into its grip before he could decide to let go.

He turned from the window, the city's reflection still clinging to his vision, and looked down at the display. *Caller ID: Unknown.*

His pulse jumped before he could stop it. Malik reclaimed the posture the office demanded of him and picked up the phone. "This is Chairman Sahar."

"Dad?"

Malik dropped into his chair. "Eren? Son, is that..." He tried again, swallowing against the burn in his throat. "Is that really you?"

Silence answered, only a faint hiss on the other end of the line.

"Are you safe? Eren, talk to me. Let me speak with Ghost."

"I'm no ghost. Your son is fine if you listen carefully to my instructions."

"Who are you?"

"Who I am is none of your concern. What I want is."

"I know I'm far from perfect," Malik said. The words came out too practiced, as if his mouth had memorized them in committee rooms. "I have a family to protect. My position demands loyalty. I must choose what keeps them safe."

"I think you already know what keeps them safe."

The sentence slipped under his ribs like a thin blade, finding the exact pocket where fear collected near his heart. With one careful twist, it fractured his control and let everything he had dammed up start to spill. "Zaheen Mandisa," he said. "You are the one who took Eren."

Silence proved no denial. "I'm sorry. For what they've done. For what I've helped allow."

"Prove it. Help us liberate Nova Angeles, and you get your son back."

The line went dead. Malik stood very still. He stared at the phone in hand. A chairman would call security. A good father would desperately try to call back. He did neither.

PART THREE
VOW

In the depths of Mars, I've battled shadows seeking to consume my resolve. Every trial has shaped me into an indomitable comet, hurtling through the stars with a fiery energy that refuses to be extinguished. My love, like gravity, will pull us together across the vast expanse of space until we're reunited under the same boundless sky.

—ARAYA, CITIZEN OF NOVA ANGELES, MINER AND
PRISONER OF TERRALUX MINERALS

42

ARAYA

"Keep breathing," Araya said. Blood slicked her hands. "Bren, stay with me."

The room smelled like metal scrubbed too hard and antiseptic used as incense. Overhead lights buzzed with a tired electrical whine that suggested they outlived their warranty years ago. Ten minutes passed. Maybe more. Time got slippery when Araya was kneeling in someone else's blood.

The medic who dumped Bren into her care was already gone. He was back down the tunnel hunting for survivors. Araya stayed exactly where she'd been told. Knees welded to the floor. Hands planted on Bren like she could physically veto death.

Blood found new places to be. It slicked her palms, crawled over her wrists, climbed her forearms. It looked like it wanted to keep going until it reached her throat and engulfed her.

The door sighed and slid open.

A woman strode in and snapped gloves on mid-step. Pale latex stretched tight over long fingers. Amber hair was pinned back, a few strands loose and ignored. Wide blue eyes locked on the wound as she crouched beside Araya. "I'm Dr. Astron."

Dr. Astron pressed two fingers near the point of entry. "He's bleeding out. Do exactly what I say and he may survive."

Bren jolted. His back bowed off the bed, and Araya flinched like the pain had jumped into her. His scream came out thin and torn, the sound of a person trying to be quiet and failing.

"It's deep," Dr. Astron said, and pushed harder. She looked up at Araya for the first time. "What's your name, outsider?"

"Araya."

Every outsider knew the medics on Perihelion were flunkies and dropouts—there to provide a thin, theatrical sense of security for anyone unlucky enough to arrive on the red planet. Araya trusted old plastic wire and sand-caked bandages more than this woman's supposed expertise.

But choice was a luxury she didn't have. "Whatever you need, I'm here to help."

Dr. Astron tipped her chin to the supply rack. "Middle shelf. Silver canister."

Araya grabbed it and thrust it forward, but Dr. Astron shook her head. "I'll be extracting. Spraying will come down to you."

Bren jerked again, sweat pouring off him, jaw clenched so tight it looked like it might crack. His head rolled side to side. "Quit talking and do it."

Dr. Astron tightened her grip. "Mineral dust is in your bloodstream," she said, almost bored by the fact. "Picture a thousand blades scraping and slashing at you. Leave coordination to me and stay quiet."

Araya twisted the cap with shaky hands. "What is this?"

The seal broke with a sharp little hiss.

She hadn't expected emergency medicine to sound like junk food, but there it was—same noise as one of her favorite finds back home. The canister even had the same stubborn, twist-and-pop cap. For one stupid second, her brain supplied the image on its own: spray cheese. Press, dispense, pretend it counted as dinner.

Then she looked at Bren, and the comparison stopped being funny.

Dr. Astron glanced at the canister. "Protein-bond catalyst. Slows blood loss. Buys us time until we get medication from Los Angeles."

And real doctors.

Bren spasmed again, muscles jumping under Dr. Astron's touch. She leaned her weight in and braced him with her forearm. Her gloves shone wet, slick with blood.

"Stop squirming," Dr. Astron said. "I'm trying to keep you alive."

Araya winced at the scene. "No sedatives?"

"Insiders only."

"He's bleeding out and you're still sorting people by loyalty?"

Dr. Astron snapped her fingers. "Hand towel," she said. "His mouth. Now."

Araya yanked the cloth from Dr. Astron's waistband, folded it and jammed the cloth between Bren's teeth. He bit down like it was the only thing in the universe he could still control.

Dr. Astron leaned over the wound. Shoulders squared. Hands planted like anchors. "On my mark."

Araya's heart hammered a frantic drum solo against her ribs. Bren was the plan. The key. The only path she could see off Mars and back to Zaheen. The realization twisted her stomach tight. She hated herself for the part of her that needed him alive for that reason alone.

"Now!" Dr. Astron yelled, and broke Araya from her trance.

Araya yanked.

The shard came free and the wound opened like a busted pipe. Blood surged out in a violent rush.

Bren's whole body seized. His legs kicked, and heels slammed the table hard enough to rattle the frame. His scream reached the towel and died there.

From the stars above to the sand below, save this man. Araya squeezed the trigger.

The silver canister hissed and spat a thin mist into the open wound. The spray clashed against blood and bubbled into pale foam. It crawled outward in hungry rings, filling gaps like it had a map of where blood wanted to escape. A sharp, synthetic tang cut through the antiseptic and tightened her throat.

Bren convulsed. Tears carved clean tracks through the grime on his face. He locked up, every muscle clamping down under the shock.

"Hold him," Dr. Astron said and threw an arm across his chest.

Araya leaned in, palms flat on Bren's shoulders. The foam shifted from pale to translucent and hardened over the wound like cheap glass.

Bren's sobs came in ragged, ugly gulps. But relief flickered across his face anyway. He was still here, and for that Araya felt thankful to Dr. Astron.

"He's stable," Dr. Astron said. She wrapped gauze around his leg. "Good work, Araya."

The canister slipped from Araya's hand and clattered across the tile, rolling into the shadow under the shelf. Araya sank onto the floor. Her arms trembled with leftover adrenaline that didn't know where to go.

One breath. Then another. Then another. He's alive. She did that. Somehow.

Dr. Astron peeled off her gloves. "The spray will hold. But if he's going to survive long term, he needs Los Angeles."

Araya looked at Bren. His skin had gone gray. Sweat beaded along his hairline. His lashes fluttered like he couldn't decide whether staying conscious was worth the effort. Every breath hitched on the way in.

His eyes found hers, and they flicked to the tray beside the bed. Araya got the message right away. She snuck the surgical scissors and pressed them into Bren's hand as Dr. Astron cleaned the station.

Bren slid off the table. His injured leg dragged like dead weight, but he lurched forward anyway and launched himself with whatever strength pain hadn't stolen. One arm wrapped across Dr. Astron's torso and pinned her. The other hand came up fast; blade angled toward the soft line of her throat.

"Kill the cameras and open the doors," he said.

"You're making a mistake," Dr. Astron said, pinned and still maddeningly calm. "You won't make it out alive."

"Are you going to do what I say or not?" Bren said, nearly out of breath.

Dr. Astron reached into her pocket and produced a compact control pad. "Turning them off," she said. "This won't end well for you. You can't even walk."

Araya snatched the crutches from where they leaned against the shelf and traded him for the scissors.

"Take us to Director Sorev," she said, sliding the blade to Dr. Astron's throat. "It's time we met on equal ground."

43

MALIK

Malik listened to the same argument dressed up in a dozen polite variations until the pressure behind his eyes pulsed.

A motion floated onto the record. A colleague asked for clarification that was provided twice. Another suggested an amendment engineered to sound bold while changing nothing at all.

Every turn of language orbited the same quiet terror. No one wanted to be the first to advance legislation that might inconvenience TerraLux Minerals, especially with Victor Kol in audience.

The hearing room glowed with restrained grandeur. Curved mahogany desks formed a horseshoe beneath a vaulted ceiling; each seat wired with microphones that caught even the softest throat clear. Chandeliers scattered warm light across marble walls etched with civic scripture.

Transparency. Balance. Order. Words carved to outlive the people who betrayed them.

Victor Kol stood alone by the rail, his charcoal suit perfectly tailored. His hands were folded, wearing black leather gloves, and his silver watch caught the chandelier's glow.

"And the outsider?" Victor asked. "Zaheen Mandisa."

"The Zaheen matter," Malik said, his voice level, "has not yet reached the action phase of today's docket."

Malik watched the committee as he spoke. No one met his eyes. They looked anywhere else. At their tablets. At their notes. At the microphones. Anywhere but the man holding the room from the gallery.

"Of course," Victor said. "Process deserves respect. Still, the city watches. Nova Angeles too. Delays have a way of looking intentional."

Performative politics at its best. Malik tipped his head a fraction, offering Victor recognition without giving him surrender. "Public confidence is preserved through consistency. Not haste."

Across the horseshoe, faces tightened. A few members shifted uncomfortably, not at Malik's argument, but at how it might sound to the man above them. Malik could almost hear the private calculations clicking behind their eyes. TerraLux Minerals funded campaigns, wrote grants, and provided access.

Most importantly, Victor Kol remembered names and actions alike.

Victor placed both hands on the rail. The gesture read as casual from afar. Malik knew better. It was a claim, made without a word, reminding them whose approval mattered more than any vote taken in this chamber. "Though history tends to reward institutions that act before disorder hardens into precedent."

Several members nodded.

"And history," Malik said, "also records what happens when power abandons restraint. Systems built on impulse tend to collapse under their own rules."

Victor's eyes brightened with quiet satisfaction. This was what he came for. Not a vote. A public measurement of Malik's spine. "Then I trust that when the matter reaches your action phase, it will reflect the urgency of the moment."

Malik lifted the gavel. "It will reflect the law. Nothing more. Nothing less."

He slammed it down, but Victor ignored its authority. "Perhaps the Zaheen matter should move up on the docket."

Victor's civility hardened like armor. But his eyes stayed honest. They always did. Malik watched them with the same focus he used on votes, on margins, on the places where the system showed its seams.

"I want her in my custody," Victor said, descending the gallery, past the committee table, and right below Malik's podium. "No more delay."

"What is your basis for overriding the chair's discretion over the agenda?"

"Because waiting has cost us time. And lives. I thought you were a man of the people, Chairman Sahar."

"This is my committee. I will control it as such," Malik said.

If he handed her over, Zaheen would lose leverage. If Zaheen lost leverage, Eren became expendable. That was the shape of the trap, and Malik refused to step into it blind.

"It follows my lead," Malik said and looked down to Victor, "not yours, respectfully, Mr. Kol."

Eyes flickered like startled birds and froze the instant Malik's gaze found them.

"Choose your next move carefully, Chairman Sahar."

Malik checked guard placements. Just as he thought, the walls were full of them. Every exit sealed. He had fallen into yet another trap. He failed Victor's loyalty test.

Malik dropped the gavel and it struck marble with a clatter by Victor's feet.

Victor retrieved the fallen gavel as though he were returning property to its owner. "What a shame," he said and sighed. "Your tenure ends here."

The guards closed in and dragged Malik away before he had any options to flee.

44

ARAYA

"This is it?" Araya asked.

Her voice held. That surprised her. Inside, everything rattled, like a tin roof hammered by a Nova Angeles windstorm.

She kept the scissors tight against Dr. Astron's throat, trusting pressure more than composure. If her hands shook, she told herself it was fatigue, not fear of killing.

The corridor offered no reassurance. White walls, seamless and unmarked, stretched ahead in identical panels, each one breathing out a faint electric hum. Even the air felt manufactured, scrubbed clean of anything natural.

Araya watched Dr. Astron as they walked, reading her face for the small leaks betrayal always leaves behind. Trusting an insider to guide her to the command center was the kind of gamble that got outsiders killed. She had no other options.

Dr. Astron marched with tight, practiced speed, driven by survival rather than belief.

Perihelion was built for compliance. It stacked backups on every task so it never had to depend on one person for long. Insiders were parts, not partners. If one failed, the system replaced them. That was why Araya could use her. No ideology pulled the doctor toward loyalty, and none pushed her toward betrayal. The system would discard Dr. Astron as quickly as it would discard an outsider, and she understood that.

Bren's plan was the only path that gave her leverage.

"This is it," Dr. Astron said.

The command center door waited at the end of the hall. Reinforced alloy. No insignia. No warning. Just a silent slab that looked ordinary on purpose, as if Perihelion knew its most dangerous rooms should never announce themselves.

"I held up my end, outsiders," Dr. Astron said. "Now be sensible and let me go. I have no intention of dying in this hall."

Araya looked at her properly. Sweat gathered at Dr. Astron's hairline, her throat working carefully beneath the edge of the scissors. The fear was real, stripped of performance. For a moment, pity pressed up in Araya's chest, unwelcome and dangerous.

Bren stepped in before it could take hold.

"Our demands aren't met," he said. His crutch struck the tile with a sharp tap that carried down the sterile hall. "Not until Director Sorev speaks with us."

Araya shot him a look. They had no further use for Dr. Astron. The alarm answered before she could speak. Shrieks rumbled her eardrums. Red light flooded the corridor.

The floor tremored.

Araya mistook it for her own body, dragged up by adrenaline and fatigue. The groaning tiles said otherwise. Perihelion shifted its weight as if it could feel every tremor.

The vibration climbed through her boots, into her legs, steady and relentless, shaking loose balance and certainty alike.

She widened her stance, but Bren's crutch skidded sideways. He went with it, shoulder-first. The impact knocked the air out of him in a single, brutal exhale. Bren folded inward, and pain etched itself deep as he slid down the wall.

"Emergency alert," the system announced. *"All personnel evacuate to designated safe zones immediately."*

Perihelion stilled, and the tremors died. For now, the facility had held against the structural damage from the tunnel blasts.

Bren stared at the command center door like he could see through alloy, wiring, and whatever lies were stacked behind it. "Everyone should be in the hangar by now," he said and rose with support from his crutches. "Structural instability pulls guards off patrol. Ore containment will outweigh their search for outsiders."

He looked at Araya. "They'll save Perihelion first. That's our window to get the hell out. Buys us twenty minutes to get override codes for our ship and fly off this collapsing rust rock."

Dr. Astron laughed. "The minute you open those doors, Director Sorev will gun you down. You're replaceable, so am I."

"If Perihelion is collapsing, they'll need outsiders to rebuild this mess," Araya said.

She reached for Dr. Astron's pocket and took her keycard. The reader chirped, and the locks disengaged. Metal seams split with a hydraulic sigh. "But only one way to find out."

45

ARAYA

Araya locked her breath into rhythm—steady in, slower out —as the blast doors groaned open. Metal screamed and ricocheted down the corridor like a warning too late to heed.

She stayed close to Bren, their arms brushing with every cautious step. Not for balance, she was past needing that, but for proof. Proof they were still here, moving forward, pretending control was something they possessed if the plan was executed.

The doors parted.

The far wall was a vast pane of reinforced glass, a cold, silent witness to the sky beyond. It stretched wide, painted in a bruised gradient—rust bleeding into amber, thinning to gray. Jagged ridgelines tore across the horizon like old scars.

It looked like Nova Angeles.

The thought cut clean through her. For a breath, a blink, the mission vanished. The scissors in her hand meant nothing. Her body stood in enemy steel, but her eyes were home.

Console stations traced the perimeter in clean arcs, each screen alive with data streams too dense to read in passing.

Operators stood at attention, fingers dancing in smooth, silent rhythms, eyes locked forward. Not one turned to look. They didn't need to.

Araya felt it. Every keystroke was measured. Every breath monitored. The room knew where she and Bren were before they stepped through the door.

At the chamber's center, a raised circular platform dominated the space. Its surface shimmered, cover with embedded lights that pulsed in calibrated gradients. Touch panels blinked in waiting loops. Every architectural line curved toward it—rails, desks, sightlines, even the polished seams in the floor.

Los Angeles had been built the same way. Every road and rail track bent inward to feed the dome. She'd crossed the stars to get here, and yet, the shape of power hadn't changed. No matter how far she ran, TerraLux Minerals pulled everything back to center declaring itself the gravity well at the heart of every human orbit.

Director Sorev stood on the platform with his hands clasped behind his back. The pose read like restraint, but only because no one here had ever tested the alternative. Calm settled on him the way authority sat on Victor Kol: worn like a second skin. Panic was for people who didn't already own the room.

His silver suit caught the platform lights and fractured them into clean, surgical flashes—too pristine for a facility that trembled on the verge of collapse.

Araya studied his face for anything, an involuntary twitch, a blink held too long. Something human. But there was nothing. Director Sorev looked brainwashed, engineered for obedience, more directive than man.

Flanking him, the two guards held their rifles low in that precise, ceremonial posture that promised death. Their barrels hovered at her center mass, both men carved from the same silence. Statues with triggers. Her glare locked on Dante's killer.

The memory surged up, raw and sudden, blood smearing the tunnel floor, Skye's hands slick as she dragged him back.

Araya's throat closed around a scream she refused to let him earn. Rage clawed at the edges of her control. But rage led to impulse, and impulse got people killed. She needed precision and calculation.

"I suggest you release Dr. Astron and surrender," Director Sorev said.

Araya pressed the scissors tighter to her throat. "Tell your guards to drop their weapons."

Bren limped forward. "Or she dies."

Director Sorev's gaze flicked to Dr. Astron, then back to Araya. One clean motion and angles were assessed, distance measured, outcomes tallied. He looked like a man who reduced people to variables in a long-running equation and never lost sleep over rounding errors.

"You misunderstand me," he said. "I'm not here to negotiate with outsiders."

Bren raised his crutch. "We're not bluffing. We'll carve her up right here. Guts and all."

Director Sorev's mouth twitched, something close to amusement. His eyes slid to Araya. "An interesting threat. But you've put the blade in the hands of someone who won't finish the job."

"I'll do what I have to," Araya said.

His smile widened. "What exactly do you have to do?"

"She doesn't owe you an answer," Bren said.

"You tore through my tunnels like a demolition team on borrowed time. Now you're sprinting toward a fantasy, what was it? A light cruiser waiting in the hangar? A clean jump to the stars? You even pictured it, didn't you—flames in the rearview, a dramatic exit."

His fingers drifted across the console.

The lights dimmed. In an instant, the room dropped into silhouette. A hologram flared to life above the platform, blinking once, then snapped into focus.

The camera feed shook violently. Skye hauled Iman by the wrist, the others scrambled behind them. The corridor pitched like a sinking ship. Overhead, a light strip exploded in a shower of sparks. A support beam came down like a judge's gavel, jarring the image.

"You were right about one thing. My teams are stretched thin." Director Sorev applauded. "Well played. But you mistook that for weakness. You storm in here to steal override codes and break the flight path on a light cruiser. You run. You imagine the universe forgets your names? Even if you go back to Los Angeles, our forces will be waiting for you there."

Director Sorev glanced at Dr. Astron. "She understands. TerraLux Minerals is *the most essential asset* to life on all planets. I won't trade proprietary control for one doctor," he said and shrugged. "Kill her."

"You will do no such thing," Dr. Astron said.

Araya turned to Bren and met her with a single look. *End it.*

Her grip tightened. But something inside her refused. Carmine Kurier rose like a ghost. The order. The signature. Victor Kol deciding her fate in a room she never entered.

What right did she have to make Dr. Astron vanish the same way?

"I said kill her, then!"

The room answered him with violence.

"Emergency alert," the system announced. *"All personnel evacuate to designated safe zones immediately."*

An explosion tore through the chamber. Consoles burst, sparks screaming. Somewhere to her right, a voice cried out and vanished under the crash of falling steel.

Araya hit the tile. Pain cracked up her spine. The scissors flew from her hand and disappeared under a collapsed panel.

A second blast pitched her sideways. A light fixture ripped loose and slammed beside her, shattering on impact.

She threw herself over Dr. Astron, hooked an arm around Bren, and pulled them in tight. Arms up. Heads down. Bodies flat. Dust burned her throat. The world fractured in strobe-light flashes. Too many things happening at once. Too much to track.

The glass wall gave way. Air ripped out of the room in a single scream. The workers closest to the window were gone in seconds, suffocated before the emergency panels slammed down and sealed the breach.

"Bren, don't," Araya said.

He answered with motion instead of restraint. With a grunt, he hauled himself upright, grabbed his crutch, and hurled it at the closest armed guard. It spun through the smoke and struck the guard's rifle. The weapon discharged.

Araya dropped, throwing herself behind a fallen workstation as Bren lunged for the guard. Her elbows scraped across tile, skin burning as she slid. The air filled with the bite of scorched wiring, sharp and metallic, heat riding it until breathing hurt. Bullet fire took the space and held it.

"Emergency alert," the system announced. *"All personnel evacuate to designated safe zones immediately."*

When the gunfire stopped, Araya lifted her head.

Bren stood in the open with the rifle braced in his hands.

Two guards lay sprawled near the platform, their armor punched through and blackened. Smoke lifted from them in slow, lazy coils.

Across the room, analysts fled in blind panic. Chairs lay overturned. Consoles sat abandoned, screens flashing warnings to no one. The corridors swallowed the runners, metal groaning as sparks fell from stressed seams.

Director Sorev emerged from behind a half-melted console, pistol held level and steady, its barrel fixed on Araya.

"Outsider," he said. "Let me show you the difference between bluff and action."

Bren brought the rifle up to Director Sorev's chest. "You stole my years," he said. "Now I steal yours."

Araya closed her eyes and waited for the shot.

46

ZAHEEN

The air met Zaheen like a held breath finally released—dust and salt and heat, heavier than she expected.

She stepped onto the porch outside Holly's bar and let the screen door snap shut behind her. She folded her arms, more from instinct than comfort. The movement pulled at the familiar burn along her body, skin never quite healed from sun and wind. Pain grounded her. It reminded her she was alive. At times, numbed by constant conflict, it was hard to remember what living meant.

Recognition kept circling her thoughts like a pesky vulture.

Zaheen had always known in the back of her mind that confrontation was inevitable, that order like Victor Kol's only held until enough people stopped pretending it was normal. What she hadn't expected was how quickly the knowing spread.

Like a virus, it touched everyone in Nova Angeles, all infected with a strong desire to take down TerraLux Minerals.

Nova Angeles awakened from a coma inflicted by systemic oppression. And the town wanted justice.

The porch door creaked.

Holly stepped out and leaned against the frame. "You're smiling. She approached and draped an arm around Zaheen. "Didn't think I'd live long enough to see that come back."

Zaheen huffed. "Don't get used to it if Araya never comes back. Nova Angeles is united though. I don't think we've ever achieved hits level of cohesion."

"That's momentum of exposing harsh truths."

"Momentum must produce results," Zaheen said. "I don't know if I can carry what they're putting on me."

Up close, Holly's eyes were pits of steadfast energy. "You already are, Zee."

Zaheen sighed, gripped her necklace, and looked back at the road. "We can't slow down now. I don't know when it happened, but this stopped being only about Araya's return."

She glanced at the horizon, or what passed for one now. Collapsed shacks shot up like broken ribs, dust drifting between them in sandy sheets. Haze ate at the sun, spit it out, and allowed only faint rays to poke through polluted clouds.

"It's about what comes after," Zaheen said. "You. Jude. All of us. Whatever replaces this mess won't be built by systems or a dome. It'll be built by people. Community is where the power sits."

Holly snorted. "You're starting to sound dangerously inspirational."

"I wonder where I picked that up."

"Definitely not Jude," Holly said and settled into the chair beside her.

"You've done more than I ever managed," Holly said.

"This town listens to you. The Sand Alliance started with, what, ten people and a hole in the floor? Maybe fifty by the time you gave your speech. Now we have merchants, smugglers, over half the scavenger crews quietly backing you." She shook her head. "You didn't get here by shouting louder than anyone else. You got here by holding a line no one else could."

Zaheen let out a breath that was almost a laugh. "I wouldn't have gone after Araya if you hadn't pushed me." She finally turned, meeting Holly's eyes. "Whatever this is, it doesn't belong to me or you. We didn't get here alone."

Holly's expression softened. "Do you think Chairman Sahar folds?"

"If he values his son more than Victor Kol," Zaheen said, "the choice isn't hard."

Holly mumbled out a laugh. "An insider making a choice that benefits the outside, historically, is not great odds."

Zaheen didn't argue with logic like that.

"Sorry to interrupt," Jude said, stepping onto the patio. "I've been thinking."

Holly wasted no time teasing. "You, thinking? That usually ends with something on fire."

"Very funny," Jude said, eyes rolling. But his expression hardened. "We need an army."

Army meant ranks and commands and bodies counted as acceptable loss. It meant blood made ordinary. Zaheen saw that path on the train tracks once before and refused to repeat the same mistakes. "You're assuming Victor Kol comes back."

"He always comes back," Jude said, knowing he was right. Zaheen couldn't deny it either. "Outsiders with power always return to put themselves on top."

"We threaten. We cut deals if we must. We build leverage. But no one wins if the streets become a war zone."

"Zee," Holly said in a tone that meant siding with Jude, "think it through. If he shows up armed and we aren't ready, people die. I know where your line is. I respect it. But maybe this isn't the moment to plant your flag on it."

Jude watched outsiders pass by. "Leadership often means choosing the decision everyone hates. If blood spills, it won't be because we want war. To put it simply, everlasting peace has a cost, and we're out of credit."

If I give the order once, there is no taking it back. I'll live beside the phantoms of my decisions. That is no peace. Zaheen looked down at her hands. They were rough with work and weather, scarred in places, capable of gentleness. They were also capable of issuing commands that would not come back clean. She didn't want to see what they looked like stained red.

A man stepped out from the fringe of the crowd, boots stirring sand plumes with each unhurried stride. A leather cloak hung from his shoulders, scuffed and sun-hardened like armor worn too long. A wide-brimmed hat cut his face in half, shadow covering one side, but his eyes were fixed with interest on Jude. "You have something I want. Jude, is it not?"

His right hand drifted toward his hip, and people scattered. Doors slammed. Someone cursed and ran.

Jude placed himself in front of Zaheen and Holly. "Do I know you?"

Zaheen clocked him as an insider from the lack of sunburn and grit on his skin. "What do you want from us, insider?"

"There is nothing I want from you," he said and eyed Jude. "I want Eren Sahar. Jude, I believe you have him."

Zaheen was on her feet before the chair finished scraping back. "Name yourself."

"I'm a ghost," he said. "I track. I hunt. I finish what I start." His eyes returned to Jude. "I came to Nova Angeles for the boy. I'm not leaving without him."

Jude unslung the rifle on his back and brought it to his shoulder in one smooth motion. "Wrong target. There's nothing here for you."

"So that's how it's going to be," Ghost said.

He revealed a pistol at his hip and fired. Glass exploded from the bar window in a spray of shards.

Zaheen ducked and hauled Holly inside, splinters tearing from the porch rail as they hit the ground.

Jude answered with fire.

47

ZAHEEN

Zaheen pressed her palm to the cracked glass. Heat leaked through the split frame in dirty breaths, thick with smog and grit. It coated her tongue and scraped her throat raw. Nova Angeles never let anyone witness violence cleanly. It insisted on involvement. On friction. On making sure every sense paid its toll.

Jude fired again. And again. Too fast. Four shots tore into the dirt, kicking up useless plumes of sand around Ghost's boots.

"He's rushing," Zaheen said, and Holly nodded in agreement.

Her pulse spiked, a frantic drumbeat hammering behind her temples. She knew that pressure. Zaheen had felt it coil inside herself before every irrevocable moment. Araya's taking. Vivian's death. And now this.

Jude dragged the scope back into line, but the window had already closed.

Holly gasped beside Zaheen, dropping her face into her palms. "I can't watch."

Ghost broke into a sprint and landed full force, shoulder to gut, driving Jude into the street hard enough that Zaheen felt it shudder through the porch boards. Sand exploded around them in a dirty bloom as they hit, bodies locked, momentum still trying to carry them even after the ground stopped them cold.

Zaheen's hand remained on the glass, useless pressure, as if she could shove time backward through sheer will. *Get up Jude, get up!*

Ghost's foot slammed onto Jude's chest, and he laughed as Jude cried out.

Jude swatted the fun free from the insider's grip.

Ghost didn't even look at the pistol as it spun away. His knife flashed instead, already aiming for its target.

Jude rolled as the blade plunged, sand erupting where his throat had been a heartbeat earlier. He came up on one knee, coughing, his red knife clenched tight in his fist. Breath tore out of him in ragged pulls, but his eyes never left Ghost.

Jude swung.

Ghost blocked with his forearm, steel kissing steel, and Jude answered with his knee. The strike sank into Ghost's ribs, folding him forward. Jude carved a quick slash across Ghost's cheek. Not deep enough to kill. Just sharp enough to put him in place.

The insider froze, bent over, breath heaving. He lifted his eyes, measuring Jude through blood and dust, weighing pride against survival.

"The gun!" Zaheen shouted through the window.

Jude snatched the weapon near his foot, brought it up, and swung the stock in a hard, efficient arc. Ghost dropped face-first into the dirt.

The street tried to reset itself. Vendors pried open shutters. Someone dragged a cart back into place. Doors unlatched, and faces reappeared, while Zaheen and Holly sprinted out of the bar.

"Are you hurt?" Zaheen said and halted beside Jude.

A bright streak of blood cut through his collar. Jude huffed a laugh that sounded more like pain than humor. "Compared to him," he said, "I'm dandy."

"I've never seen this insider," Zaheen said.

"Me neither, but he knew Jude," Holly said. Her eyes fixated on the body, then flicked down the street, already searching for the next shadow. "It seems we're not as safe from Victor's reach as we once thought."

"This seemed to be Chairman Sahar's work," Jude said. "Why would Victor care about Eren Sahar?"

Zaheen pulled her hood up. "One attack means more will follow. Whether I like it or not, you may be right. This won't end quietly."

Jude crouched beside Ghost, checked him for anything useful. "I'll take him back to the cargo crate. He'll wake up soon. We need answers."

"I'll spread the word of a mandatory town meeting. In the plaza. Full community turnout," Holly said.

She looked directly at Zaheen, no softness left to cushion the truth. "We vote for an army."

Zaheen opened her mouth, instinct already rising to fight the idea of an *army*, but Holly's look stopped her.

"You need rest," Holly said. "Take it while you can. Everything's going to be much harder than anything we've faced."

Jude hoisted the unconscious man over his shoulder. "I'll see you both soon."

Zaheen let them go. *If this was Malik Sahar, what does it mean for Eren? What does it mean for leverage?* Too many fires. Too many directions.

Araya was the point of every compromise. Every lie. Every threat made Zaheen feel like she was swallowing glass. She kept that in mind. Araya was the reason she still believed there was a line worth holding, even as the world—and her closest allies—had finally dragged her across it.

War was coming, and Zaheen understood that was the way to Araya. She nodded to herself. *Blood will spill then.*

48

ARAYA

Blood spread across the deck.

Director Sorev's abdomen had collapsed into a wreck of torn fabric and exposed flesh, pouring dark and wet across the tile floor like fuel bleeding from a ruptured cruiser. He clamped both hands to the wound, fingers sliding, failing to hold anything in, and his breath stuttered as his knees gave out. He hit the floor hard.

Each inhale splintered into ragged bursts. His eyes, already clouding, lifted and found Araya. His focus sharpened on her, and drifted past, just over her shoulder, and a satisfied smile tugged at the corner of his mouth.

She glanced behind her, fighting off tears for the inevitable.

Dr. Astron lay crumpled on the deck, limbs slack, unfocused eyes staring at the flickering lights. A single wound stained the front of her suit, red spreading across her chest and flowing down both arms.

This wasn't supposed to be your end. Another death slipped into the decision matrix Araya had built, another consequence stamped into the plan as if it had been waiting there all along. *How many more to find my own peace?*

"She's gone," Bren said.

His hand closed around Araya and guided her away, not gently, but with the instinctive urgency of someone trying to block a blow that had already landed. As if turning her body could spare her from the pain sprouting inside her heart.

The command center shuddered. Metal groaned. Walls flexed. Consoles rattled loose from their housings and spilled wires and glass across the deck like exposed organs. Somewhere deep in the station, something structural gave way. Collapse. In the tunnels. In the corridors. In the systems. In her.

This isn't my doing. This is a hatred I've survived. Araya repeated that over and over, forcing her breath to stay even.

Bren limped to the control station, favoring his good leg, fingers dancing over layers of controls. After mere seconds of random tapping, he slammed his fist onto the console. He swore under his breath and grabbed Director Sorev by the collar, hauling him upright as if force alone might shake answers loose. "How do we access the override codes?"

Director Sorev's eyelids twitched, struggling to stay open. His pupils failed to settle on anything. Red emergency light swept over him in pulses, turning his skin into alternating shades of warning and ruin.

"Tell us," Araya said. "You've lost at your own game. Die with dignity."

Director Sorev coughed. Blood dotted his mouth and clung to the corner of his lips. When he finally spoke, the words scraped out slowly. "If I can't leave this place," he said, hacking, "you don't either."

Bren let go, and Director Sorev hit the deck. "This is it," Bren said.

Araya ran for the console. "We've come too far to give up."

The interface flared alive under her hands, a cold bloom of symbols and shifting menus. Layers of security stacked and restacked, walls rising, rerouting, sealing. Pathways threaded open and snapped shut as if Perihelion enjoyed watching her chase it.

She dropped beside Director Sorev, grabbing his chin to keep his focus on her. "Listen to me," she said. "TerraLux Minerals won't remember you for loyalty. Victor Kol chooses who lives and who gets buried under his profits. He pulls your strings the same way he pulls ours. Men like that don't care about devotion. They care about output. Hell, if he cared about you, you wouldn't be stationed on Perihelion."

"*Emergency alert,*" the system announced. "*All personnel evacuate to designated safe zones immediately.*"

Another tremor rippled through the floor. Araya steadied herself with a palm on the plating of the console.

"Give me the codes," she said, calmer now. "Let me end this machine's grip on all of us. Yours. Mine. Everyone caught in between."

Araya couldn't tell if he heard her at all, or if her words had already become part of the facility's dying noise.

His lips parted. "Kilo," he said with a wet inhale. "Oscar... Lima... nine-one-seven... Delta."

Bren was already on it, and the console responded with a scream.

Director Sorev laughed, accompanied by blood spilling

down his chin, streaming from the corners of his mouth, and pooling around his crumpled frame.

"Attention," the intercom announced. *"Security breach confirmed. Shutting down all systems."*

The console lights dimmed one by one. The room's steady hum, a sound Araya only recognized once it vanished, cut out like an engine losing power. Red strobes blinked twice and died. Darkness rushed in and swallowed the command center whole.

Bren moved anyway. Rage gave him direction.

His fist snapped into Director Sorev's face with a crack that felt too loud in the sudden quiet. The insider's head whipped back, struck the side of the console, and his body went slack on impact.

"You coward," Bren said, chest heaving as he stared at what remained of the man's expression. His shoulders hitched as he drew back for another blow.

Araya caught his arm.

He jerked toward her, fury burning so hot it looked borrowed from someone else, and he registered her face and froze.

"He's gone," she said. Her voice came out steadier than she felt. "Bren. He's gone."

Bren's eyes flicked past her to the ceiling. "Araya, run!"

Araya dove. Air punched out of her lungs as she hit the deck. Shards and dust rained down in a choking sheet. Something screamed as it tore free and slammed hard enough to make the floor jump.

When the debris finally settled, the silence returned in pieces.

Araya pushed herself up, blinking through grit, and that was when she saw him.

Bren lay half buried in broken panels and wires. A light fixture jutted from his chest, spearing him clean through the center like the room had decided to finish what Director Sorev started. Blood spread beneath him in a slow, unstoppable tide, darkening the floor in widening halos.

"No," she said, voice cracking. Araya crawled to him, hands shaking so violently she could barely find his. Tears came hard and ugly.

Bren's fingers closed over hers, warm for a second, then slipping colder.

He managed a smile that didn't belong in a place like this. "I wasn't meant to leave," he said. His eyes searched hers, urgent and soft in a way that frightened her more than the collapse. "But you... you still can."

"We find a way. We leave together."

Bren's lashes fluttered. He tried to turn his head, tried to look down at the damage, and the motion stole what little breath he had left. Tears slid from the corners of his eyes, cutting clean tracks through the dust on his cheeks.

"Iman," he said. "Skye. Get to them." His head tipped to the side.

She sat there for a second too long, frozen, his blood warming her palms. She forced herself to rise, as the ceiling crumpled down around her. "I'll carry you with me," she said. "Always."

"*Emergency alert,*" the system announced. "*All personnel evacuate to designated safe zones immediately.*"

Another tremor tore through Perihelion.

She wiped her face with the back of her wrist, smearing dust and tears, and ran—out into the corridor—while the room behind her finished dying.

49

ARAYA

Heat clawed up Araya's throat as she tore through the collapsing corridors.

Her breath came jagged and dry, scraping hot against metal that tasted like dust and rust. Her heart slammed her ribs like it was trying to break out and run ahead of her. Every step triggered ghosts—Dante, Bren, even Dr. Astron—flashing behind her eyes in ruthless, high-definition loops.

Perihelion was a symphony of moaning steel, joints shifting under stress, and bolts popping one by one. Each groan behind her was a shove forward. She lengthened her stride, lungs screaming, boots slapping a floor that no longer trusted itself.

She burst through the final hatch.

The hangar yawned open—vast, ruined, exposed. It looked like the dunes around Nova Angeles after a storm tore through and left everything it touched scattered like scrap.

Light cruisers lay gutted across the bay, scorched hulls split wide to reveal sparking innards of fractured alloy. Walkways sagged over wreckage. Cables hung in shredded loops like torn sinew. Fire prowled the walls in slow waves, turning the smoke into a shifting mural of molten orange and violent shadow.

The smell of fuel and hot chemicals burned her nose. A bitter metallic tang settled at the back of her throat and refused to leave. A nearby console spat a few weak sparks and died.

Araya scanned through smoke. *There!*

Skye stood ahead, planted like an anchor in the chaos. She barked orders and shoved survivors toward a squat, boxy ship whose engines bucked and rattled like a furnace on the verge of mutiny.

She ran toward Skye.

"Araya!" Iman came sprinting across the shaking hangar. A support beam groaned overhead and split the wall behind her in a spiderweb of fractures. Iman reached Araya and crushed her into a fast, fierce hug. "You made it!"

She pulled back, hands gripping Araya's shoulders, eyes scanning her face like a diagnostic readout. "Tell me you have the override codes."

Her gaze flicked past Araya, sweeping the hangar. "Where's Bren?"

Araya opened her mouth. Nothing came out.

"He's gone, isn't he?"

Araya looked at the line of soot-streaked survivors being shoved into the ship. "We're doomed."

The whole slab of ceiling on the opposite side of the hangar let go and dropped like the universe was swatting a fly. It hit the deck and the sound punched through Araya's teeth. Screams ricocheted by outsiders across the bay.

Another set of cargo containers snapped free. They

slammed down hard enough to make the floor jump. That yanked Araya back to Bren. He would have kept going, so that's what she decided to do.

She bolted to the ship. "We can at least get to space."

Iman matched her stride without a word. They sprinted for the cruiser while fire chased their shadows and smoke reached for them like a huge hand.

At the threshold, Araya caught Skye and crushed her into a hug, but she tore herself free just as fast because hugs didn't fly ships.

They piled into the cockpit. Iman first. Skye right behind. Araya last, lungs already sandpapered raw.

Araya slapped her palm on the console. For a heartbeat, nothing happened. Then the screens shivered awake, coughed up static, and stabilized into jittery feeds.

The cargo-hold camera filled the center display. Outsiders packed shoulder-to-shoulder, faces smeared with red lustronium dust, eyes wide and searching for instructions the universe didn't provide.

Araya dropped into the pilot's chair and yanked the harness across her chest until it clicked. The navigation panel flickered under her fingers—lights dimmed, flared, dimmed again—the ship couldn't decide if it wanted to help or just die dramatically.

"Without override codes," Araya said, "we get one route. Los Angeles."

Skye snapped her harness in and grabbed the engine lever and hauled it down. The cruiser answered with a furious roar. The cockpit rattled in protest, like every bolt was filing a complaint.

"Then we take what we get," Skye said.

Iman, strapped into the second row, pointed through the cockpit glass.

The hangar exit was sealed by a blast shield: two interlocked panels fused shut, rails dead, hydraulics dead, the whole thing sitting there like a final middle finger made of alloy.

"Not even a battering ram is getting through that," Iman said, panic finally cracking through her control. "How are we supposed to—"

"I'll do it." Skye unbuckled.

Araya's stomach dropped. "No." She lunged across the console and grabbed for Skye's arm. "Skye, don't."

Skye barreled past her and shoved Araya back into the pilot's seat hard enough to knock the air out of her lungs.

"Get the ship ready," Skye said. "And catch me."

Araya's pulse detonated in her ears. "Skye, get back in the ship."

Skye didn't slow. "Don't miss," she called over her shoulder. "I'll be back in one piece."

Araya eased the cruiser into position.

Through the cockpit glass, Skye tore down the platform while fire climbed the walls and smoke churned. The manual control stand waited ahead, bolted beside the blast shield. It was an old emergency rig with a simple promise: if the systems failed, a person got to be the backup.

Skye glanced back once and flashed a thumbs up. She held the wheel and hauled. The panels shuddered, lurched, and began to grind open.

Mars rushed in.

Air howled through the growing gap, ripping smoke, dust, and loose tongues of fire toward the void. The force slammed into Skye like a freight train. Her body snapped sideways until she was nearly horizontal, boots scraping uselessly as she clung to the rig with everything she had.

Araya shoved the throttle and swung the ship around, fighting the crosswind screaming through the now fully open hatch. The controls bucked in her hands.

Araya pressed the ship's speaker for Skye to hear. "Let go!"

The wind tore Skye loose. For a split second she was nothing but velocity and chaos, tumbling through smoke and fire, and then she was inside.

Araya slammed the seal. The cockpit door locked with a heavy *thud* as flame and debris surged through the hangar behind them. Skye hit the deck in a breathless sprawl, and Araya pushed the throttle.

The cruiser screamed forward.

Engines howled as they blasted out of the hangar and away from the collapsing Perihelion, leaving fire, wreckage, and Mars's fury clawing at nothing but open air.

"You're insane," Araya said, eyes locked on the flight path, hands still fused to the controls.

"You caught me." Skye coughed and laughed. "You caught me just in time."

"No one else is jumping in or out of any other ships," Iman said, pressing a hand flat to her chest. "That nearly killed me too, Skye."

Behind the cockpit glass, Mars loomed vast and wounded. Its rust-red surface was scarred with fire and collapse as Perihelion burned, a bright, furious wound against the planet's skin.

Araya forced herself to breathe, and take it all in. The fire.

The rubble. The lives left behind on the red planet. Then the sky went black.

The last of Mars slipped from view as the cruiser punched free of the atmosphere and burst into open space, the burning world shrinking behind them until it was nothing more than a dying ember in the dark.

50

ZAHEEN

Moonlight smudged through a curtain of haze, offering only a thin spill of silver. It was just enough to sketch a path across the midnight dunes. The desert breathed around them, warm wind curling past Zaheen's face. Sand hissed over her skin like tiny, needling doubts.

Zaheen drew her cloak tighter and tucked her chin against the bite that still lived in the night.

Holly trekked beside her. "We're here, Zee."

The outpost crouched in the sand like a relic half-devoured by time. Beige stucco walls were split with long fractures, dry as old riverbeds. Drifts banked against the front steps, close to swallowing them. A battered stone path led toward a detached garage where the roof sagged, and the corners gave up grain by grain.

Zaheen eyed the dilapidated structure. "Everything set the way we discussed?"

"To a tee."

Zaheen felt off balance, like she had not fully arrived in her own body yet. An hour ago, she had been asleep. Then

Holly was at her door, dragging her into the dark. Strategy whispered between dunes. Miles of desert crossed. "And you're sure it's them?"

Holly caught her hands before Zaheen could pull away. "Would I bang on your door in the middle of the night just to guess?" Holly said, forcing a smile. It wobbled, but the point landed. "It's them. I'm sure."

"I'm getting everything I can out of them," Zaheen said. "Including commitment."

Holly smiled and gave Zaheen's hand one last squeeze before letting go. "Of course you will," she said. "I'll be right here when you're done."

Zaheen walked up the steps of the outpost door. *Araya, I'm coming for you.*

The door creaked open on a tired hinge. Jude stood waiting, rifle in hand. "They're all yours," he said. "I'll stand guard. If this is a setup, we'll see it coming."

"Thank you, Jude."

He stepped aside and slipped back into the night.

Zaheen was alone now.

The room glowed in muted yellow. Peeling stucco walls closed in around a single table. Wood-boarded windows trapped heat and secrets alike. Four lanterns burned in the corners, their flames unsteady, throwing shadows that climbed and tangled across the figures waiting inside.

Zaheen took the empty chair across from them and leaned forward, forearms pressed to the rough wood. She let her gaze move from face to face, mapping the room and every threat inside it. *Know your enemies. Know them well.*

She felt the imbalance in her bones. Not long ago, they would have bound *her* hands, asked the questions, and decided what she was allowed to say. Now she held the center of the table.

The gunman who had tried to shoot Jude sat bound, a fresh cut running from cheek to jaw. Blood and sand clung to his leather like medals he had never earned.

Beside him sat Chairman Sahar, spine straight, posture calm. His robes were earth-toned and unassuming, the kind that allowed him to belong anywhere. Wealth hid easily beneath restraint.

And then there was Leila Sahar. Arms crossed tight. Brow drawn. Obsidian robes drank in the lantern light and gave nothing back.

Zaheen felt the familiar pull of guilt tighten in her chest. None of this had happened to her directly. She had not been taken. And still she sat here, speaking for the disappeared, for the silenced, for Araya. She reminded herself that proximity was not a prerequisite for justice. Someone did not have to be broken by a system to stand up to it.

Zaheen folded her hands on the table and met their stares. "We have a lot to discuss."

51

ZAHEEN

"I grew up watching you hide behind walls," Zaheen said. "You fed on fear and claimed it as loyalty. You built a system that strips people down until they forget they're human. Even you started believing your own lies."

Her gaze locked on each of them. "You thought you were untouchable. Sand doesn't care about your boundaries. It finds the smallest crack. It gets in and grinds. Wears the machine down until it erodes."

Zaheen lifted her hands and opened her palms up to the ceiling. "Welcome to my land. Sand and haze. Brutality seared down to truth. There's no hiding. Not anymore."

Chairman Sahar shifted in his seat. Of course he did. He reached for control the way politicians always did. Sympathy first. Soft words meant to soothe the room and make her feel cruel for holding the line. Zaheen hardened. She had no use for his pity.

"I want to express," he said, voice slick with practiced remorse, "that what Ghost attempted to do to your friend was my order. But long before our call, I instructed him only to search for my son. I would never intend—"

Zaheen lifted a hand. "Enough," she said. *Always words with you.*

Leila slammed her fist onto the table, hard enough to make the lanterns jump, and the shadows tremor across the walls. Zaheen had expected it. Predictable. It made it easier to stay perfectly calm.

"Where is my son?"

"He's here. One of mine is with him. I want him returned to you."

Leila shot up from her chair. "I want to see him. Now."

Chairman Sahar's hand caught her shoulder, nervous, trying to pull her back down. Leila shrugged him off like he weighed nothing.

Zaheen held her ground. "You don't get demands," she said, meeting Leila's glare head-on. "Not after what you've taken."

"You have no idea what it's like to be a mother."

"You're right, but I do know what it's like to have someone ripped away." Zaheen gestured to the seat. "We have much to discuss. Don't waste your son's time."

Leila hesitated, shaking with anger and lowered herself back into the chair.

"Listen carefully," Zaheen said, thousands of outsiders riding on this outcome. "I didn't bring you here to trade threats or chase power. I want peace. Every one of us carries scars from Victor Kol. Every one of us has lost someone, or lives with the fear that we will."

Her voice softened and snagged on the truth she could not forget. Chairman Sahar's policies had made this possible.

Ink on paper that turned into doors kicked in, names pulled from lists, Araya taken. Fury surged up, hot and rising. Zaheen extinguished it and steadied her tone.

"We're looking toward the same horizon," Zaheen said. "A future worth living with the people we love beside us. Do you choose Victor or the people you love?"

Chairman Sahar answered without hesitation. "I chose my family over the inside. I walked away from the power he promised me. The comforts. The life I was told I deserved."

He held her gaze. "I want to stand with you. The threats, the violence, that wasn't who we were. It's what Victor turned us into."

Turned. As if the rot had arrived on its own. As if it hadn't been fed, protected, and rewarded for his selfish record.

Chairman Sahar drew a breath like a man breaking the surface after staying under water too long. "Let me help you get Araya back."

"If you stand with us, you do it on my terms to prove loyalty," Zaheen said. "We keep this clean. You help me get her back, and then we'll see what else you're capable of."

Only then did she turn to Leila. "And you," Zaheen said. "Where do you stand?"

"Did you hurt my son?"

"He was kept like a prisoner," she said. "Shelter. Food. But there was pressure. I needed to know what information he carried."

Lanternlight caught the fury building in Leila's eyes. "I should hate you for it. But I keep replaying it. What could I have done? What did I fail to do?"

Leila sighed. "I want to build something better for the people I betrayed."

Zaheen nodded. "Then we understand each other."

Ghost shifted in his chair. The rope bindings creaked as he leaned forward. He rolled his shoulders once, like he was setting down a weight he'd carried too long. "I cut ties with Victor long ago," he said. "I hate him as much as you do. Maybe more."

Zaheen studied him closely. Every scar. Every hardened line. A man shaped by choices he could not undo. Ghost seemed honest, and she had to trust her gut. "Then let the past sink beneath the dunes," she said as she pushed back from the table. "Bring him in."

The door groaned open.

Holly stepped through first, one steady hand anchored on Eren's shoulder, Jude bringing up the rear. Eren froze when he saw his parents. Shock crossed his face, then disbelief and a sound that broke loose from his chest before he could stop it. He ran.

Malik and Leila caught him at once. Arms wrapped tight. Hands gripping like they might lose him again if they let go. They folded around him, a family pressing itself whole, as if holding him close enough could erase every second they had spent apart.

"Now comes the morning vote," Holly said, stepping beside Zaheen.

Jude slung his rifle across his back. "You've done well, Zaheen."

Zaheen heard them, but both drifted past. She couldn't look away from the reunion.

Will that ever be me? Will the universe ever grant me that kind of mercy?

Millions of eyes fixed on Victor Kol and held him steady at the podium, like a cathedral waiting for its god to speak. Los Angeles was his proof, spread beneath an artificial sky that never dared to misbehave.

In a city this polished and engineered, doubt had nowhere to take root. He had molded chaos and hammered it into order until the streets flowed on his timing and the crowd breathed on his cue. Even the weather obeyed, sunlight dialed in by technicians until the atmosphere learned restraint.

Today must be flawless. Whatever he demanded next would only take if perfection surrounded him first.

Victor lifted his chin and let the silence stretch one second longer, long enough for the people to remember who owned the air and water in Los Angeles.

His army had swept the districts clean and funneled civilians into the square until the crowd became a single, contained body. Now Victor stood at the podium between Officer Nakamura and Deputy Durand, close enough that their uniforms read as extensions of his will.

Armed guards lined the perimeter in measured intervals, a ring of discipline that told everyone the same thing: duty flowed toward Victor first, and everything else came after.

He smiled, more rehearsed than genuine. "I have summoned you under emergency decree," Victor said. "An attack has been made on our collective future."

As faces hardened along the promenade, Victor's satisfaction deepened. The walkway gleamed. Golden statues of his likeness watched from every angle, each one caught mid-victory. The gardens sat clipped into obedience, every hedge trimmed to the same measured curve.

He let his gaze drift to the screens on sides of buildings. Not for the crowd. For himself.

There he was again, magnified above all in his armored obsidian suit. A ruler wrapped in the image of a warrior, untouched by struggle yet crowned by its symbolism.

"You've felt it," he said. "The disruptions. The rumors. Some look at what we've built and dare to call it tyranny."

He scanned the crowd and savored the desperation stamped across their faces. Desperation was survival instinct made visible. Survival was the one promise he'd branded as his gift to Los Angeles. That was why they clung to him, and he knew how to turn that need again and again until the city could only see one solution. His leadership.

"The outside is rising against us. They want our resources and our homes. They believe your children should inherit a world engulfed by sand. I will not allow it."

Murmurs rolled through the crowd. Victor leaned toward the microphone, not hurried, not strained. Controlled. Intimate, like he was offering them a truth they were lucky to receive.

"I was nearly killed by an outsider named Zaheen Mandisa. Remember that name. She will perish." He paused and let the next words drop heavier. "Worse, she acted alongside the fallen and disgraced Chairman Malik Sahar."

Shouts spiked. Panic flashed across faces. Victor lifted one hand and the noise bent around it, shrinking under his quiet authority. "Don't worry. Malik Sahar and his family have been banished to the outside."

A subtle nod from Victor, and the guards lining the promenade snapped their rifles skyward.

"We must remain vigilant. Unity is not a gift of destiny. Unity is a discipline. It must be defended. At all costs. That is why, today, I have declared war on Nova Angeles. Be assured it will end as swiftly as it begins. We are powerful. We are united. We are civilization made real, and we will crush the barbarians beyond our walls."

Patriotic orchestra music blared across the speakers. Victor bowed and held the pose until the applause swelled. He rose into waves and practiced grins and slipped backstage and into a convertible for the short drive to his penthouse, letting the spectacle keep rolling.

Officer Nakamura and Deputy Durand cleared his path, shoving back reaching hands, squalling babies, anything the crowd thrust forward in hopes of a kiss or a blessing, until the motorcade finally peeled away and parked at his penthouse.

The reinforced glass doors of the penthouse lobby hissed shut behind him. The air changed immediately. Cooler. Filtered. Scented like money and disinfectant. Polished stone gleamed under recessed lights, and every surface reflected order back at him.

Victor's smile dropped like a switch had been flipped. *Fools. All of them.*

"Leave me," he said, facing forward.

Boots scuttled across the floor and faded. Silence, at last.

He pressed the elevator button. The chime answered. Victor let out a breath he hadn't realized he was holding. The doors slid open and revealed Mr. Kurier inside.

"Sir. I was hoping to speak to you."

Victor rubbed his temples. "Mr. Kurier, now is not the time."

"Sir." The messenger didn't step out. "It's Perihelion."

Victor's interest piqued. And with the doors closing behind him, he was trapped.

"It's gone dark," he said, and Victor held down a gasp. "No communication in or out. The final transmission was a facility shutdown protocol."

Impossible. "Set up a line with Director Sorev," Victor said.

"I'm afraid we can't. Everything is gone. Cargo crate tags, light cruiser shipment data, and even tunnel feeds. It's as if Perihelion was never there. All that remains is a single ship, already in transit, with coordinates set for Los Angeles."

"Thank you, Mr. Kurier." That's all he could manage, or he might snap Mr. Kurier's neck right then and there out of frustration.

The elevator chimed again, and Victor stepped off but held a hand to keep the messenger inside. "Prepare me a convoy. I want to meet whoever is on that ship face to face."

53

ZAHEEN

To an insider, the streets of Nova Angeles at dawn would feel empty. Dead even. Zaheen knew better.

The town only looked abandoned. Wind threaded through the alleys, softening footprints left by hungry people and shuttered vendors alike. Sand lifted and spun across shacks and rusted carts, reshaping the ground with every passing gust. Desert rats owned the shadows now, darting between road and rubble, quick to scurry away when Zaheen approached.

The quietest I've ever seen it. Zaheen walked alone toward the central plaza. Holly had asked to come with her. Zaheen smiled and told her no. What she meant to ask of her people already carried enough weight. Sharing it would have made it heavier. She needed time to think, and Holly would best soothe the crowd of the idea of having new insider allies.

The sun climbed over the dunes like a verdict being read aloud. Its glare spilled across buildings worn down to their bones, walls pitted, paint flaking, history exposed. Corrugated tin roofs rattled under the wind, the sound sharp and dry, a brittle rhythm of ruin answering the desert's breath.

She lifted her eyes to the smog-choked sky and tried to picture Mars beyond it. *Araya, am I making the right choice? Are you even there anymore?*

She turned the corner, and the plaza opened before her, packed tight with her people. They sat shoulder to shoulder, quiet, waiting.

At the center stood Holly, Jude, and the four insiders.

I'm leading them toward a war they didn't choose. I hope you're still out there to save.

Holly saw her first. One by one, heads followed, the motion rippling outward until the whole plaza was looking at her.

Zaheen nodded and stepped into the open space, circling the perimeter of the seated outsiders. Every face held expectation, fear, and determination that there was a better life waiting for them beyond this conflict.

All futures balanced on what she would say next.

She hated it, the authority resting in her hands. It didn't come naturally. She didn't command by force or spectacle. But giants didn't fall on their own. To bring one down, someone had to be willing to leap first, blind to the landing, and trust their people would follow.

She gestured for the insiders to sit as well. Malik, Leila, Eren, and Ghost lowered themselves into the circle. Zaheen trusted them enough to stand beside her, if only because there was nowhere else for them to go.

Still, she would not let her people mistake necessity for loyalty. She would not let anyone think she had chosen insiders over outsiders. For now, they were simply four more bodies in the movement.

"Whether we like it or not, the inside is coming to destroy us. Victor Kol is on our heels, ready to strike," she said, pacing the ring.

"I don't trust Malik Sahar or the others, either. But he brought us this warning, and we would be fools to ignore it. The insiders in this circle are to be treated as equals. They have the same enemy as we do. Anyone willing to stand against Victor Kol is a companion for as long as that stands. I won't hear dissent today. Not when the goal is bigger than pride."

She slowed, letting her eyes sweep the faces near her. "Our people must return. That is why I gathered you here."

Zaheen stopped pacing and planted herself at the center of the circle.

"Sand Alliance," she said. "Some of you know the name. Others may not. A secret group that grew day by day with one purpose: to break Victor Kol and TerraLux Minerals. Now you're part of it. All of you. We're standing at the edge of our hardest test. War is coming. And we decide together how we stand."

Zaheen expected murmurs, but voices surged, flooding the plaza with agreement, disdain, and everything in between. She glanced at the insiders. They stayed stoic and unreadable as most insiders do.

Zaheen looked at Jude and Holly, both waiting for her to take the plaza back.

"We fight." Zaheen held their stares—from supportive to far from it. "I have a plan. I won't lie to you. It might fail. But it's the best chance we have to survive."

Zaheen gave a glance at the sky. *May this plan be the reunion we seek.*

"Victor Kol wants me dead, so I'll meet him at the train tracks with Malik Sahar for one last attempt at negotiation. It'll buy time for the rest of you to get your loved ones, anyone who can't fight, out of Nova Angeles and into the dunes until this is over. A scouting party will prep for the train's arrival. Holly, Jude, Eren, Ghost. The rest of you lay traps, fortify your homes, and shape the sand until the insiders stop understanding where the town ends, and the desert begins."

A voice rose from the back. "What if their forces are too strong?"

"Then we die," she said. "Those are the choices. We fight, or we run and never come back. I will not run and surrender my home. Who will stand with me?"

Holly's hand lifted first. "I will not abandon Nova Angeles."

Jude joined in. "I fight for those who cannot."

The crowd began to move with them. Hands rose one by one. At first it was careful, unsure, fingers trembling in the early light. Then more joined, quicker, steadier, until the plaza seemed to stand on its own again.

"Build your traps," Zaheen said. "Sharpen your weapons. Victor Kol will show no mercy."

Sunlight pierced the clouds overhead, and Zaheen felt its warmth on her face like Araya's hand in hers. *We will bring you home, my love. I promise.*

54

ARAYA

Araya pictured herself as a shooting star.

Not the romantic kind. The *physics* kind. Something moving too fast to argue with, dragged into a gravity well, heated until it failed, and forgotten five seconds later.

That was the thought that hit her the moment Earth slid into view on the forward glass.

Earth didn't look like home from up here. It looked like Mars's spiteful cousin. Beige and rusted and bruised. Araya searched anyway, a stupid reflex, for the blot of Nova Angeles. For the dome. For anything that said *you survived long enough to see this again.*

She forced the thought of Zaheen down before it could soften her. Softness got people killed. Los Angeles came first. She was far from Zaheen.

Araya tapped the intercom. "Approaching Los Angeles," she told the cargo hold. "Brace for turbulence."

Skye rested her hand on a panel she didn't need to touch. Autopilot already had them. "I wish Dante and Bren could've seen the dune sea once more."

Araya didn't answer. If she opened that door, grief and guilt would rush in and refuse to leave.

The ship punched into atmosphere, and the view vanished behind a swirling wall of gold. Sand hammered the hull. The cruiser bucked hard enough to rattle her teeth. Araya pressed her palm to the window. Heat bled through the reinforced glass.

The absurd part was how familiar it felt. Comforting, even. Like an old scar proving she survived the worst.

"When we land," Iman said from the second row, "we surrender. It's the only way to avoid bloodshed."

Skye made a sound that wasn't quite a laugh. "You're assuming surrender means they don't execute us the second we step off the ship."

"I'm assuming we don't have better options," Iman said.

Araya kept her eyes on the display as the altitude bled away. "Iman's right," she said, and hated how true it sounded. "Even if I wish she weren't. We don't have weapons or intel. We land, disembark, and we find the next step."

"If we had the override codes—"

"Well, we don't," Araya said.

Bren's face flared behind her eyes, half-buried, blood spreading with slow intent. Heat climbed her neck. She forced it back down.

Skye shrank into her seat. "That wasn't fair of me. I'm just scared."

"We all are," Iman said. "That's why we lean on each other. Stay calm. Stay quiet when the insiders interrogate us. We've come too far."

The ship screamed.

A series of warnings stuttered across the display, red text

chasing itself like it was panicking. Araya's stomach dropped anyway, even though she'd known this was coming from the moment they left Mars.

"We're landing," Araya said.

The sandstorm thinned, suddenly, into cleaner air. Ahead, a hard ring of metal rose out of the haze: the perimeter of Los Angeles. The ship cut through and dropped into a hangar so massive it swallowed sound. A stadium of steel. A floor that gleamed like a star.

The cruiser slammed into the docking cradle. Magnetic clamps rose up and locked onto the hull with a final, absolute *thud*. The dome sealed behind them with a seismic boom. It might as well be a coffin lid deciding Araya didn't get a second opinion.

Skye leaned forward and pointed through the cockpit glass as the last dust settled. "It's him."

Victor Kol stood at the far end of the bay. Arms folded behind his back, posture relaxed enough to be insulting. He waited the way predators do—patient, confident, deciding exactly how much fear to let their prey feel before closing in.

Soldiers fanned out around him in a wide crescent. Row after row of polished armor. Rifles angled up, ready but not rushed. Exits sealed before anyone even touched the ground.

"Head of the snake," Araya said.

Victor Kol raised a hand, and when he closed his fingers into a fist, the soldiers charged the ship.

Araya stuck to the plan. She didn't fight. She gave them nothing to justify what they were already going to do. The cockpit door tore open. Hands clamped onto her arms and yanked her forward.

They forced her down at Victor Kol's feet. Her knees

struck the grated floor, the impact jolting up into her skull. Crimson dust burst around her in a choking cloud.

Victor stepped back. Just a half step. He waited for the dust to settle and returned to his original position.

Araya lifted her head. To either side, outsiders—including Iman and Skye—were being shoved into a rough line. Shoulder to shoulder. Measured spacing. Cattle for slaughter and prisoners for display.

"Hold," Officer Nakamura ordered as she strode along the line.

Every soldier mirrored the same posture. One rifle. One target. Officer Nakamura stopped beside Victor and fixed Araya with a hard stare.

Victor remained silent until a door slid open behind him. A familiar face stepped through, and Araya nearly lunged on instinct. Rage flared, white-hot. Every order. Every signature. Everything taken from her. From Zaheen.

"Mr. Kurier," Victor said, his voice smooth as polished stone. "Is this the one associated with Zaheen Mandisa?"

"Yes, sir." Mr. Kurier stopped at his side. "Araya Santera. As expected."

Araya wrenched her focus back to Victor. "Where is Zaheen? Why say her name?"

Victor Kol raised his chin and stared down at Araya. "She is exactly where you left her. You'll be joining Zaheen soon enough."

"I don't fear you, Victor Kol."

"You will in due time. Did you destroy my facility? Are you no better than Zaheen?"

She answered with a smile.

That did it. The pleasure drained from his face. Veins rose

along his temple. The corners of his mouth pulled tight as frustration finally punched through the mask.

He turned his back on Araya.

"Officer Nakamura," he said. "Prepare the assault on Nova Angeles. Make sure Zaheen watches Araya and her companions die before we move in. Then burn Nova Angeles to the ground."

Outsiders screamed as guards tore blindfolds from their belts and shoved them over heads. Bodies were yanked from the line and dragged away. Araya used the last scraps of sight she had to find Skye and Iman.

She met their eyes. Held them. Long enough to pass the look they'd shared a hundred times before. *There's a way out. We just haven't found it yet.*

The world went black. Hands tightened around her arms, and Araya was hauled forward into the unknown.

55

JUDE

"This is where we split," Jude said.

The desert immediately disagreed. Wind came at them from every direction at once, as if the dunes had decided to attack. Sand tore across their robes in horizontal sheets, stinging exposed skin. The ground refused to stay solid—ridges collapsed, reformed, and collapsed again.

Jude crouched by Holly, Ghost, and Eren. He glanced back toward Nova Angeles. Or tried to. The city was gone, erased by sand and distance.

"In this?" Ghost shouted. His scarf swallowed half his words, but not his attitude. One gloved hand clamped his hood in place. "I can't see five inches ahead. Is it always like this out here?"

"The outside is dirty," Eren said. "And angry."

Sand scraped across the boy's face, but he didn't blink and tucked his chin in robes. His eyes stayed locked on Jude.

You should be thankful I let you borrow that. The robes snapping around Eren's frame belonged to Jude's daughter. He hadn't said that. He wouldn't. The fabric cracked in the wind like a torn banner, every gust threatening to lift the boy clean off the sand. Eren looked less like a teenager and more like a badly secured kite.

He still hated Jude. That part was clear. Jude learned to live with it.

He wished Eren wasn't here at all, but Malik insisted. Said the boy needed exposure. Immersion. As if the desert were some kind of lesson instead of a meat grinder.

Jude argued to leave him behind. Zaheen shut that down fast. Trust went both ways, she said. And they needed Malik just as much as Malik needed them.

"The outside is more than what meets the eye," Holly said. She raised her hiking stick toward the horizon, steady despite the wind. "It can be powerful. Full of energy."

Her voice tightened. "But there's a storm coming. A big one. See the clouds?"

Jude followed her line of sight. The storm wall rose beyond the dunes like a sleeping giant. Dark coils churned through a bruised sky, blotting out what little blue still survived. Rust-colored haze devoured the sun.

A hand landed on Jude's shoulder, and he dipped to avoid further contact.

"Relax," Ghost said, pulling his hand back. "I've told you before. It wasn't personal. I help outsiders too. Same as you."

"That doesn't make us friends," Jude said.

Holly stepped in before it could get worse. "Give us the plan. Zaheen and Malik are counting on us."

Jude reached into his coat and pulled out four small canisters. "One each," he said, handing them out.

Eren turned his over in his palm. "What is it?"

Jude grabbed his wrist. "Careful. Don't open it yet." He pointed to the cap. "When you see the train, twist it like this."

He demonstrated. Ghost and Holly mirrored the motion. Eren hesitated but followed.

"Then you throw it in front of you," Jude said. "And you run until your legs scream and then a little farther. Straight back home. We split into pairs and circle the perimeter."

"I'll go with you," Holly said, but Jude shook his head.

"No offense," he said looking to Ghost and Eren, "but you're insiders. That alone makes me cautious. One of you is coming with me. The other goes with Holly."

Ghost folded his arms. "You're kidding."

"Zaheen gives out trust like water," Jude said. "I don't. If you want mine, you earn it."

Eren stepped back, sand sliding under his heel. "I'm not handing my trust to you either."

Ghost laughed and clapped Jude on the back. Jude resisted the urge to flinch. "Well. Guess that settles it. You and me."

Holly drove the end of her staff into the dune. Sand burst outward in a sharp spray. "Eren and I head east," she said. "May the sand shift your way."

"May the sand shift your way," Jude said. He turned and led Ghost into the storm.

56

ZAHEEN

Zaheen stood at the edge of Nova Angeles.

The desert gave way to open silence and train tracks stretching endlessly ahead. She waited nearly an hour before smoke plumes rose on both horizons, thin at first, then thickening. Victor Kol was on his way.

The storm arrived. A wall of sand lifted and gathered with patient anger, rolling in layers as it folded over the desert like a ravenous beast ready to devour both inside and out. Wind drove it forward in long breaths, each gust testing the ground, tasting for weakness.

Zaheen watched the dunes shiver and reshape. She watched the world erase its own footprints without apology. That was what she envied most. A storm never second-guessed itself or asked permission. It never mourned what it buried.

Pressure rose in her chest, that same restless churn. Zaheen drew a breath through grit and heat. When the train arrived, she would show Victor Kol the coward he was. Nova Angeles would not sit like a carcass waiting to be picked clean.

She didn't notice the footsteps behind her until a hand settled on her shoulder.

"Those who can't fight are safely out of harm's way," Malik said. He let his hand fall and stepped beside her, pulling his hood up to match hers. "Your people out there know what they're doing. They'll make it back."

"Your son is in good hands. Why send him at all?"

"Because he's spoiled to the core. He won't learn from me and his mother."

Thunder cracked again. Zaheen turned back to the storm, to the tracks, to the thin black smears of smoke announcing Victor Kol's near arrival.

Malik shifted with the wind, his coffee-colored robes snapping hard against his legs. "Is that going to be a problem?"

There isn't a moment of my life that isn't littered with problems. The storm barely made the list. Kol's vanguard. Jude and Holly somewhere in the blind. Nova Angeles bracing for impact. And the nagging sense that something would slip when they needed it most.

Zaheen didn't look at him when she answered. "The storm is the least of our worries."

"That doesn't sound promising."

"You know," Zaheen said, sand slicking her lashes and coating the stillness of her face, "I never thanked you for joining our side. I know we need each other to survive right now, but what we build here can outlast this. We can become stronger together. It doesn't erase what you've done, but I believe in second chances."

"That's generous," Malik said, and bowed his head. "I'd

rather move forward than backward. Let this be the start of a real shift."

"Good," Zaheen said. "And don't expect me to apologize for taking Eren. I hated doing it. But to get Araya back, I'd do it again. Every time."

Malik's mouth tightened. "I like to think I'd do the same in your place. You're stronger than Victor. Just in case you needed to hear that."

She did, desperately. Without Holly and Jude, loneliness pressed in at the exact moment she needed them most. "Whatever happens today, always remember we're stronger than Victor Kol. If I fall, the fight does not."

Malik's mouth parted as if he meant to answer, but the ground shuddered. Steel sang through the sand. From both directions, two trains surged toward the platform like blades drawn and slammed to a stop a mere meter from one another.

Hatches snapped open. Soldiers spilled out in a silver tide and fanned across the platform and onto the sand. At the front marched Victor Kol. He glided through the storm like it belonged to him, one hand lifted to guard his face while sand scoured his polished armor. His black cape cracked behind him, sharp and violent in the wind.

Victor stopped at the edge of his formation and fixed his gaze on Zaheen.

Beside him, who Zaheen recognized as Officer Nakamura, handed him a megaphone.

"The outsider and the traitor," he shouted into the device, stepping closer so his voice rode the wind. His other hand tightened around the grip of his pistol.

"We don't have to end this in bloodshed," Zaheen shouted and addressed Officer Nakamura instead. If there was a chance of rebellion in his ranks, she thought her previous mercy might be enough to sway the officer. "Don't let vengeance dig graves for your soldiers."

Victor answered with a slow blink and a roll of his eyes. "Positions."

The command sent soldiers spilling off the trains in a steady stream, grips locked around outsiders. They shook and sobbed, crimson dust smeared across their mining uniforms in bruised bands.

One by one, the soldiers shoved them to their knees and raised their rifles.

Zaheen scanned faces. *No Araya. Maybe she's already dead.*

Malik removed his hood. "Insiders, do you really want to kill the innocent? Put your rifles down. Save these people. Save yourselves, before he spends you like red lustronium."

Victor answered in a low, oily drawl, like a blessing dipped in poison. "These outsiders will die. This entire line will suffer from your defiance. My mines lie in ruin, and my soldiers have no mercy left to spare."

His expression tightened, predatory and pleased. "I brought a surprise. Someone special."

Victor turned toward the train, and out came Eren, escorted by Carmine Kurier and a duo of soldiers. "Your son's a clever one, Malik. Smarter than you, perhaps. He found me on the dunes."

"Eren!" Malik's cry tore loose, more wound than word. He surged forward, but Zaheen locked her grip around his arm and held. He shook under her hand, pulled between fury and fracture.

"Don't worry, Zaheen," Victor said, like he spoke to a child. "I brought someone for you. Two outsiders, actually."

Zaheen fell in shock when Holly stepped down from the train. Deputy Durand yanked Araya out next and threw her in front of Victor.

"Let them go!" Zaheen shouted at what could've been a brick wall, because Victor drew his pistol instead.

Eren stood at Victor's side, Deputy Durand at the other.

Holly and Araya sank to their knees in front of the barrel, sand drifting around them in slow, cruel waves.

"Which one?" Victor asked. "Who do you want to watch splatter first?"

Holly's face looked swollen and raw, one eye darkened, her mouth split at the corner. She tipped her chin, a small, stubborn plea in her stare. *Choose me. Save Araya.*

Zaheen couldn't choose. Her hand rose to her chest, fingers closing around the necklace beneath her robes like it could keep her heart from breaking open. This was supposed to be the moment she earned. The reunion she bled for. Not this. Not on his platform, under his gun, with her people watching.

Araya looked thinner than Zaheen remembered, all bones and cuts, red grime ground into her skin. Still, she held Zaheen's gaze and smiled.

"This is what you signed up for?" Zaheen shouted over the roaring wind. The words tore out of her throat and vanished almost instantly, shredded by the storm piling itself against the dune's crest. Sand stung her cheeks and teeth. The ground beneath her boots shifted with every gust, the ridge threatening to give way at any second.

Zaheen ignored it. There was no space left in her body for fear of failing. "You swore to protect civilians. Instead, you shield the ego of a man who thinks law bends to his moods. That makes you complicit."

Victor's rage shoved the end of his gun at Holly's head. "I said choose!"

Zaheen locked eyes with Officer Nakamura. "I let you walk away."

Victor angled the pistol again. "Officer Nakamura owes you nothing. Choose!"

Zaheen's breath caught. She felt it, how precarious everything was, how close the balance sat to collapse. One decision to change the fate of life and leave the other in the sand.

Victor's arm snapped toward Araya. "This ends now."

Zaheen sucked in a breath. She saw the alignment of bodies, the geometry of death arranging itself in front of her. The muzzle leveled. The trigger tightening for Araya.

Officer Nakamura pivoted with brutal efficiency, aimed at Victor, and fired.

The sound punched through Zaheen's chest, a concussive force that stole the air from her lungs. The recoil of it seemed to ripple outward, shaking sand loose from the dune itself.

Deputy Durand hurled himself into the line of fire.

Zaheen saw it all in sharp, unforgiving clarity—the split second of realization on his face, the way his body twisted as if speed could undo physics. The round struck Deputy Durand. Blood burst from his forehead in a violent bloom, dark against pale sand. He collapsed and the windstorm covered his body in sand sheets.

Araya dove for Deputy Durand's fallen pistol. "Fight! Outsiders, fight!"

All Zaheen heard were screams and the howling wind as the sandstorm fully collapsed onto them. She couldn't see Victor. Officer Nakamura. Holly. Or Araya.

57

ARAYA

Gunfire stitched the air around Araya in ugly, overlapping bursts. She stopped trying to count. Counting was for people with time and intact nervous systems.

She stayed low and let the sand do what sand did: hide, grind, swallow. On all fours, she crawled through the churn with Deputy Durand's pistol welded to her hand.

Zaheen. Skye. Iman. Their names climbed up her throat like they wanted to scream. She forced them back down. Anything louder than a whisper was an invitation for doom.

Through the grit-haze, Officer Nakamura snapped into view. One knee down. Magazine swapped. Efficient. Casual. Her silver armor caught what little light existed and flashed it back in sharp, bright insults.

Araya lunged in close and clamped her hand around Officer Nakamura's forearm. "Come with me."

The sky smeared into orange. Wind swept a fresh skin of grit over the dunes, erasing the battlefield as if it never existed. The landscape looked like Mars, and that was no comfort. It was just as lethal.

They pushed forward, shoulders hunched, eyes stinging. Araya tried to offer the train as cover and immediately filed that idea under suicide. The cars would be crawling with insiders. Nova Angeles was the only direction with even a tiny, pathetic sliver of probability attached to survival.

"Your six!" Officer Nakamura shouted. She fired twice without breaking stride. Two soldiers charging out of the storm dropped like their strings got cut and collapsed into the sand. The dunes swallowed them halfway before their blood finished deciding where it wanted to be.

A shape broke out of the storm—one person hauling another, their bodies blurred into a single, frantic silhouette.

Araya squinted. Her stomach dropped. She slapped Officer Nakamura's barrel down and stepped into the line of fire, planting herself between the muzzle and the figures before the next shot could find the wrong target.

"Araya." Holly stumbled out of the haze.

Eren sagged in Holly's arms, his shirt soaked through with blood and sweat. His breaths were shallow.

Holly's strength gave out. Eren slipped from her grasp and folded into the sand. "We need shelter. He needs a medic."

Araya dropped beside them. She forced herself to look past Holly's swollen eye and split mouth, and the tremor in her hands hovering over Eren like she could plug bullet holes with hope.

"What happened?" Araya asked.

Officer Nakamura crouched in, all business, scanning the damage. "Gunshots to the abdomen."

Eren shivered despite the heat. His skin had gone that awful pale that said the body was turning off nonessential systems. His teeth clacked in small, helpless taps. He turned his head toward Holly like she was the only landmark left on the planet.

"I'm sorry," he rasped. "I—I see now."

Holly leaned in fast, desperate, like she could hold him in place by sheer will. "You did what you thought was right. I forgive you, Eren."

Eren's breath caught and didn't come back.

Tears poured from Holly. "This is my fault."

Araya wrapped Holly up and held her. "None of this is your fault."

"If I hadn't taken him from Los Angeles, he wouldn't be here," Holly said, words spilling faster now. "He wouldn't be dying in the sand. Eren returned the favor. Beat me with my own walking stick. Handed me to Victor to prove loyalty."

Her voice collapsed into a whisper. "But I planted the resentment the moment I allowed his taking. Victor shot him as Eren ran to his arms for sanctuary."

Araya shifted her body, angling herself in the storm. Sand hammered her back in sharp bursts, and she took it without flinching because it protected Holly from the onslaught.

Holly winced, fingers pressing to the gash at her temple where blood had dried dark and brittle.

"How's your head?" Araya asked.

Holly's eyes drifted back toward Eren.

Araya blocked the view. "Can you walk?"

Holly nodded. Tears pooled, stubbornly refusing to fall.

Officer Nakamura raised her pistol and swept the haze. "We can't stay here," she said. "The insiders will regroup. And when they do, they'll target Zaheen and Malik."

"Araya!"

All three of them turned.

Relief washed over Araya as Skye burst through the grit, Iman right behind her, both of them coated in sand. Araya grabbed them and pulled her friends close. "Thank the seven sand seas," she said.

Iman looked to Officer Nakamura and nodded. "You saved all of us. I won't forget it."

"I did what was right."

Skye's gaze caught on Eren's body. Then on Holly, folded inward with grief.

"We mourn later," Araya said. "Nova Angeles needs us."

Another burst of gunfire cracked through the storm. The sound pulled at Araya like a line tied around her chest. "I'm heading toward the shots," she said, shifting her stance, ready to run. "Zaheen needs me. I won't ask you to jump into another fire."

Iman stepped in front of Araya and caught her hands. She held Araya's gaze until the rest of the world blurred out. "You're trying to carry this alone."

"I can't leave her. I won't again. And I won't risk getting another friend killed."

Sand clung to Iman's lashes, but her eyes stayed steady. "If the insiders regroup at Nova Angeles, we can sweep the wounded and get them onto the train. If we don't, the storm will bury them. Everything they survived on Mars. Everything you bled for on Perihelion will be gone under the dunes. What would Zaheen do?"

Araya didn't hesitate. "We save who we can," she said, stubborn and certain. "Then we go find Zaheen."

58

KOL

Victor Kol entered Nova Angeles with a smile.

He drove the long silver spine of his army into the maze of tin and ruin, and the formation obeyed him the way metal obeys heat. At each corner, he split the column cleanly—two files peeled away, another tightened, and the whole mass flowed around debris without breaking cadence. He never raised his voice. He didn't need to. He had built these men to read him like code.

The wind tore through the streets as if it wanted to strip the city to its studs. Abandoned carts skittered through intersections, slammed into slouching buildings, then spun away again, clattering like tumbleweeds made of scrap and hunger. Loose signs whipped on their chains. Shutters banged. Somewhere overhead, a sheet of metal flapped like a slow, panicked wing.

The storm punished everything equally.

Victor walked through Nova Angeles with the ease of ownership. Everything here belonged to him. These dwellings, and the people inside them, amounted to nothing more than bodies to feed Perihelion.

He kept his pistol low, muzzle tilted toward the ground—not because he feared a misfire, but because he refused to waste posture on threats beneath him. He swept his gaze across alleys and doorways. He didn't so much hunt as inventory.

He measured distances. Marked exits. Calculated angles.

He identified choke points and blind corners. He noted where outsiders would hide—behind sagging doors, beneath awnings, inside the dark guts of half-collapsed shacks. He also noted where they would die: in open stretches where armor could advance and bodies could not scatter fast enough.

Nova Angeles offered him no surprises. The city had always advertised its own ending.

He pictured it with the clean satisfaction of inevitability: Zaheen and Malik dragged into the plaza, wrists bound, faces forced upward for the crowd to see. Their heads severed cleanly from their bodies.

"Mr. Kurier," Victor said as he stopped at a crossroads where alleys braided together like veins.

"Yes, sir." Carmine held position at his flank, close enough for Victor to hear each shift of breath beneath the scarf.

"You're with me," Victor said. "Send the rest out. Capture Zaheen and Malik alive. I want the honors."

Carmine turned toward the waiting ranks. "Zaheen Mandisa and Malik Sahar come in alive for Mr. Kol. One squad with me. The rest of you clear the city. Street by street."

A ripple moved through the soldiers as the orders settled into them. Helmets turned. Boots shifted. Rifles rose. Teams broke off in bursts and slipped into the alleys with the crisp precision of practiced violence.

Victor drifted forward while his squad sprinted ahead and split into the passages like water pouring through a broken gate.

He watched them go. Every outsider he sent into the city bought him something: information, pressure, panic. He didn't care which one, so long as it ended with his targets in his hands.

"Mr. Kurier, where does this desert rat fester?"

Carmine yanked his collar higher over his mouth. Sand clawed at his teeth, and he fought it back with fabric. "Zaheen's place sits just past the plaza. I can lead you."

"Then lead," Victor said, and sand ground between his teeth as if the city itself wanted to make him chew grit.

He let Nova Angeles watch him move through its rot. He wanted the outsiders to see him. *Victor Kol walks your streets. Victor Kol does not fear you.*

He studied each branching passage the way a surgeon studied a wound. He tracked the city's circulatory system— alleys feeding into narrower cuts, paths looping back toward the plaza, dead ends stinking of ambush. Each alley felt like another vein in a dying body, and he cataloged which ones he would cauterize first.

Victor and Carmine didn't make it ten more paces.

A guard shouted through roaring wind. "Watch out!"

Too late.

The first row of insiders hit the tripwire and crashed down hard, boots tangling, rifles clattering, while tin cans strung along the line erupted in a metallic rattle.

Outsiders rose on the rooftops. Their silhouettes cut

sharply through the sand-haze—ragged coats, wrapped faces, makeshift weapons. They hurled rocks and splintered chair legs in a brutal curtain.

The first impacts slammed into armor with hollow thuds. Then the blows found gaps. A chair leg struck one soldier in the neck and snapped his head sideways like a breaking hinge. A rock smashed into another man's armor and spiderwebbed the plates until they became useless.

His guards surged forward. The men still standing formed a canopy over Victor and Carmine, shields raised, bodies angled to absorb the blows. Men turned themselves into architecture. A moving roof of armor.

"Break ranks," Victor said. He threw an arm over his head as the hail rained down. "To the alleys!"

The formation shattered into survival at once. Soldiers sprinted past him in search of cover. Snares cinched around ankles and yanked bodies sideways. Hidden pits swallowed legs to the thigh. Men toppled forward, lost their rifles, and opened their mouths in brief animal shock before the next trap finished them.

Trip lines snapped taut and triggered spears that punched up from the ground. Rusted metal drove through limbs and pinned soldiers in place like desert scarecrows.

Bones snapped. Blood squelched. Screams ripped free and vanished into the wind as if they had never existed.

A soldier stumbled backward into Victor's path, eyes wide behind a cracked visor. Victor shoved him aside. The man hit the sand and rolled, and another rock smashed into his face with a dull crunch that cut off his cries.

Victor darted into a rusted tin shack and slammed his shoulder into the door hard enough to rattle the frame loose.

Carmine followed a heartbeat later, dragging one guard with him. The guard tore free and stumbled toward the wall, shield still raised as though he believed it could stop the outsiders' assault.

Inside, hot metal and old dust choked the air. The storm hammered the walls and turned the structure into a trembling drum. Sand hissed through the seams and gathered in thin drifts along the floorboards. A broken table lay on its side, half-buried. A child's shoe rested in one corner like a relic from a life that had ended quietly.

Victor pressed his back against the tin, raised his pistol, and listened.

"Stay quiet. Stay still. Let them butcher our men. Their deaths buy us seconds, and those seconds buy us a path toward Zaheen."

59

ZAHEEN

"It's all-out war," Zaheen said inside the Sand Alliance headquarters.

The words barely cut through the noise beyond the walls. Outside, gunfire and sand tore Nova Angeles apart. Smoke dragged low through the streets, thick and bitter, stinging her eyes even through the cracked windowpanes. Bullets stitched the air where homes had once stood and punched holes through tin and memory alike. The assault shook what little remained of the city—metal screamed, structures buckled, and the ground itself trembled with impact.

Zaheen turned from the window and found Malik frozen beside it. He locked his posture tight and drew his shoulders up as if bracing for a blow that never came. He clenched his hands at his sides until his knuckles went pale, his fingers trembling like they might splinter if he let himself breathe.

"They're fine," she said, though the words scraped on the way out. "You have to believe that."

Even as she offered it, belief felt thin. It didn't stop bullets. It didn't drag people out from under rubble. It didn't keep the people she loved breathing when the world came to collect its pound of flesh. Belief built a bridge out of fog, but sometimes that bridge kept her from falling.

Malik's face tightened as grief carved deeper into him by the second. He stared past the window, eyes glassy with a future he couldn't control.

"Leila will be fine," he said, as if repetition could reinforce reality. "But Eren..."

The name collapsed in his mouth.

He swallowed hard. "What am I supposed to tell her if something happens to him?"

"It's best not to think like that," she said and headed toward the door. "I've been there. It almost destroyed me."

"Where are you going?"

"To find Araya."

"That's a death wish," he said. "They're hunting us."

"Then stay here," Zaheen said. "That's one less target for them to spot."

She yanked up her hood and burst into the storm.

The wind hit her like a wall. Fabric snapped tight across her face, and the scarf bit into her cheeks as sand found every exposed inch of skin. Gunfire cracked through the streets. She couldn't tell whether the outsiders regrouped or the insiders closed in.

Either way, the desert gave her no answers.

Zaheen forced herself to breathe evenly as she scanned the shifting landscape ahead. The dunes rose and fell, their peaks swallowed by haze, their slopes sliding beneath her boots. Out here, Nova Angeles unraveled fast. Buildings gave way to sand and half-buried wreckage.

Somewhere beyond the storm's veil, she hoped Araya still

fought to survive and had not already disappeared beneath layers of sand and silence.

A hand clamped onto her shoulder.

Zaheen spun, fist ready to fly.

"Figured I'd find you here." Jude braced himself against the gale with his rifle raised, stance wide and grounded, eyes scanning past her into the storm. Ghost held position at his side, weapon angled low but ready. "Where are you going?"

"Araya's out here." She tried to push past him, but Jude shifted with her and blocked her path.

"Then you're not going alone," he said.

Ghost nodded. "We have rifles. You have fists."

"Then use them. Malik's in there, and he's one bad second away from falling apart. Go guard him."

Ghost barked a short laugh. "Hear that, Jude? Somebody trusts me." He peeled off toward the shack without another word.

Zaheen turned back to Jude. "Come on."

He fell into step beside her without argument. "Any sign of Holly?"

The wind struck from every direction, hard and hungry, but Zaheen kept her focus pinned forward. "She'll be fine. It's Holly."

Jude guided them through the alleys. They slipped around collapsed stalls and splintered siding and passed the first bodies where the traps had bitten true. Sand had already started to bury insider armor.

Zaheen's stomach tightened. Insider or outsider, they all bled the same.

"I want Victor alive if he's still out here," she said. "No more killing."

Jude shot her a sharp look as they ducked into a narrow corridor of rusted metal and torn wood. "Alive? Why spare him?"

"Because if he dies, he becomes a story people kneel to," Zaheen said, her voice steady through grit and gunfire. "A martyr keeps wars alive. I want this to end today."

"Oh, it will," Victor said.

The click of a pistol stopped the world cold.

Zaheen turned toward the sound and slid a hand across Jude's chest—a quiet command to hold, wait, and trust her.

Victor Kol stood ahead of them, arm extended, barrel aimed at her head.

Carmine Kurier hovered close to his side.

"You've already lost enough," Zaheen said. "Lower the gun."

"You're not in a position to make demands," Victor said, and clicked off the safety.

Zaheen flicked her eyes toward his flank. "You'll always be an errand boy climbing a ladder that was never built for you."

Carmine responded with an arrogant smirk. "And people like you will never touch the bottom rung."

Victor kept his arm locked and the barrel steady at Zaheen's temple. "Mr. Kurier is a patriot," he said. "You, Zaheen, are what failure looks like. Small. Cornered. Pitiful. Dirty."

"You keep telling yourself that," Jude said. "You can tear her apart piece by piece, and me after, but the sand still gathers and surrounds your dome with its fury."

Something shifted at the edge of her vision.

Figures rose along the rooftops—outsiders, bloodied,

sandy, and very much alive. Insider rifles gleamed in their hands. Ghost waved, and Malik stood beside him.

"Your reign ends here, Victor," Malik said. "It's long overdue."

Victor's face tightened. Rage yanked his aim toward Malik.

Jude fired first.

The shot tore through Victor's hand. Bone broke. Flesh split. Victor screamed as the pistol clattered into the sand. He dropped to his knees, clutching his ruined hand to his chest, breath breaking into ragged bursts.

Carmine dropped with him, disbelief written stark across his face.

Zaheen rushed over and snatched the fallen weapon and leveled it at Victor's head without hesitation. She stared down at both insiders. Not gods or monsters, no... just men who spent far too long believing the world bent to their will.

"Both of you will watch Nova Angeles and Los Angeles rise together from a prison cell."

She lifted her gaze to Malik and Ghost. "Free any prisoners. Treat their wounds. Feed them. They were misled. This was never about the insiders. It has always been about TerraLux Minerals and Victor Kol."

Zaheen looked back down at Victor. Sweat streaked through the sand on his pale face as he cradled his shattered hand.

"Greed ravaged our world," she said. "It infected you a long time ago. It will not claim me."

Victor moaned in pain, and Ghost giggled from above.

"There has to be a better world for all of us," Zaheen said. "No one life weighs more than another. So we stop this. We go home. We end the violence. Insiders will return to the domes and tell their people change is here. I'll tell mine the same. Then we rebuild until life feels worth living, *for everyone.*"

Zaheen placed the pistol in Jude's hand.

She stepped past Victor and Carmine without looking back, turned toward the dunes, and walked into the storm to find Araya.

60

ZAHEEN

The storm passed as suddenly as it arrived, dragging its fury away as if it had grown bored.

In its wake, the desert settled into something almost reverent. The sky shifted from bruised gray to pale blue, and the clouds pulled apart like reluctant curtains. Light washed across the dunes, turning them gold. Their curves stretched smooth and endless, brushed clean by wind and time.

The sand caught the sun and scattered it back in soft halos. Each grain flashed briefly before sinking into the whole again. Ridge and hollow, crest and trough—the entire expanse looked painted into place, impossibly calm, as if the world had paused to remember what beauty looked like when no one tried to own it.

Zaheen stood on the outskirts of Nova Angeles and let the quiet settle around her.

She lowered her hood. The wind softened into a warm breath against her skin. Moments earlier it had lashed at her face, furious and sharp. Now it slid past her gently.

She closed her eyes and breathed deep, filling her lungs with heat, dust, and something that felt like mercy.

The desert endured. So did she.

Now that the danger had passed, pain crept into her muscles. The ache arrived late, after adrenaline loosened its grip. Her hands trembled faintly at her sides. She flexed her fingers and grounded herself in sensation—sand under her boots, sun on her face, the steady beat of her heart drumming loudly in her ears.

Four figures crested a low rising dune and hiked toward her.

Zaheen squinted, her breath catching. Recognition came in fragments: a familiar posture and stride.

A laugh burst from her throat, startled and bright. She stepped forward and broke into a sprint. "Araya!" she cried, her voice tearing through the open air.

Araya opened her arms.

Zaheen crashed into her. The impact knocked the breath from both of them. She clung tight, her fingers digging into fabric, into warmth, into the undeniable proof of a living body beneath her hands.

Araya smelled like chemicals, dust, and something faintly metallic—Mars, maybe. Zaheen lifted a trembling hand to Araya's chin. She needed more than sight. She needed touch to believe this was real.

Then she kissed her.

The kiss tasted like salt and endurance, like fear finally releasing its hold. Zaheen laughed into it and cried at the same time, the sounds tangling until she couldn't separate them. She pulled Araya into a hug so tight it hurt, ribs pressing together, arms locking as if she could anchor her there through sheer will.

"You're home," Zaheen said. "You're home for good."

The words broke as soon as they left her mouth. She cradled Araya's head between her palms and brushed dust from her cheeks with her thumbs, holding her like something sacred. "No one takes you from me again."

"Every second without you hurt more than Mars itself," Araya said.

Zaheen leaned forward until their foreheads touched. The world narrowed to heat, breath, and the quiet certainty that this was no mirage. Her hands trembled again, but this time she didn't fight it. She let herself feel the enormity of what she could have lost.

"I watched the stars," Zaheen said. "I begged them to bring you back. I told them I'd give anything."

Her fingers slipped to the gold at her throat. She unclasped it and held it out, the chain catching the sun and flaring bright.

"Your pendant found me when we were at our lowest," she said. "When I didn't know if we would survive." Her voice steadied as she lifted it toward Araya. "Now I give it back when we're at our highest. Happy birthday."

She chuckled softly and fastened it around Araya's neck. Zaheen leaned forward and kissed her again, slower this time, unhurried, a promise instead of a plea.

"I love you," Zaheen said.

"I love you, Zaheen." Araya squeezed her hand. "There are people you need to meet."

Zaheen glanced past her and spotted the others. Her gaze landed on Holly, and she rushed straight into her arms.

"We did it, Zee," Holly said.

She pulled Zaheen into a tight embrace and began to cry.

61

ZAHEEN

Zaheen still hadn't let go of Araya's hand since their reunion.

At some point, holding on had stopped being reflex and become a choice. At first, instinct drove it, an anchor against the leftover terror that Araya might vanish again the moment Zaheen loosened her grip.

But now Victor Kol had fallen, and Zaheen knew peace.

Together, they stepped into Holly's bar.

Narrow bands of sunlight slipped through fractured windows and cut the air into warm ribbons that drifted across the room and settled over faces marked by exhaustion. The space had changed without trying to. Noise, smoke, and the sharp edge of survival had given way to bliss.

Survivors filled the room. Outsiders, insiders, and those who had once belonged to both or neither. They sat, stood, and leaned wherever they finally allowed themselves to rest.

Zaheen took it all in with a soldier's awareness and a lover's hope.

At the center of the room, Victor Kol and Carmine Kurier sat bound to rusted chairs, ropes biting deep into their wrists. They worked their mouths uselessly beneath their gags, their protests reduced to strained sounds that barely rose above the murmur around them.

Zaheen felt no satisfaction when she looked at them.

She felt only a quiet certainty that this was how power ended. It ended up restrained, reduced, made small beneath the gaze of those it had tried to erase.

Officer Nakamura stood watch between them, pistol ready, posture steady and unyielding. She met Zaheen's eyes and gave her a nod.

They were not going anywhere.

At the bar, Ghost, Jude, Iman, and Skye drank from bronze steins. They had earned each swallow.

Holly stood behind the counter with fresh bandages wrapped over her wounds. Tiredness weighed on her posture, but it had not broken her. She spoke with Jude and braced one hand against the bar, as if reminding herself that she still owned the ground beneath her.

Zaheen scanned the room again.

She found Malik in a corner booth with Leila.

They sat close but did not touch. Grief had hollowed them both and carved deep marks into their faces. Leila's eyes looked red and distant. Malik's shoulders slumped forward as if he carried the entire desert across his back.

It wasn't my fault, Zaheen told herself, even as her gaze snapped back to Victor.

It was his.

She stopped in front of Victor. "Your end, marks our beginning."

Victor thrashed against the ropes, fury flashing in his eyes before pain dragged it back down.

Araya loosened her grip on Zaheen's hand and pointed at each bound man in turn. "Your hands are stained with blood," she said. "You both will stand as a reminder of the path we never take again. Officer Nakamura. It's time."

Officer Nakamura seized their wrists and hauled them upright, the ropes creaking under the sudden strain. She held them with an iron grip. "You will face justice. Your trial will happen in full view. The inside will rebuild under a council, and you will watch your empire collapse from behind a cell."

At the bar, Ghost drained his cup in one pull, refilled it, and drank again as if he needed the burn to prove this was real. "Back to steel and glass."

He stepped close to Carmine, fisted a hand in his collar, and yanked him forward just enough to snap the ropes tight. Carmine choked on a muffled sound.

"A special cell awaits you, Mr. Kurier."

Nakamura and Ghost dragged Victor and Carmine out of the bar.

Zaheen met Araya's eyes. A silent permission passed between them. *Breathe. Live. There is no more fear.*

Zaheen slid into the seat across from Malik and Leila, careful not to crowd their grief. "Eren's legacy will live in what we do next. You saved so many outsiders. I won't forget that."

Leila lifted her head. When she spoke, grief broke open inside every syllable. "Los Angeles will open its arms to anyone who needs refuge. The trains are ready. We'll take the wounded first."

Malik threaded his fingers through hers. "From this moment on, choice belongs to the people," he said, sweeping his gaze across the room. "Any outsider who wants the dome is welcome to it. Any who wants to stay can stay. No more quotas. No more takings."

Zaheen nodded. This was how change began.

She crossed back to the bar, where Araya spoke with Iman and Skye. "Are you sure you don't want to stay?" Zaheen asked Skye.

"Malik offered to teach me politics," Skye said. "If we're rebuilding, outsiders need to understand how the inside works."

Iman glanced at Jude. "He asked me to go with him," she said. "People need to hear the truth, that the inside is safe now. That the rules changed. I also want to find Dante's family and give them the news."

Araya pulled them both into a tight embrace. "Our paths will cross again."

"I don't mean to interrupt," Malik said.

Exhaustion and humility softened his expression in a way that still surprised Zaheen. "I forgot to say thank you."

Zaheen shook her head. "Don't," she said softly. "This victory was everyone."

"My council will reach out to yours once we draft the constitution," he said. "We'll put peace back where it belongs. Power to the people and far from the extractive corporations."

Zaheen watched him walk toward the door with Leila and the others gathering to leave for Los Angeles. As the room thinned and the voices softened, she drifted toward the doorway and stood in the spill of light and sand.

"Tomorrow, I'm leaving with Iman," Jude said, clapping a hand against her back.

Then Holly laid a hand on Zaheen's shoulder, and the familiar weight of it drew a smile she had not expected.

"Jude," Holly said, "promise Zee and me you'll visit often."

Jude chuckled, and the sound carried the truth that it might be a while. "I'll be back when you've got fresh stock behind that bar."

He pulled them both into a hug, then slipped out into the day.

Zaheen caught Holly's hands and held them, grounding herself in their callused warmth. "I love you, Holly. We did it."

"I knew we would." Holly squeezed her hands once, then turned to see off those preparing to cross the dunes.

Araya stepped close and threaded her fingers through Zaheen's. "Our future will always be sand," she said, "but our children won't live chained to what chained us."

Zaheen looked out toward the desert. "Sand flows freely. As long as we're together, we'll build the world we've been reaching for."

Zaheen smiled, quiet and sure. "A place fit for a family."

ACKNOWLEDGMENTS

Writing a novel is often described as a solitary act, but this book exists because of a community of people who shaped my thinking, challenged my ideas, and reminded me why stories matter.

I also owe a great deal to the writers, scientists, and story-tellers whose work has expanded the way I think about the future. Science fiction gave me a language for asking difficult questions, and your work challenged me to imagine what humanity might become.

To my friends and family: thank you for your encouragement and belief in this project!

Finally, thank you to the readers who picked up this story. If *Escape From Perihelion* does anything, I hope it reminds us that the future is not something that simply happens to us; it's something we choose to shape.

ABOUT THE AUTHOR

Diego Tovar is an environmental advocate and writer originally from Austin, Texas. He holds a bachelor's degree in Ecosystem Science and Sustainability from Colorado State University, and a master's degree in Global Environmental Policy from American University. Now based in Washington, D.C., he brings together his work in environmental policy with his passion for telling stories that imagine more just and sustainable futures. Learn more about his books, speaking engagements, and upcoming projects at diegotovarbooks.com.

READER'S GROUP GUIDE

1. At the beginning of the novel, what motivates Araya and Zaheen to keep going despite the risks around them? How do their motivations evolve by the end of the story?
2. How does Araya's and Zaheen's relationship toward community change throughout the book? What moments most strongly shape their adjusted mindsets?
3. Several characters are forced to make difficult choices in order to survive. Which character decision stood out to you the most, and why?
4. Were there moments when you disagreed with a character's actions? How did those moments shape your understanding of them?
5. In a world shaped by crisis and inequality, what does loyalty mean to the characters in this story?
6. The society in *Escape From Perihelion* reflects deep environmental and social divisions. What

aspects of this world felt most believable or realistic to you?

7. The book portrays powerful institutions that shape who survives and who suffers. How do these systems influence the characters' lives? What systems in real-life have similar effects?

8. How does the setting influence the tone of the story? In what ways does the environment itself feel like a character?

9. The novel explores the consequences of technological advancement alongside environmental collapse. What message do you think the story sends about the relationship between technology and responsibility?

10. If you lived in the world of *Escape From Perihelion*, which choices made by the characters do you think would be hardest for you?

11. A major theme in the novel is survival. How do various characters define survival differently?

12. The book raises questions about sacrifice. When, if ever, is sacrifice justified in the pursuit of a larger goal?

13. How does the story explore the idea of hope in a world that often feels hopeless?

14. Many moments in the novel force characters to choose between personal safety and helping others. What does the story suggest about responsibility to others?

15. How does the novel explore the tension between individual action and larger systems of power?

16. *Escape From Perihelion* is a work of climate fiction. In what ways does the story reflect real environmental challenges facing the world today?

17. Which elements of the book made you think differently about environmental justice or climate inequality?

18. Do you see parallels between the world in the novel and current political or environmental realities?

19. What scene or moment in the book stayed with you thc longcst aftcr finishing it?

20. After finishing *Escape From Perihelion*, what questions about the future of our planet or society linger with you?

21. If this story continued beyond the final page, what do you imagine happens next for the characters?

IN ORBIT WITH DIEGO TOVAR

A Fast Orbit Press conversation about Escape From Perihelion, climate fiction, and the future of storytelling.

Q) What inspired you to write *Escape From Perihelion*?

The idea came from a question that has been sitting in my mind for years: what happens when the environmental decisions we make today finally catch up to us on a mass scale? Don't get me wrong, environmental injustice is present and has been, but some of us face the severities more than others. I wanted to explore a world shaped by those consequences, but through a deeply human story about survival, trust, and the choices people make when systems begin to fail. Science fiction allows us to imagine those futures while still asking questions about the present.

Q) Your work often touches on environmental justice. How did that influence this novel?

Environmental justice is at the heart of the story. Climate change doesn't affect everyone equally, and the communities that contribute the least to the problem often experience the worst impacts. I wanted the world of *Escape From Perihelion* to reflect that imbalance and ask readers to think about who benefits from power structures and who is forced to live with their consequences.

Q) What exactly is climate fiction, or "cli-fi"?

Climate fiction, often called cli-fi, is a genre of storytelling that explores the impacts of climate change on people, societies, and ecosystems. It can take many forms—thrillers, survival stories, dystopias, or even hopeful visions of the future. At its best, cli-fi is about humanity. It's how we respond to crisis, how we treat one another, and whether we can change course.

Q) What did you want that relationship between Araya and Zaheen to represent?

At its core, the relationship between Araya and Zaheen represents trust and love in a world where those things are incredibly fragile. When systems collapse and power becomes concentrated in the hands of a few, the most important thing people have left is one another. Their relationship is about learning to rely on someone else even when the world has taught you not to.

Q) The world of *Escape From Perihelion* feels harsh and unequal. Was that intentional?

Absolutely. One of the goals of the novel was to show how environmental collapse doesn't happen in isolation. It interacts with politics, economics, and inequality. In many ways, the world of the book is an exaggeration of trends we already see today. Science fiction allows us to stretch those realities far enough that we can examine them more clearly.

Q) What do you hope readers take away from the story?

More than anything, I hope readers walk away thinking about the future differently. Climate change can feel overwhelming, but stories remind us that the future isn't written yet. The choices people make—both individually and collectively—can change the trajectory of the world.

Q) Do you see climate fiction and science fiction as a form of activism?

Yes. Stories shape how people imagine the future. If we only imagine dystopias (which I'm cognizant of that feeling in *Escape From Perihelion*), it can feel like collapse is inevitable. But at the same time, storytelling can also challenge people to think critically about systems of power, responsibility, and possibility when put in situations of peril. Fiction can open the door to conversations that statistics and reports sometimes can't.

Q) What's next for you as a writer?

I'm always interested in exploring stories that sit at the intersection of science fiction, environmental justice, and human resilience. The future is full of questions whether it be about technology, power, social justice, and about how humanity will adapt to a changing planet. Those questions will continue to shape the stories I tell.

www.ingramcontent.com/pod-product-compliance
Lightning Source LLC
Chambersburg PA
CBHW060516160726
47991CB00001B/62